Praise for Jaguar Beault:

"If Phyllis Diller had married Sam Spade, their kid would be named Jaguar Beault. If you are a fan of detective novels, you've probably noticed that after a while, the plots and the author's styles all begin to sound similar. Enter John Thom - a bright new voice in the mystery business. Wicked dialogue, a touch of noir, a unique brand of humor and a fresh take on an old genre, Thom's tongue-in-cheek delivery is a delight. The plot is engaging and packed with local San Francisco color and old-time references from the author's eclectic past. As a lead character, Jaguar Beault is unique, offbeat and refreshing; *The Madagascar Pigeon* is pure entertainment."

– Brian Neary, award-winning author of
"Hawk," "Twenty-Seven Million"
and "5 Seconds to Chaos."

A Minority View:

"If I had half a mind...I do, I do have half a mind...I would make a formal inquiry into why these writer types always look on the underside of San Francisco. All they see is crime and guns and fog and gridlock and all those potholes and no parking and exorbitant prices and sleep-walking pedestrians and rocketing bicyclists. Why don't they look at the good stuff I...we do, like flying the banner of ecological salvation? Like how we are at the forefront of federal grants to take the pain out of the lives of the unemployed, the homeless, students, corporate donors, and other misfortunate voters, er, citizens."

– Nancy P.

TERMINATION DETERMINATORS

John Thom

The Jaguar Beault Thriller Library so far:
The Madagascar Pigeon
Termination Determinators

There's more to come from the exploits of Jaguar Beault. Watch for future thrillers currently in the literary pipeline from **Bat & Ball Press**. Like...
The Nuclear Armageddon Endgame
Evil in Silicon Valley

Order Jaguar Beault Thrillers:
E-reader version on your Kindle
Print copies from Amazon.com

Contact the author at: **jaguarbeault@gmail.com**

ISBN-13: 9780961124229
ISBN-10: 0961124229
Library of Congress Control Number: 2014919811
CreateSpace Independent Publishing Platform
North Charleston, South Carolina

Bat & Ball Press
San Francisco

Cover photo by Kimberly Suydam. She provided the cover photo for *The Madagascar Pigeon* as well. Nice shots, don't you think?

A note about the publisher: **Bat & Ball Press** opened for business in the 1980s when it issued the second best book ever in the vast library of baseball history. It is entitled *Champion Batsmen of the 20th Century*. That was a time before the steroid plague sullied the game and many of its hitting and pitching stars. All the employees of **B&B Press**, great fans of the game, lost their innocence and sadly – but filled with hope – set out to find a new voice in the publishing game. They found that voice in the series you are now enjoying – the Jaguar Beault Thrillers. Jaguar Beault does not do steroids. It is nature that dealt him his imposing size and strength, not banned supplements used by cheaters. **Bat & Ball Press** moved from Los Angeles to San Francisco and has not looked back. Well, you asked.

This work is dedicated to the seven and one-half billion people on Earth who have not bought a copy of *The Madagascar Pigeon*, which puts them behind the curve if they want to have helpful background about Jaguar Beault as he collides with more crime in *Termination Determinators*. This dedicatory sentiment is offered to you, if you are one of them, as a reminder to go do the duty you have not performed. Buy the book. Do not fret, copies of that first mystery in this series remain available for purchase. It is for your own good. Any bubblehead knows thrillers ought to be consumed in chronological order. Because it just makes sense, that's why. A child could figure this out. Criminy, this is like pulling teeth.

1

This was not Mickey Truke's lucky day. Typical, if you want to be let in on his recent history this early in the story. The fact is he hadn't had his lucky day since he left the police force and took up his new career.

"Son—of—a—bitch," Truke dictated as he tripped over a sleeping dog, accidentally squeezing off a burst from his Glock automatic after pounding through the French doors into the drawing room. Bullets cracked against a wall and more climbed up into the ceiling. "Shit," Mickey agreed with himself.

Recovering some nimbleness, Truke scrambled to his feet surveying the room. No one had drawn a weapon against him. That was a good thing. Mickey wore a three-quarter-length overcoat the color of desert sand. It covered a holster along his right thigh. The gun in the holster was a .22 caliber Ruger six-shooter. A silencer stuck out of the hole in the bottom of the holster. Mickey seized the gun and pulled it free. As he did, the silencer fell "clank-clank" to the floor. "Oh, man," Mickey complained. He reached down to grab the device while watching the room. He tried to screw the silencer onto the barrel of the Ruger while his hands were full of guns but that proved impossible. So he tucked the Glock into his left armpit then he got the silencer onto the Ruger's barrel.

The crescendo of the gunfire retreated, leaving the lingering odor of telltale cordite. The dog put his head down and went back to sleep.

The man was sitting in a leather-looking chair. The woman was standing against the mantel. He was sipping a colorless drink. She was not. He was graying around the temples. She was gorgeous. He was in the uniform of a Marine colonel. She was gorgeous. Oh, and in a black

1

sheath dress that revealed nothing. And everything. Curiously, they both sported New Balance running shoes. He spoke first, sneering at the intruder.

"Who in hell are you and what are you doing here?" His face was martial, his tone commanding. He did not bother to stand. He glared at Truke.

Mickey Truke said sternly, "Which one of you is Svetlana?"

The answer came in a dumbfounded silence. "Aha," Truke said a moment after recognition, "it's you."

"No," she said, "my name is Seakrit."

"Secret? Why is your name a secret?"

"Not *a* secret, Seakrit."

"Huh?"

"My name is Seakrit, Vickie Seakrit."

"Oh," Mickey absorbed. Then turning to the soldier, he said, "Then you must be Svetlana."

"Uh, no."

"But I was told there would be a Svetlana here."

"Who told you that?" the colonel demanded.

"I can't tell you."

"Why, because you don't know?"

"I know, I just can't tell you."

"Why?"

"It's none of your business, that's why. And stop asking questions. I'll ask the questions."

"What do you want with Svetlana?" the colonel asked with a smirk on his face.

"That's for me to know and...hey, I said to stop asking questions."

"Well, how will we know why you are here shooting up the place if we don't ask you why?" the colonel questioned.

"I already told you why I am here," Truke testified.

"No, you did not."

"Yes, I did."

Here Ms. Seakrit chimed in. "No, you did not. You simply barged in shooting that dreadful gun of yours."

"That was a mistake. It was an accident. I didn't see your dog."

"It's not my dog," Seakrit said.

"His then," Mickey said, pointing the Ruger at the Marine.

"It's not my dog," the colonel said.

"What's it doing here if it's not your dog?" Truke asked.

The colonel said, "It probably lives here." The woman seemed to agree because she nodded.

"Lives here? Don't you live here?" Mickey asked. The question was aimed at both of them or either of them.

"Who is Svetlana?" the soldier answered.

"Exactly!" Mickey said excitedly. "Where is she?"

"I have no idea," the colonel said, sipping his drink, looking at Truke, glancing at the woman.

"Will she be back soon?" Mickey pressed.

"Why would she be back here?"

"She lives here."

Ms. Seakrit said, "Perhaps the dog is her dog. That would make sense. Does this Svetlana have a dog to your knowledge?"

"Wha...I don't know! Forget the dog! Does Svetlana live here?" Mickey pressed further.

The colonel looked at Vickie and said, "Any idea?" She shook her head.

Truke looked around. "This is too weird. What are you two doing here?"

"We..." Ms. Seakrit started. "Say, if we tell you, are you going to hold it against us? You're not a cop, are you?"

"No. Well, not anymore. Was once. Not now."

"Oh, good. We...shall I tell him?" she said to the Marine.

He laughed. "Sure, why not?"

"We're...you won't tell, will you?" she said to Mickey.

"Just tell me," he sighed.

"We're taking stuff from the house."

"You're robbing the place? You're burglars?"

"No, well, yes, but that is such a coarse way of putting it," she said.

"Yes, coarse," the Marine agreed.

"Isn't breaking into a house a little beneath a Marine colonel, Colonel?"

The colonel laughed. "Oh, this," he said, looking down at the uniform, "I found it in the bedroom. Fits real good. Makes me look official, don't you think?"

Truke stared at him, then at the woman, then around the room. "So you don't even know who Svetlana is, am I right?"

"Yep."

"You don't even know if she lives here?"

"Could be she does, could be she doesn't."

"Hmmm."

It was instances like this that gave Mickey Truke moments of doubt about his career change decision. In the past, he could call his desk sergeant and ask for further instructions. This one would have been fairly evident. "Arrest them, Truke," he would be advised, "they are committing a felony." Not now. Now he was an independent consultant hired to...consult. To act independently. To take a job and get it done. The kind of dream job he dreamed of during those boring nights on morning watch motoring through the streets of crime-free Beverly Hills wondering if anything criminal was ever going to deal him in so that he could do the police work he trained for.

"What did you want with Svetlana anyway?" the fake soldier asked Truke.

"Never mind about that," he answered.

"You brought that gun. It has a silencer. You are planning to shoot her. I thought so."

"Never mind about that either," Mickey said. "I gotta go." At which point he holstered his Ruger and brandished his automatic as he backed toward the French doors with a nimble sense of where things were. It would have been a clean exit except for the dog, the presence of which as a part of his situational orientation Truke neglected to remember. This time as he went toes up and backside down over the dog, the stream of bullets tore along the ceiling. "Son—of—a—bitch," he was able to observe. The dog got up and walked over and sniffed Mickey's crotch.

4

There was no mistaking the fact that MacKenzie Urban Truke, known all his life as Mickey, could not have borne the more obvious appellation – "Mack" – for the good reason that he was always a little less than average height and weight for each of his ages. He barely made it on the BHPD, slipping in with just the minimum physical requirements. He was, however, a determined little fellow...and good on the written examinations.

Police work in Beverly Hills proved to be grueling. Monotonous hours watching law-abiding behavior. Even with the tempting riches of the wealthy and famous who lived in the city, the criminal element mostly steered clear. Social media sites, good for instantaneous communication if for nothing else, informed bad guys of the not-yet-court-challenged heavy-handed police responses to the rare burglar or speeder or panhandler. Better to do your scofflawing somewhere else where cops actually adhered to their codes of conduct and not to the lower standards appreciated by Beverly Hills taxpayers.

That was then, this was now. Now was a promising though still virginal line of work that put Mickey in an orbit transiting the contradictory and mysterious conceits of the San Francisco Bay Area: the hustle and bustle of the money-grubbing millionaires who live off the sweat and toil of the poor; the street clans who try to live off the orts spilled by the money-grubbing millionaires; the artisans who covet playing Symphony Hall instead of on the street corner where they are tolerated by cops whose code of conduct is a progressive's wet dream; the Chinese community whose activities are so deep-rooted that its structure is almost impenetrable to outsiders as it glides into political power;

tourists who actually rave about the food on Fisherman's Wharf; sports fans who dream annually for a Joe Montana and a Jerry Rice to re-join the 49ers; strip club owners who sponsor entrants in the Gay Pride parades; and a former San Francisco mayor who must have been cloned to be able to appear at every event in every square mile of the city. Like he is still mayor. He isn't.

A notion less contradictory, depending on how your moral compass is calibrated, was the brokerage firm Mickey Truke consulted for. As a brokerage firm, it, well, it brokered matters. Today it might introduce a wannabe sailor to a nice man selling a yacht. The nice man might even own that yacht. Yesterday, it maybe could have persuaded an office-building owner to put the asset up for sale. To a friend of the brokerage firm. Tomorrow, though this is just a guess on your author's part of the brokerage firm's processes as a go-between, it maybe might help a San Francisco supervisor change his stance on police patrols near his...well, these are just examples of brokering processes.

When it brought in Mickey Truke, the brokerage firm assigned him to its new division, the one that brokered finality. As in, "Mickey, shoot Svetlana." If you have read Chapter 1, you will remember that Mickey did not shoot Svetlana. Mickey did not see Svetlana. Mickey may not have been in Svetlana's house. Mickey's orbit that day did not cross Svetlana's orbit at the expected time and place. So much for Mickey's situational orientation.

Inside Grace Cathedral on San Francisco's Nob Hill, you are struck by the traditional Gothic styling, by the volume of stained glass windows, the flanking chapels, the labyrinths for reflective walking, the organ and its more than seven thousand pipes, the High Altar, and the surrounding silence. The perfect place to discuss assassinations. In a whisper.

"You didn't shoot her," the suited man whispered.

"I didn't see her," Mickey Truke whispered back.

"We brokered you to shoot her."

"She wasn't there."

"Where was she?"

"I don't know."

Discussing assassinations usually includes a lot more specificity and precision. That's an assumption your faithful author makes only after dipping into other sources. I have no personal experience with assassination. But based on what I have read – or have chosen to take as reliable, at least – I believe the discussion inside Grace Cathedral about Svetlana's fumbled assassination ought to have taken a different turn. Such as:

"You didn't shoot her."

"I didn't see her."

"We brokered you to shoot her. You are a useless piece of cow dropping who has yet to complete one assignment correctly. Our reputation is on the line every time we take on a job. You have single-handedly driven our Termination Division reputation down the toilet. Customers will certainly migrate to that new conglomerate down in South San Francisco we've been hearing rumors about. They're going to get all the good kills, I just know it. We may have to go kill *them*."

That is more likely how it would have gone.

"But back to Svetlana," the suited man said softly.

"She wasn't there," Mickey Truke reaffirmed softly back.

"The police found her tied and gagged in a chair upstairs. Did you go upstairs? Evidently not. Whoever stole every last valuable she owned apparently went upstairs. The police said the house was stripped clean. Oh, and somebody shot up the drawing room. Probably the thieves to show they meant business."

"That was..."

"One more chance, Mickey. Do it right or you're off the team."

"I'll try my best."

"Good God, not your best, just get it done right. Right?"

"Right, Uncle Ben," Mickey sighed.

One more chance, Truke thought, one damn last chance. Crap, he added. The Jackal never had to hear this shit, Mickey thought further.

"This is your last chance, Jackal, even if you are the top-rated assassin in termination history." The difference, Truke admitted to himself, was that the Jackal shot people. Shot them dead. Shot them dead according to the job specifications. Mickey, on the other hand, did not have a spotless record. Of his five consultations, five targets are still walking around and breathing, enjoying the sights and sounds of the Bay Area. Trying to console himself by remembering that even the great Willie Mays sometimes went 0 for 5 in a ballgame, Mickey thought, was just plain blather. Uncle Ben would have seen right through that Willie Mays thing if Truke had dared to bring it up. Mickey was unlucky, not blind, so he did not bring it up.

"Yes, Uncle Ben, I think I have it all."

"You think or you do?"

"I do."

"Go over it again for me."

"I wait for him on a remote stretch of the bike path in the Presidio..."

"In Lincoln Park." Uncle Ben said, rolling his eyes.

"In Lincoln Park and dispatch..."

"Shoot him."

"And shoot him, making sure we are alone and then covering his body..."

"Pushing his body down a hill."

"And pushing his body down a hill where it won't be seen."

"And?"

"And?"

"Yes, and?"

"Oh, using a silencer."

Uncle Ben stared at Mickey. "I told you you get one more chance. This is it."

"You can count on me," Mickey said.

"I've already counted your five failures on this hand, now I'm starting on the other one." Uncle Ben stared at Truke and said, "Mickey, you are giving contract kills a bad name."

"Sorry."

"You damn well should be," Uncle Ben said angrily. "Now, any questions?"

"What's with this guy?" Mickey asked. "From what I've heard he's harmless enough, a big-time private eye. Came up with a sensational murder collar and got a bunch of sleazebags tossed in jail for a long time. Sounds like he was just doing his job."

"Just doing his job? That's what you've heard? Harmless enough? A big-time private eye? Well, let me tell you something. Seems he walked away with a fortune from that harmlessness. A sockful of jewels and a beautiful dame. The swag didn't belong to him. He took it anyway. That's knavery in my book," Uncle Ben huffed and puffed.

"So we're going to terminate him for showing a little initiative?" Mickey asked.

"We're going to ter...you are going to term...you are going to shoot him because we will be paid to terminate him. That's what we do. We are a brokerage house. You are going to terminate Jaguar Beault."

"Is that how it's pronounced? I thought it was beault."

"It just looks like that, but it's Beault."

"Doesn't make sense to me," Mickey said.

"You just do your job the way you are supposed to and we'll make sure his name is spelled properly on his headstone."

"That's a good one, Uncle Ben."

3

Jaguar Beault is a San Francisco private detective. Perhaps you have heard of him. Gosh, you may have read that book about him and the curious bird statue. If not, you are referred to this book's dedication. Mickey was correct when he said that Beault pulled off a high-profile murder case. Made the news in no small part because his inamorata – she is now – is a well-known TV news reporter who had loads of inside information. Some people say she is rather pretty.

Beault works out of an office in the Outer Richmond on San Francisco's west side. He's had space there since he went into business for himself. His building is just a short way off Balboa Street where he can satisfy his needs for caffeine and sugar as well as nutritional foods with a convenient stroll to a nice array of eateries. His office is in the frequent embrace of the fog from, in large part, the close-by Pacific Ocean. You'd know this if you had a copy of his book.

His caseload increased in proportion to his reputation after he did what Mickey learned from Uncle Ben, that Beault really had cornered more than a few gun-totin scums for the police to take into custody and the courts to take off the streets. Beault did in fact pocket a fortune from the deal. He earned it. And now with a bigger roster of clients – admittedly none so dramatic as *The Madagascar Pigeon* caper – he found he was slowly losing ground to the unfamiliar administrative duties a busy office typically puts in front of the boss.

"Hon," Beault called to Nadine, "I think I need to hire a helper."

"I have a job, babe," Nadine called from another room, reminding the private eye. Nadine is Nadine Berry, the KSFG-TV investigative reporter known throughout the Bay Area for her hard-hitting work. Nadine is Beault's aforementioned inamorata. They are in love.

"Not you, sweet," Beault clarified, "someone else. Someone who could take over the daily chores of my office."

"I know what you meant, Bas."

"Oh. Um, but I need a secretary or receptionist or whatever they're called nowadays."

"How about office assistant?"

Bas thought about that and then answered, "Office assistant, yes, that sounds good." Bas is Jaguar Beault. Jaguar Beault is Bas's professional name. His *nom de guerre*. Bas is Basil Protherington. Beault has to explain all this from time to time when people ask about his name. Following that he tells them why his business is not known as Basil Protherington Investigations. "It just wouldn't command the attention and respect from clients that Jaguar Beault Investigations does," he says. Everyone agrees with him.

"Just be sure she's not pretty. You know how jealous I can be," Nadine said when she saw that Beault was warming to the idea of an office assistant.

"That's only because I spend all my days giving you reasons for the green-eyed monster to come spewing out of you."

"Don't brag, dearie, when there's nothing there to brag about."

Beault coughed.

"What was that?" Nadine asked.

"Nothing, my love."

"Good," she laughed. She came in from the other room. "Bas, what you should do is put a notice in with the state employment department. There are loads of qualified people still looking for jobs. You're sure to get some experienced candidates. Need any help from me?"

"Naw. I'll do what you said, though. I'll do up a notice. That sounds like the best route to take."

And so he did. The note read: "I need an office assistant for my office. Call me at (his phone number.)

When Nadine had put the finishing touches – the beginning touches as well – on the revised job description notice, Beault drove to the state employment office, parked a half mile away at the only available spot, walked to the building, entered, and took a number. The notice he held now read: "Wanted: Office Assistant for a one-man private investigation operation. Skilled on phone, computer, filing. Must have good judgment and discretion." There was the necessary phone number. Beault felt that Nadine's version was better than his own. He had said as much to Nadine before leaving the house, exhibiting his own astute grasp of good judgment and discretion.

In the employment office, Beault watched people of every stripe come and go, carrying hope, looking for change – from joblessness to employment – but unable to conceal their despair. Their faces told him they wanted jobs. Nothing else was important. Beault felt good that he was in a position to make the hopes come true for one of them.

When his number was called he sat down in front of a woman about fifty years old who showed the strains that came with dealing with the jobless. "Good morning," he started.

The woman nodded and said, "Do you have your forms filled out?"

"Yes, here."

"This is just..." She looked up. "You have a job notice. You aren't looking for work? You don't belong here." She was not scolding, just trying to enlighten this man that he needed to be somewhere else. "We find jobs for people. At least we try."

"I know," Beault said, "that's why I came here today. I want to post this. I need a helper, er, an office assistant."

"You know what?" the clerk said, "I'm going to do this for you. It's not often we get somebody in front of us who has a job to give instead of the other way around. The rule here is for people to be begging for a job. I will take this card, darling, and I'll set it in motion."

Beault smiled and said, "Thank you."

"You're a private eye?" she asked. Beault nodded his answer. "Is this work dangerous?"

"Sometimes, yes, but I do all I can to avoid the danger."

"I meant is this office assistant job going to put somebody else in danger?" she asked.

Beault hadn't thought about that. He said, "I hadn't thought about that."

"Well, it's not our responsibility here to warn people about any dangers in job openings," she admitted. "You should do that yourself, you know, when you are interviewing. You use a gun in your business?" she asked bluntly.

Beault leaned in and said, "Uh-huh."

"Well there you are. Danger," the clerk said. "You be sure to spell that out to anyone who applies with you."

The lecture went on a short while longer until the nice lady felt she had admonished this private eye enough. Beault was all too happy to leave the building and begin the long walk back to his car.

4

Lincoln Park occupies about one square mile of wooded hills on a rise above the ocean near San Francisco's northwest corner. It is popular with runners, dog-walkers, bicyclists, painters, photographers, and others who enjoy the out-of-doors even when it is foggy as hell. Old Fort Miley is out there, the Legion of Honor, a tribute to the World War II stalwart destroyer, USS San Francisco, a golf course, and you can throw in the nearby famous Cliff House, too. Old shipwrecks are rusting in among the rocks down below, probably victims of the covering of a blinding fog. Now, happily, there are some nifty foghorn buoys dotting the entrance to the bay to help ships and things navigate with more confidence. San Francisco still has fog.

Mickey was told that Jaguar Beault likes to stay in good physical shape. He has a routine with the machines in his gym, but he is not a gym rat by any stretch although he is partial to a good health regimen. Riding a bike was something fairly new. He knows a police detective in the city who is an avid rider and where Beault got the idea to take it up.

Mickey Truke may have had a crummy termination record, but that did not mean he was not thorough in his planning and preparation. (How in hell did I miss Svetlana that day, Mickey kept wondering.) For this Beault job he carefully followed the private detective several times as he rode from his Victorian home near Lafayette Park where he and his girlfriend resided. Beault liked to pedal out to the coast on streets with the fewest hills. Truke thought Beault was being very practical, avoiding San Francisco's lung-challenging climbs on steep hills so that he could add more miles to his rides. Smart guy. Too bad I have to kill him. As Truke identified patterns in Beault's bike rides, he believed he could predict a route that would take him to Lincoln Park – the agreed-on place to kill him and hide the body – instead of some other destination favored by the private eye. Lincoln Park would be Beault's *final* destination, Mickey congratulated himself.

On this occasion, Truke saw his opportunity. This route, Mickey noticed, takes Beault to the park. Zipping ahead, Mickey parked his car and made his way through the large cypress trees to a spot where he was a classic killing distance from a turn on the bike path. On the farther side of the path, the terrain sloped quickly down into a tangle of brush and scrub and trees where it would be days or weeks before the body was found.

Willie Mays may have gone 0 for 5 yesterday, Mickey dreamed as he waited for Beault to pedal by, but today he is going to hit a grand slam homer.

Truke had on his customary daytime termination ensemble. Brown. Not black. Black would be a dead giveaway. Brown shoes, brown chinos, brown sweatshirt with a brown hoodie he pulled over his head. If he were seen, folks would assume Mickey was dressed against the fog that might settle damply over Lincoln Park. San Francisco has fog sometimes, which I know I have mentioned a couple of times, but it's important here to show you what Mickey was up to.

"Where is he?" Mickey muttered. It was taking this private eye a lot longer to pass this spot than it should have. Several times Truke had raised his silenced Ruger to passing riders only to see it wasn't Beault. Not a lot of bike riders today and that was good. Not Beault either which was not good. Straining against the damp air and the subtle shifting of the surf a short distance away, Mickey tried to hear oncoming bikes. Not so easy to do because generally they are noiseless. Dang my bad luck again, he scolded.

Yielding to the urge to see what the heck was holding up his prey, Mickey slipped from behind a tree, and with the gun held in one of the sweatshirt's deep pockets, he scrambled down to the path to sneak a look. He could see a short way up the path where Beault would be riding to this point as it turned abruptly to the left where Mickey's back was facing. He could not see Beault coming *down* the path because – at this very moment – Beault was coming *up* the path from the other direction. Mickey was leaning into the pathway. Beault was leaning into his bike on the pathway. Mickey did not hear what was coming. Beault did not see what was coming. The bike converted the arc of the pathway's turn into a tangent right through the on-duty assassin. Just more of that old refrain of this not being Mickey Truke's lucky day.

A retelling of what happened on that pathway at that moment beginning with the "oh no" shouted by Jaguar Beault and the resounding "wha..." partially asked by Mickey Truke and ending about five seconds later would demand a graphic description that you male readers would declare gruesome and you female readers would, well, you good ladies might just faint away. I'm not being a pig here when I say that, it's just how things stand. Or how things collapsed for Mickey in pain and blood and failure once again.

A couple or so salient facts, however, should be recorded. One, the gun Mickey was gripping in his sweatshirt pocket discharged. He should not have had his finger in the trigger housing, something he knew from his police academy training years before. Two, Beault's bicycle took expensive damage. Three, Mickey bled from more than a few places where his brown outfit was shredded and where a bullet had hit his leg. Four, Beault was grateful for the many safety accoutrements he was sporting as a bike rider, these protecting his head, his elbows and his knees, places he would otherwise bleed profusely for want of those protections. Five, Mickey thought he had joined those sunken boats below and become his own coastal debris. Six, this was the beginning of a useful friendship. Unusual, but useful, yes. Also, Beault picked up Truke's gun after it bounced loose during Mickey's interaction with bicycle and pathway. Beault is nobody's fool. That gun meant something even if Beault hadn't got it figured out just yet. He was distracted because he was sore all over his body.

5

Truke and Beault got back to Beault's Victorian on the edge of Pacific Heights, on the somewhat-less-expensive edge of the glamorous district away from where prices are out of reach for everyone except for the heady billionaires who can buy whatever they want whenever they want and wherever they want. They got back after Beault called Nadine and asked her to bring the car to Lincoln Park because, he fibbed, he had a flat tire. Also to bring some gauze and tape and some iodine. "Just some scrapes is all," he assured her. Nadine did what Beault asked. She wasn't surprised by the call. She had seen Jaguar Beault in action before and knew how his profession and his hobbies sometimes put him in the path of pain.

Nadine Berry is that TV reporter we have already talked about. Perhaps you have seen her on KSFG. That is, if you live in the San Francisco area. She is a terrific reporter and a real looker. In the Victorian, Nadine spent a while cleaning Mickey's many bloody cuts, swabbing them with iodine and re-taping them. She had done a quick triage in Lincoln Park mostly to minimize how much blood was going to get on the car seat. Lucky for Mickey, the bullet that hit him in the leg was just a wing job. "This is not my lucky day," he lamented several times.

Alana, Nadine's toddler daughter, stared at Mickey and at her mother's ministrations to Truke's bloody splotches. Between bites of her strawberries, she saw red splotched all over the stranger and asked, "Did the man spill his tawberries, too?"

Beault snickered at this, Nadine smiled, and Mickey said, "Not my lucky day at all."

Beault said, "Your unlucky day didn't make it any easier on me, you know." Truke did not respond. "And it could have been a lot worse if that bullet went somewhere where it would do some real damage." Truke looked at Beault and still said nothing. "Which brings me to this," Beault went on, "why did you have a gun with you and why does the gun have a silencer? I thought silencers are illegal. Who were you going to shoot?"

Truke looked at Beault then at Berry then back at Beault.

"Me," Beault said. "You were going to shoot me."

Before Mickey could say anything, Nadine patted Truke on his arm and said, "There, all patched up, Mr. Truke, the bleeding has stopped, you are loaded with anti-infection creams, and you'll be good as new before you know it."

Mickey said thanks and tried to stand. "Ouch, ow, that hurts."

"Well, no kidding," she said, "you just lost a fight with a bicycle. You should hurt."

Mickey slumped back into the cushion on the sofa. "You don't have to hurry, Mr. Truke," Nadine told him, "just sit a while and get yourself back to normal and tell us why you were out to shoot Bas."

Truke looked sharply at Nadine. "Bas? Who's that?"

"That is Bas," she said, nodding at Beault. "Bas is short for Basil. Basil is his real name. Jaguar Beault is his professional moniker. I call him Bas. If I am going to be Mrs. Basil Protherington, I can't really call him Jaguar, can I?" Bas smiled. Alana chomped another strawberry, red juice dripping down her chin.

"You were going to shoot my future husband, Mr. Truke. That I cannot forgive. You are a murderer, and..."

"Umm," Mickey interrupted, "no, I am not."

"You are an assassin, self-admitted by wielding a gun with a silencer," Nadine corrected him.

"Not exactly," Mickey counter-corrected her. "I haven't closed the deal yet. Uncle Ben told me this was my last chance. Five assignments, five duds. This was number six. I didn't get to shoot anybody even when I was a cop. So no, ma'am, I am not a killer, not an assassin. Hell, now I'm not even employed. Uncle Ben will drop me like a hot rock. And all the termination jobs will go to that crowd that's just setting up shop in Daly City or Brisbane or South Frisco or wherever Uncle Ben said they were."

"Uncle Ben, he'll let you just walk away, knowing what you know?" Beault asked. "Won't he have to kill you? With a code name like Uncle Ben and a business like assassinations, you have been up to your eyeballs in intrigue – dirty intrigue – with that fellow and you'd be a walking-around liability."

"Uncle Ben's not a code name. Uncle Ben is my uncle...Ben. He's my mom's brother, and if he even thought about reprisal against me, mom would invent new ways to dismantle him."

"I like the sound of her, Bas," Nadine said.

"Me too," Beault answered. He looked at Truke. "You were a cop? Not here in the city."

"No. In Beverly Hills."

Beault laughed. "To protect and serve the rich and famous."

Now Truke laughed. "A crime spree down there was a Latino family driving through town after eight p.m. Not that we profiled, mind you."

"What in the name of Penny's loafer made you go into the assassination business? From being a cop?" Beault asked with amazement. "That is bizarre."

"It was Uncle Ben. He can be persuasive. He is in a bunch of different businesses and had this expansion plan idea. Termination Division, he called it. He knew I could shoot. He talked me into it."

"As I said, bizarre."

"I can see how you would feel that way. You know what else?" Mickey asked.

Nadine said, "There's more to it?"

"Yeah, well, sort of. We haven't killed anybody."

"I'd say that's a good thing," Nadine pointed out.

"I agree...now...you know, in retrospect. What if I had killed Beault here after he's been so nice to me? And you, Miss Berry, nursing me the way you did. I'd feel awful. I think the Jackal would feel the same way if he was in my shoes."

"The Jackal?" Beault said.

"Yeah, you know the Jackal. The LeBron James of assassins."

"Oh."

"Of course, I'm not in the same league as the Jackal. The more I think on it, the more I believe that I have failed on six attempts because I really don't have the killer instinct, that down deep I just made sure that I didn't snuff anyone. You know, in my subconscious. Wow, Uncle Ben would be furious if he heard me saying that."

That silenced the room for a moment.

"Now what?" Mickey asked.

Beault looked at him, turned to Nadine, looked back at Truke and said, "You have just confessed to attempted murder, conspiracy, and more, all of which puts you behind bars for a few centuries. You have also implicated others in these crimes."

"Uh."

"And here's the funny thing. You confessed these things to a private investigator who has contacts in the San Francisco Police Department's criminal investigations units and...this is even funnier, you have confessed these things to probably San Francisco's top-rated investigative reporter."

Nadine jerked her head at Beault. "Probably?"

Beault began a defense of his misspeaking, but Truke went ahead with "I...uh...I didn't mean to...uh..."

"To talk so much?" Beault said, looking back at Nadine with a sheepish grin.

"Well, yeah. Boy, am I a dumb sh...slob," Mickey turned the word when he glanced at the toddler in the room.

"This is a royal mess, Nadine," Beault said. "What we should do is just cut our losses, drive Mr. Truke up to the bridge and push him off. The way he's bruised and battered right now he couldn't put up any resistance. Then the whole affair would be over and done with."

"Um..." Mickey dissented.

"No," Nadine interjected. "No way. That's no answer," she said, giving Mickey a boost of hope. "Too many witnesses," she added. Beault laughed. Truke did not. "We'll drive him up to the bridge," Nadine went on, "but we will keep going up to the hills above the Marin Headlands and we will shoot him and leave him to the mountain lions."

"No..." Mickey started to object.

"We'll use his own gun," she said. "There's some poetic irony in that, I'd say."

"Shall we make it look like a suicide?" Beault asked.

"Sure," Nadine agreed. "No, hold on a minute. If we do that, won't that let Uncle Ben off the hook?"

"Oh, yeah, I see what you mean." He didn't see what Nadine meant, but he said it anyway.

Mickey now. "You two aren't really going to kill me, are you? You're just funning with me, right? Cuz you seem like really nice people." Mickey's eyes misted.

"Are you crying, Mr. Truke?" Nadine inquired.

"No...I..."

"You should cry, Mr. Truke," Beault said, "because you are in a lot of trouble."

Mickey looked at Beault, turned toward Miss Berry, and then stared straight ahead. "I am in a lot of trouble." After a moment he said, "Maybe you should shoot me. Get it over. I think I would make a pathetic prisoner." Then after another moment, "Oh Jesus, oh Christ, oh God. Oh."

The toddler in the room said to her mother, "Mommy, that man is praying just like Uncle Grenville." Alana caught on quickly to things. She is, as mentioned, Nadine's daughter. Alana's father died in an auto accident when she was an infant.

"Yes, Alana, just like Uncle Grenville."

"Don't tell me you have an assassin in your family," Mickey said. "Uncle Grenville?"

"He's my brother," Beault said. "He's in the religion business. He has a congregation over in the Castro. He's a minister."

"Does he perform miracles? Can he perform one for me? Like make me disappear, change my appearance, get me a new name?" Truke put his elbows on his knees, reacted to the pain there, and put his head into his hands. "I must be going nuts," he announced.

"Mickey," Nadine said, "what did you mean when you talked about a new crowd going into the termination business? Are you serious?"

"What difference does that make," Mickey began out of context, "they wouldn't hire me either."

"Focus, Mickey," Beault said, "that is not what Nadine is curious about. What do you know about this?"

"Only what Uncle Ben told me. Just what I told you. Rumors of a new group getting into the business. He isn't too happy about it. He thinks because I can't do it right this new crowd will be getting all the choice assignments. Uncle Ben is really annoyed about that, I can tell you."

"Uncle Ben is annoyed about that," Beault said to Nadine.

"Yes, I heard that," she said back to Beault. "I wonder if we can do anything about that. You know, because Uncle Ben is so annoyed."

Beault smiled. "Do you think if we put our heads together we might be able to, oh, I don't know, do Joe Blough a good turn?"

"What the..." Truke gulped. "Who's this Joe Blough?"

"Joe Blough?" Beault said, "Did I say Joe Blough? I meant your Uncle Ben."

Mickey stared at Beault. "Oh."

Nadine smiled. Then she turned serious and said to Beault, "First things first. Where are we going to shoot Mickey? We've got things to do. We have to buy you a new bike, give Alana her bath, figure out who this Joe Blough is you just spoke of, and find Uncle Ben."

"Wait," Mickey gasped, "don't say you're going to shoot me."

"Why not? You were going to shoot Jaguar Beault," Nadine said dramatically. "Fair is fair, Mickey."

"Oh, God," he whimpered. Beault and Berry laughed.

6

Finding Uncle Ben was easy. Jaguar Beault is a first-rate and insightful detective and Nadine Berry is an experienced and resourceful investigative journalist. Both have an intimate knowledge of the City by the Bay. How they did it was they told Mickey to take them to Uncle Ben or else they would tie him up and pour salt into all the cuts and bruises he was wearing from his collision with Beault's bicycle. "I know where they all are, I patched them all up," Nadine said slyly to Mickey. Beault and Nadine also mentioned the police and how police forces take a dim view of assassins. Even in San Francisco. Mickey took them straight to Uncle Ben.

Uncle Ben was an inch or two taller than his nephew and should have been – maybe he was – embarrassed by his weight problem. He stuck out in front, posing challenges to the buttons on his shirt. His cheeks jiggled. He had lost a good portion of his hair and wore what was left a little longer than was complimenting. He admitted he was not married. "Not anymore, anyway." When he talked at any length, he huffed and puffed, his paunch competing with his lungs and voice box for air.

"This is real awkward," Uncle Ben admitted, whispering. "I don't normally talk to cops and reporters."

"This is real awkward for me, too," Nadine whispered. "I don't usually talk to assassins in such hallowed halls."

"Hallowed, yeah. Grace Cathedral. Good place to talk...if I gotta talk at all, because nobody's gonna overhear us. Like that's gonna matter. Here I am talking to a private cop and a reporter."

"We did not give Mickey a choice in the matter," Beault said. "Better you talk to us about this than to Joe Blough."

"There's that name again," Mickey butted in. "Who is that?"

"Stay out of this, Mickey," Uncle Ben told him. Then back to Beault and Berry. "What am I looking at here?"

"Unequivocal capitulation," Beault said.

"What if I say no?"

"Ben, Uncle Ben," Beault sing-songed, "let's not talk what if. Rather, let's talk what is as in Joe Blough."

"Who in hades is Joe Blough?" Mickey again.

"Someone your uncle happens to know about," Nadine answered. "That's true, isn't it, Ben?" Ben nodded. "Good, but we'll leave him aside for the time being. Instead, let's see how we can help each other. Let's talk."

And talk they did in soft tones respectful of the holy silence cannonading throughout the famous religious edifice, and also so they would not be overheard by the prayerful and small groups of tourists. That is, Jaguar Beault and Nadine Berry talked. Uncle Ben listened. Mickey Truke did not interrupt. Berry and Beault decided on a goal they had sketched out after Truke failed to kill Basil Protherington and before Mickey delivered the pair to his uncle. The goal was as simple as it gets – put an end to assassination associations, starting, of course, with Uncle Ben's own fledgling Termination Division. Uncle Ben's agreement to that condition came easily, but not without a long sigh as he sized up his nephew.

"We can't call you Uncle Ben, Uncle Ben," Nadine said. "What's your name?"

"It's Ben. Ben Franklin."

"You're joking."

"No. I was named after him. No relation, just some admiration on the part of my dad. I'm Benjamin Franklin. My sister is Beatrice. Mickey's mom. She's Bea Franklin, or was until she became Bea Truke.

It was just too easy for dad to do that with a last name like ours." Ben huffed and puffed. He added, "I'm Mickey's uncle. Uncle Ben."

After a short gawk at Ben's explanation, Berry and Beault went back to talking. Franklin listened. Like before. They talked about needing to find a way to bring down the upstart assassin ring supposedly based in South San Francisco that had been dropping hints and innuendos here and there about their killing expertise even if there had yet to be a corpse to call their own. Bring it down, Beault and Nadine argued, with an armful of evidence that even a jury in the ultra-liberal all-forgiving Bay Area could not mangle. That got a laugh from the four of them in the church pew. Furthermore, retire Uncle Ben's other activities that might be colored with suspicions of possible wrongdoing. That got a gasp from Uncle Ben and more huffing and puffing.

When Beault and Berry were finished talking, Ben Franklin had a turn. "I can see my hands are tied over this whole business. Yes, I'm done with the termination thing," he huffed and puffed and coughed. "Yes, I should not have started the termination thing. Hindsight, you know. And since my back is to the wall, I will do what I can to cooperate. In fact, I may be able to deliver some helpful information. I know someone in the city who has sweeping business interests. He could prove to be valuable. If he wants to be, that is. He's the one who has heard the rumors about new assassins in town. He told me about them. He thought I'd be interested from the competitive standpoint since I was...uh, you know, getting into that sort of thing. He tried to talk me out of it, by the way. Don't ask me why I did not heed his advice. I'm a schmuck, I guess. I'll have a talk with him."

"That's promising, Ben," Beault said, "you do that." He looked at Ben and Mickey and said to Nadine, "We should go."

7

South San Francisco is a real city. It may be the dumbest city name there is...if you do not include Intercourse, Pennsylvania, and Truth or Consequences, New Mexico. Happily, most people call it South City. This is not the place to discuss whether that gives it any more cachet than it deserves. They may be nice people and all, the ones who live and work there, but all they can come up with is South San Francisco? All that proves is they can read a compass. Then, on top of choosing that name, they plaster it in these huge letters on a hillside facing a whole atlas of other nearby cities, busy freeways, and in easy sight of the noisy flight patterns to and from nearby San Francisco International Airport so everybody can read about them. Read about them? It says "South San Francisco – The Industrial City." Not "A City With a Heart" or "A City of Welcomes" or "Come Visit Us" but "The Industrial City." Why don't they just write "Smokestacks R Us"?

It gets better. Unfortunately for South City, there are some low-rent commercial zones that tend to attract business enterprises with imbalanced balance sheets and the profit-challenged managements who labor over them and ignore their responsibilities to neighborhoods and community. You know, deadheads. Among them at the time of this reporting was a family recently relocated from another country. Like most immigrants, they viewed America as a destination where they could work hard, get ahead, improve the lot of their children and enjoy the freedoms the U.S bestows on everyone who behaves. The family's skills were limited, so they went into a business segment, which, despite being very competitive, is ripe with promise: crime.

Scott and Zelda Menzies are the elderly patriarch and matriarch of the family from Australia, elderly enough so that the day-to-day chores and decisions are shared with the children, four boys – Bryce, Bruce, Bert and Burt – and, somewhat less so, with three girls, the triplets, April, May and June. April and May, born just before midnight on November thirty, and June, just after on December first, are married to three ex-Aussie Rules footballers from Perth in southwest Australia. The odd juxtaposition of the girls' birthdates gets a lot of raised eyebrows whenever it comes up. June likes the separate attention she gets on her exclusive natal day.

Three of the four boys married Russian beauties. From a catalogue of other Russian beauties. Bryce is unmarried. Six marriages had produced fourteen children. Three cousins had joined the Menzies when the trip to America was decided on. That made thirty-two people in all, a housing challenge in their adopted Bay Area where limited turf and unmet demand made population densities high, very unlike Australia where land is plentiful to build on if the money and the inclination and needs are present. Crowded double-and-triple-up in scattered rentals in South City was just one more motivation for the Menzies to try their hands at some get-rich-quick schemes. Tough cookies, they said, if some of the schemes were unlawful.

It did not start off that way for the Menzies. The able-bodied buckled down and got jobs or opened businesses. Bert and Burt got separate territories to deliver the San Francisco Chronicle each morning. They cleverly piggybacked other newspaper routes in their territories for some added revenues. Bruce got a job as a limo driver, keeping his sanity in the maze of roads and hills and cities and traffic in the Bay Area by relying heavily on a dash-mounted GPS mapping system. It even talked to him.

April and May leased a roach coach, or lunch wagon, and lucked into a couple of lucrative business complexes in the Silicon Valley where they had steady customers.

The three ex-footballers were snapped up by nightspots in San Francisco's North Beach as doormen. (They are bouncers.) Bryce worked as a TSA agent at San Francisco International Airport. Not possessing a U.S. passport did not seem an obstacle to his hiring into that position. Your government at work.

June heard of a Chinese man who owned storefronts throughout Chinatown and elsewhere. Some are tearooms, some are social clubs, some are souvenir stores, some are liquor stores, some are legitimate, many are gambling holes. Numbers was a favorite of the clientele. June became a bagman...er, bagwoman.

The three Russian women married to the Menzies boys worked nights for an upstanding, licensed and bonded office cleaning service. The hours were unfortunate for the family thing, the money was less than satisfactory – though a lot more than they would have earned in their depressed old country – but certain goodies they could fit in their pockets to bring home pleased everyone in the Menzies clan.

Nevertheless. You see, there were thirty-two mouths to feed, a load of beds to make, rent, plus other expenses unlike the ones they had worried over in Western Australia where there was a lower cost of living than in the world's favorite city. And gasoline. "Crikey, why is it so much more here than anywhere else in the states?" they asked. "What do they do, add Napa Valley vintage wine to the gas tanks? Who makes these bloomin rules? And us," the Menzies complained, "a limo, two cars to deliver papers, a gas-guzzling lunch truck. This is eating us bleedin alive."

Crime. That's where the money would be and that's where the Menzies headed after a series of family meetings on money matters.

The need for speed in their new venture was driven by the dwindling bank accounts they held. Even the Aussies knew that haste would make waste. Avoid missteps. Choose smartly. Study up. Study. They were used to that. The four brothers took college degrees at Western Australia University in Crawley, a suburb of Perth, and the three sisters at Murdoch in the same city. Not Crawley, Perth. The three husbands of the triplets had tried college, but left early to take up professional footballing.

Now in America they turned to new studies. They didn't read the penal codes, they just read the newspaper every day and watched the local news on television and easily detected the methods bad blokes were employing to take in tax-free dollars…if they didn't get lax like those birds in the news columns or on the tube and get themselves caught. America, the land of opportunity.

Bert and Burt, delivering papers before sunup, turned to jacking electronic gizmos from parked cars and anything else of value not tied down along their routes. The stuff was easy to fence. America, the land of opportunity. Half the riders in Bruce's limo – usually the drunk ones – were easy to shake down. ("Do you want me to dump you in East Palo Alto, in a tux, late at night? I didn't think so.") The scam worked every time, and denying any charges would be just too easy. Prove it, he would say.

June was especially generous. She offered protection. Her bag-running task put her in contact with lots of retail outlets, many run by Chinese proprietors, some of the nicest folks she had ever met and who, she observed, might be cowed by police uniforms. She believed that anyway. She was told by one of her brothers that in China, where the shopkeepers and their parents or grandparents had come from, police uniforms radiated threats and it was the same here in the U.S. Her brother was full of crap on many topics. June, dropping suggestive hints to these very shopkeepers on her route, said they needn't worry, she'd take care of things. For a modest tithe. She didn't know how she was going to protect anyone or who she was protecting them from. The shop owners hadn't pursued that. They were a most easy going bunch of people.

Scott and Zelda liked what they saw. Up to a point. That point was a net income figure still short of their needs. Oh, their fundamental needs were getting covered, you know, rent and food and clothing and fuel and such. But other – more visceral – needs were still a reach away. This was America. In America you bought stuff. Even if you didn't need it. That's how you kept score. And the Menzies were losing. What do you do when you are losing? You go to the playbook and see what you can do different. Running numbers and selling protection were okay and scamming drunks and boosting things from cars got you a little viggerish. But the family had to do more. Something to bring in some real money. One of the B-rts suggested bank robbery. "It's in our bloody bones, for Christ's sake. We're Australians. We came into being from criminals. Banks is where the cash is."

"Oh, B-rtie, B-rtie, B-rtie," Scott intoned as he patiently reminded the boy how "we have a bummed-out history with that one. We got away by the narrowest margin. Didn't get a penny out of the deal, and two of you had to lay low for months while the ink that exploded over you when you opened the moneybag wore off. It wasn't even real money. And the newspapers and the TV? They had the time of their lives making us feel like the dippiest bank robbers in Western Australian history." He paused. "Didn't get a damned penny out of the deal. No. No more bloody banks."

"How about kidnapping? Take one or two of those tech billionaires down in the Silicon Valley. Piece of cake," June offered.

Scott thought for a moment, and then said. "Maybe. The bad thing, though, is it brings in the FBI. They'd be relentless. We'd do serious jail time if we got caught. I'll think about it."

Zelda nodded and added, "Has promise, I agree. But it has big risks. But if we killed someone, we..."

"Momma! What are you talking about? Are you drinking again?" one of the girls blurted out.

"Shut your disrespectful mouth, young lady. Let me finish. I'm saying if we do hits on people there'd be good money – hell, great money – in that. And no witnesses left behind."

"Assassinations," Scott said with a thoughtful look.

"Yes," Zelda said, smirking at the daughter who had insulted her. Zelda hadn't had a drink since breakfast.

"That has even more promise than the kidnapping thing," Scott went on. Some of the family nodded. "There's always somebody who wants another somebody out of the way. Terminations. We would be termination determinators. This could be it. Momma's right, too, there'd be big money in it, I bet. Let's us give it a go."

"Yeah, but how do we get customers," Bruce asked. "I mean, can we have a big advertising campaign? Have people queue up for Assassinations, Ltd.? That'd be tricky. I think the coppers would see right through us."

"Leave that to me, mate," Scott told him. "Remember what I've already told you, we've got two things going for us, one, all of the people along your routes, and, two, the whole bloody Internet at our fingertips, haven't we? Leave this to me."

8

In his Outer Richmond office, Beault's phone message machine was blinking when he walked in. The phone recorder is a new one with state-of-the-art digital features that Nadine tried to coach him on. It was there on his desk because he could afford a new one now. The jewels from that pigeon statue, remember? Ah, Beault thought as he eyed the blink-blink-blink from the machine, this will be a couple of candidates for the job I posted. He put his keys and briefcase down, shrugged off his sweater, opened a window in defiance of the cold air outside, set his coffeemaker in motion and sat down.

The private eye got a tablet out and a pen to write down the two or three names and numbers he would need to answer. He pushed the red-blinking light and was told, "You have forty-six new messages." He shook his head and reached over to push the stop button.

Beault reflected. When he left the state employment office the other day he had newly forming thoughts about the unfortunate conditions of the job market in California, notably in San Francisco. It shouldn't be this way, he commiserated. Didn't the peninsula house the money-printing tech monoliths in the Silicon Valley and in his own city? Couldn't everybody get a job? Not being a politician or an economist or, until now, an employer, Beault had no answer.

Now, a few days since posting his job need, his new thoughts about the job market solidified, knocking him for a loop. Forty-six people wanting to see about one job with a shamus? This was disturbing to Beault. He pulled out a second pen and set it aside as a backup in the event that forty-six names and numbers and any special notes depleted the ink in the first one. He took a deep breath and pushed the replay button.

"This is (Jane Doe) and I am calling about the job of office assistant for Mister Jaguar Beault. My phone number is...I have twenty-two years experience managing offices of various types..." That one sounded pretty solid.

Next, "My name is (Jane Doe) and I am calling..." Same thing.

Next, "This is (John Roe) and I am..." Ditto.

One by one came a name, a plea, a phone number. An hour passed and Beault wasn't half way through the note taking from the forty-six messages. He hit the stop button, leaned back in his chair and bellowed, "Aaaaahh." He went to the bathroom, came out, got more hot coffee, stretched his arms and back, and touched his toes.

Basil Protherington was raised in a family that honored courtesy. Consequently, it did not occur to him that he could close his job search window right here and say he had plenty of candidates to select from. No, he felt strongly that he needed to listen to each caller's name and put a phone number to it. So he patiently pressed the lighted button.

"Hello, Mister Jaguar Beault Investigations" – that voice – "I bet you can't guess who this is" – that goddam voice – "yeah, it's me, Crystal" – that effing nitwit – "I haven't called you in a long time. How are...hey, I seen, uh, saw you did a big murder thing or something. That was so cool. I tole all my friends about it. Well, I'm sixteen now and a junior at school and I figgered I should give you a call and see how things is between us. You really freaked me out last time we talked. Oh, that was cool, too, so, you know, here's my phone number in case you still don't have it from before."

Beault wrote down the number on a separate page. He hit the stop button. He leaned back in his chair and bellowed, "Aaaaaaahhh." A moment passed and then a knock on his door.

"Mr. Beault, Basil..." a voice called through the closed door. "Are you in trouble? Do you need help?" These were intriguing questions, especially the second one. It was intriguing because from whom it came. It came from a floor mate of the private detective, one Rowena Willingham, Doctor Rowena Willingham. She is a shrink with an office a couple of doors down from Beault's. And when a shrink says to you do you need help, you become intrigued. Beault let her in.

"Look here, Rowena, you're a shrink, uh, I mean a psychiatrist and I..."

"I'm not a psychiatrist, Bas, I'm a psychologist."

"Really? What's the difference?"

"About a hundred fifty dollars an hour," the doctor said.

Beault did not know if she was making a joke or describing the state of affairs in the head medicine fraternity. Neither did Beault ask the doc which side of that hundred and a half difference she came down on. Protherington discretion.

Beault motioned the doctor to a chair and got her a cup of coffee for the accepted offer he had made. He refilled his own cup and set about telling the shrink the story of Crystal.

"It's okay for you to call me a shrink, Mr. Private Detective, if I can call you a gumshoe," she negotiated. Beault nodded his acceptance of the rebuke.

You'll remember Crystal if you read that pigeon book. She gave Jaguar Beault a real pain just below his lower back and behind his back pants pockets. He told Rowena of the slutty calls, Crystal's demonstrable shallowness, her apparent wanton ways, and how he finally ended it – he mistakenly believed – with threats if she ever called again.

"Now the empty-headed girl has called." He sighed, but his rage was not masked. "Do you want to hear her message?" he asked the doctor.

"No," she said.

"Here, I'll find it and you can listen."

Rowena chuckled. After about five minutes of fumbling through the candidates' phone messages and Rowena's polite protestations that she did not need to listen, Beault finally located Crystal. "Here, listen."

Doctor Willingham, not on the clock by the way, listened, knowing pretty surely that she did not have a choice, and commented when Crystal had finished, "She's perky, isn't she?"

"Perky? That's what you call that? You know what I want to call that?"

"No, because you will lose your temper and use language I've never heard before and then you'll want me to diagnose this girl." Rowena kept her no-expression face pointed right at Beault until she couldn't hold it and broke into laughter.

"Oh right," Beault said, "just like everybody else who thought this was so funny. You should have heard my brother. Grenville said it..."

"Grenville? I haven't seen him over here in weeks. How is he doing? I'd love to see him again. When do you think he might be stopping over here? We could all go to lunch. Well, unless you're too busy to join us."

Beault hung his head. He said, "Doctor Willingham, we have gone all over this, haven't we? Grenville and his special situation. And your own special situation. Your special medical and psychological training and experience with patients and, yes, your savvy. You should know better. Grenville is gay. This is not the first time I have told you that my brother is a gay man. God, it's like I have to give this sermon to every woman who has ever met Grenville and me."

"Well, you tell him for me that I miss him and look ahead to maybe that lunch."

"Yes, doctor. Now, where were we?"

"Here's what you do about your little Crystal there, Bas. Don't do anything."

"Nothing?"

"Yes, nothing. She's only sixteen and she's got an infatuation or a crush or whatever. She's full of hormones and I'll go so far to say she's also bored. Her life will be changing at a quick pace. She'll get over you. I know that will break your heart, but she will. This will pass. Ignore her."

"I guess so. You're the head doctor."

"Excellent. And yes I am the doctor, the head doctor. That'll be two hundred bucks for this session. We'll meet again in a week and we will..." she tumbled into a long laugh. Beault tried to laugh as well.

9

The body lay face down on a boat dock overlooking Richardson Bay in the city limits of Sausalito just to the north of the Golden Gate Bridge. Two bullets entered the head just above the right ear and a little to the back. As a consequence, the body was a dead one. Police gave out few details in the hours that followed the discovery. They identified the deceased as Byron Johnson, aged sixty-five, and a local resident, locally known also as a figure in the hip-hop entertainment scene. They did not make public that it was two .22 caliber shots that apparently killed him, nor that his spouse, aged twenty-three and extremely distraught at this time, had been called back from Lake Tahoe where she had planned to be and where she previously broadcast widely to her friends and acquaintances that she would be visiting a friend.

Nor did the cops reveal that the victim died leaving an iron-tight will, making the grieving widow sole owner of all of the loving pair's properties and money and investments and other niceties. Neither did the police explain that the poor, no, not poor, make that the weeping girl was the one hundred percent beneficiary of her husband's hefty, real hefty, life insurance portfolio. The Sausalito police kept these facts to themselves. That is, the police said nothing about the financial implications because either they did not know anything about them at the time or that it was plainly nobody else's business.

Some of Mrs. Johnson's neighbors tried to bolster the distracted girl's spirits. They were pretty sure the police were unnecessarily keeping stuff to themselves. Most people in Sausalito knew right away who the victim of the shooting was. Just not why he was a victim or who made him a victim. Separately, therefore, anonymous sources spilled their guts to the newspapers and to San Francisco television and radio stations. Some of what they said was actually somewhat factual. Tweets and text messages offering opinions proliferated throughout the scenic bayside village. Many opinions landed on the possibility that the young lady herself maybe had a hand in the sad demise of her husband. Only speculation, they confessed. The event was like a July Fourth picnic in the park but without the tables filled with organic foodstuffs grown locally and priced accordingly. Sausalito is in Marin County. Marin County is in California. California is in an orbit by itself.

Los Menendez Banda, hearing of the killing, quickly took credit for the hit via phone calls to the media. Most of the reporters fielding the calls didn't understand the Spanish name. Most of the reporters also did not give a darn. It was a lead on a story and that is all that mattered.

"Perfect," Scott Menzies proclaimed in South San Francisco. "This fell into our laps like manna from heaven. We're on our way. A rich dead wanker and we get credit."

"Was he rich?"

"I don't know. But he was about three times older than his trophy wife. You figure it out."

"Los Menendez Banda? Why couldn't we use a different name? We're not Mexican," one of the girls asked.

"That's the whole point, inin't? Throws the bloody suspicion away from us white people and gives the assassins a scary name, dunnin't. Word'll be out that there's an effective termination service now operating right here in the San Francisco Bay Area. We'll drop a few more hints here and there along our usual routes, you know, on the network we already have in place. Hells bells, June, you should be able to do a whole campaign by yourself in Chinatown, in the Tenderloin, and up in North Beach." Scott Menzies was on a roll.

Elsewhere, but with less sophistication and practically no planning, although with an equal purpose as the South City crowd, calls to the media from someone in San Francisco claimed credit for the same Sausalito shooting. The caller said the "tough-ass killing" was by the "tough-ass Haight-Ashbury Wild Bunch." Only half of the reporters fielding the calls were able to hold off laughing at the name.

When the news teams on television reported the dual credit-taking of the murder of the well-known hip-hop mogul, Mr. Byron Johnson, the on-air newsreaders had to bring years of journalistic neutrality and hundreds if not thousands of hours of facing television cameras to properly deliver hard, and in this case, sad news without splitting their sides. "Haight-Ashbury Wild Bunch?" some of them intoned, failing their honored profession with unintended smirks.

In an apartment in that very Haight-Ashbury district just east of and abutting the famous Golden Gate Park, one of San Francisco's great landmarks, a small group of young-to-middle-age men scrambled in front of a twenty-one-inch TV and whooped when their name was broadcast. "This is so totally cool," one of them said. He was about thirty years old and dressed in loose-fitting brown pants that would go for about three dollars at the Goodwill store down on Haight Street. His pullover was one that would not carry a designer's label. No self-respecting designer would own up to it. If the thirty-year-old had shoes, they couldn't be seen in the clutter of the housing unit.

"I really dig our name, Haight-Ashbury Wild Bunch," a skinny twenty-looking fellow said as he watched the newscasts. "It's totally cool."

"I just said that."

"I can say it, too."

"Find something new to say."

"I can..."

"Shut it." This came from a forty-year-old thin guy who had selected clothes off the same racks around the corner at the Goodwill store. "We don't need no bullshit arguing. Now we gotta get our asses in gear and make hay from this thing in Sausalito. We gotta convince people that we done this."

"Yeah, but how?"

"I'll do that. I'll do the thinking. You just follow orders."

"We could use Craigslist," another disheveled youth said. "I heard some women talking about how you can find all kinds of neat shit on that. I think it's on a computer. I guess you hafta pay though. We got any money?"

Someone else asked, "Do we have a computer?"

The forty-year-old didn't say anything. He was thinking. Or so it seemed. "Craigslist," he finally said. "Yeah, that might be just the answer. I'm glad I thought of that."

"Hey, I..."

"I said shut it, alla ya. I got things to think over."

Another young undernourished guy woke up from a mattress on the floor. He was in undershorts and a tee shirt. When he stood up he kicked over a guitar standing against a wall. It made no musical sounds when it fell. It had no strings. "Have we been on the TV yet? Did our name get out there? It'd be so cool if that was the case. Has it? Did our..."

"Holy shit. Are all you as dumb as you look?" the forty-year-old self-anointed Wild Bunch leader protested. "No more talk, no more of your bullshit. I got thinking to do. I gotta find where's there a computer and see about this Craigslist."

"When is rent due?" a voice spoke, cracking the good will of the room.

"Rent! Shit," said the Haight-Ashbury Wild Bunch leader. "It's covered for this month. Hey, only three of us are working and pulling in any scratch. The rest of you hafta go out and find work or steal some money or bum enough so we don't get our butts tossed out into the street."

"Maybe you could kill somebody and make some money that way. Like assassins, like," a twenty-year-old said. "Maybe that's what you should do."

"I told you idiots to shut it. Let me think. Jesus, where did I find you assholes?"

"Hey, man, eat shit and die. We ain't no idiots. Where'd you be without us? We pitch in for the goddam rent, remember."

The Wild Bunch leader stared at the kid and refused to answer.

"Oh my aching arches," Scott Menzies cried out. "Who in hell is this Haight-Ashbury Wild Bunch?"

"Father, Haight-Ashbury is a place up in the city. It's called that because..."

"I know what it is. You don't need to tell me."

"You asked."

"What I want to know is what is this Wild Bunch. Who are they? Them saying they killed the old man in Sausalito. Never heard of them before." He looked at the several family members with him in the apartment's living room. "Never needed to until now. And now they're taking the wind out of our sail."

"How?"

"By saying the same thing as we're saying. By taking the credit for this kill."

"Oh yeah, I see."

"God!" Scott huffed. "Let me think."

A twenty-something came into the apartment in the Haight and mortified three others lounging on beds and the floor. "Holy crap, do you have to bust in here like that?" he got shouted at. "Scared me."

"Scared you? All I did was open a freakin door and walk in."

"No, you busted in."

"Like hell. Here, I'll show you," he said, turning to the doorway again.

"You don't got to show me shit. I know what I saw. And what I heard."

"God, what a ding-a-ling you are. I know what we should do. We should make up a secret knock so that you know who's coming in and you won't get scared when a door opens."

"Where ya been anyway? You said you was gonna get coffee."

"I got coffee. That's what this is. I got it. God, you're a butthead."

"That's the coffee you got? A can of coffee? You gonna drink that?"

"It's coffee, man, what is your beef?"

"Okay, go make some coffee."

"I will. Where's the coffee thing?"

"You mean a coffee maker, right?"

"Well, duh, yeah, a coffee maker. Where's it at?"

"Look around."

He looked around. "Hey, I don't see it. Where'd it go?"

"There isn't one, just like your brain."

"Why isn't there one?"

"The same reason there wasn't one yesterday. Or last week. Or last month. We don't got a coffee maker. Haven't had one."

"Okay, genius, where'd all the coffee come from we been drinking if we haven't had a coffee maker?"

"How dippy are you? We go get it from places that sell it. In cups, not in tin cans."

"Really? Then what am I supposed to do with this? It's not real coffee." The can of coffee was held up as evidence.

"Hand it to me and I'll shove it up your..."

The door busted open and scared the shit out of the four tenants discussing coffee. "Did you hear? Some Mexicans say they capped that dude in Sausalito," a new twenty-something yelled into the room.

"Quit your yellin, you scared the shit out of us."

"I what? How? All I did was come in here. What's going on, anything I should know about? What are you scared of?"

"We're scared because you..."

Boom. A bedroom door flew open and pounded against a dresser pushed too close to the doorway. The forty-something came out of the bedroom wearing undershorts and a tank top. "I'm sleeping in there and then I'm not sleeping in there because you lumps are out here making enough noise to wake me up. I'm wondering why. Why?"

"Asswipe here bought coffee. Get this, he buys a tin can of the stuff."

The forty-something looked at the coffee can and said, "We don't have a coffee maker. What good will a tin can of coffee do us?" he asked, slipping into the coffee debate.

"That's what I said to him."

"What did he say?"

"He said he doesn't know we don't got a coffee maker."

"How long's he been camping here?"

"Dunno. Half a year?"

"Half a year and he don't know we don't have a coffee maker? Is he blind?"

"I'm standing right here. You act like I'm not here."

"You ain't here or else you are blind. We don't have a coffee maker."

"Okay, okay, shit."

"What was the other yelling about?"

"This one here came running in yelling about some Mexicans."

"Why, what happened with Mexicans?" the forty-something turned.

"I just heard out on Haight that some Mexicans say they's the ones who killed that guy in Sausalito."

"They what?" the forty-something shouted. "Was it on TV?"

"Hell if I know."

"Why'd they do that?"

"Maybe the same reason we did."

"Why'd we do it?" another twenty-something, who had not spoken during the coffee discussion, asked.

Everybody looked at the forty-something. He scratched his chin, scratched his head, scratched his crotch, and announced, "Goddam it." He shook his head then said, "We got any coffee?"

The guy with the unopened can of ground coffee said, "Here."

Zelda shuffled out of the kitchen with a drink in her hand. "We're out of coffee," she said into the room to no one in particular. "Someone should go to the store." No one stirred. "Shcottiee," she said to her husband, dabbing the corner of her mouth with a little finger to wipe away droplets of her third drink, "Who are these, uh, Wilder Bunchums?"

"Don't know, pet, don't know who they are."

"We should find out," one of the girl's husbands suggested. "Then we'd know." Scott stared at the man and began to say something to him but stopped. "But how do we find out who they are?" the husband added.

"That's the mystery, ininit? Who are they and how do we find out?" Scott summarized. "I just did a quick lookup on the Internet. No hits on that name. They must be hiding deep down in the clover."

Zelda swallowed the last of her drink and said, "We should try to find out who they are." She got ignored.

10

There were not forty-six applicants for the office assistant position open in the Jaguar Beault Investigations Company. Remember, one of those calls was from the pathetic Crystal. No, there were instead seventy-nine applicants because the next day Beault's fancy digital phone message retrieval machine captured thirty-four more. Beault did the arithmetic in his head: 46 calls on day one plus 34 more on day two equals 70. Subtract Crystal and you get 69. He noodled for a second and then chastised himself. That's not right, it's 46 plus 34 equals 80. Yeah. And 80 minus Crystal is 79. That's better, Beault congratulated himself on his improved calculating.

Beault wondered again, silently, why there was this long lineup of job seekers when the world-famous tech world around him in the Bay Area should be hiring people in droves, vacuuming up anyone in the idle work force. Still there was no telling answer from the boss in this one-man private eye enterprise who had not turned into an economist overnight or learned anything more since he saw that throng of unemployed in the employment building where he had the same question.

Yes, he had no answer. At the same time, he admitted, it was not for him to provide the answer. His job was to interview eighty, no, seventy-nine people for the single job opening in his cozy office. So he set about doing just that...for about two seconds before he realized that if he followed that plan he would be able to take on a new office assistant in maybe a year. With luck on his side. So he did the practical thing. He picked a phone message at random, listened to it, liked the sound of the woman's voice – grandmotherly – and called Dagmar Davos and said, "You're hired. When can you start?"

11

"**Y**our girlfriend called," Nadine said to her hubby-to-be who looked up from his book, paused for a beat, and then said, "I told her not to call here. I tell all my girlfriends not to call here."

"This one didn't get the message," Nadine said, trying to act offended.

Beault laughed. "Who was it?"

"The one who hates me."

"The one who hates you? Nobody hates you. Who...oh, Miriam."

"Yes, Miriam."

"She doesn't hate you. Not anymore. I think she's past that. Hates you? How do you know about that?"

"She told me."

Beault stared. "If I am the detective in this house, why is it I am in the dark about things so often? When did she tell you about that?"

"When you proposed to me. Remember how I had to drag that out of you?"

"That's not..."

"Don't worry, I still said yes, didn't I?"

"Hey, that's not what..."

"Anyway, I went to see her. I knew you two cared for each other, and I wanted to see how much. We talked. She told me she hated me because she thought I was trying to horn in on Grenville. She was...she probably still is smitten with your brother."

"She..."

"Miriam's a nice girl. I like her. I gather she is over you."

"My dear, the women in my life don't get over me. They carry that torch as a symbol of unfulfilled dreams. They..."

"Are you going to call her? She said it might be important."

"Did she leave her number?"

"It's the same one you have memorized, my chickadee. Go call her. Tell her hello from me."

Riding on the new tires on the new wheels on the new axles on the new chassis on his new car, Beault glided smoothly over the roadways to Sausalito except for those San Francisco moments when he tried but failed to avoid potholes. Crossing the bridge brought his spirits up high. Beault hadn't been across the mile-and-a-half-span of the Golden Gate Bridge in some time. He missed that thrill. He reminded himself that it was worth the steadily rising tolls to experience the iconic masterpiece. He was on his way to Miriam's junk store.

"You know, Basil, that check you sent me, I was overwhelmed. You had no reason to do that," Miriam said warmly.

"Grenville and I knew right away that the money we got out of those jewels was not for me alone. Among others, Miriam, you got some because you helped me – us – solve that blessed Madagascar Pigeon fiasco."

"It was very generous of you."

"Gren and I loved the letter you sent thanking us. It was beautiful. You can write."

"It came from here," Miriam said, pointing at her heart.

"We could tell."

"Coffee?" Miriam suggested.

"Sure."

"Let's head down the street. I know a place. I'll lock up for a while. Where's that clock sign? Oh yeah, here it is." The sign advised, "Back in five minutes."

Beault suppressed a laugh, remembering when Miriam handed him that same sign when they went upstairs alone in the afternoon that one time.

As they sat down in the café, Beault said, "Nadine says hello. She was razzing me over your phone call."

"I knew she would. She is special. You are very lucky you have her."

"Don't I know that. And that, Mir, is in comparison to you."

"Have you set a date?"

"We're trying to work around Grenville's church calendar. It'll be a small wedding in his church in the Castro."

"He'll be proud to marry you."

"I'll be proud it's him doing the honors. Nadine said she'd have it no other way."

They drank coffee. Beault said, "I don't mean to be nosey, but are you still seeing Ty?"

Miriam put her coffee cup down and closed her eyes. "I can't answer that, Basil. I can't say no, I can't say yes. It's complicated. He and Ping Bodie have not handled things well. Ty's mom – Ping's daughter – in prison for murder. Ty's sister in a mental institution. His real father is in the lockup. That Crabbe dirtbag is in jail. The both of them – Ty and Ping – they're still trying to live all this down. Ty," Miriam choked up, "Ty even changed his name. He changed it legally, that is. Now he's just Ty Laven, not Lavender. We talk, we see each other occasionally, but he's...he's...you know what...he's lost. I tell him I will try to help. He says okay but then he withdraws."

Miriam was crying. Beault held her hands across the table. "You're a treasure, Miriam. I hope Ty recognizes that and lets you into his life for support."

"Me too."

They got coffee refills and talked some more before Beault said, "You had a reason to call me."

"I did. It's about that shooting here. The Byron Johnson killing. Everyone here in town knows he is a bigwig in the music business. Everybody's talking about it."

"Oh yeah, that. Not the kind of publicity Sausalito wants, I'm sure. And you know what he does. That hasn't been released yet officially. I don't know why your cops are keeping that to themselves. It can't be a big secret. Just one of the things they haven't released.

Maybe it's because they haven't had a first-rate homicide in ages. They're out of practice."

"Bas, we're a small town. Everybody here knows these things. Many people know him. I know him, knew him. I know her, too. Donna-Ellie. What a lifestyle they lived in that crazy hip-hop world where there is unlimited money and power. And the jealousies. God, I bet they eat each other."

Beault convulsed. "Sorry."

"I was down at the yacht club and this is all anyone is talking about," Miriam said. "What they're saying is that it looks real bad for her. A young hottie with an old fart of a dead husband."

"She told the police she was up in Tahoe when Johnson was killed. That's what the first reports said. Are you saying different?" Beault asked.

"Bas, Donna-Ellie was not up in Tahoe when her husband was murdered."

"What about her alibi?"

"Are all alibis true?"

"Uh."

"I saw her that night – oh, she didn't see me – she was with a man who looked and dressed like a hip-hopper...if you'll excuse my stereotyping," Miriam said glancing around the coffee shop, "and the revelation that I know what hip-hoppers look like."

"I'm guessing you haven't told the police here."

"Good guess."

"Why?"

"Because there is a dead man and an on-the-loose killer. I don't want to advertise that I know what I know."

Beault gazed at Miriam. "I don't blame you. There'd be a risk."

"Can you do something about this? You're the famous private eye."

"You mean like me advertise that information while there is an on-the-loose killer on the loose?"

"Well, yeah."

"I'll tell Lieutenant Blough. I can earn some points with the San Francisco police. I really don't need to score any points here in Sausalito.

Joe can bring that information over to your chief. The cops here can take it from there. Your name won't even come up. Tell me what you can about that sighting."

"I was jogging. It was getting dark and Donna-Ellie and her, uh, companion, drove slowly by in that big gas-guzzler she drives. I guess she couldn't recognize me. But I sure as shootin saw who she was. It made no impression on me at the time, but then Byron's murdered on the same day. That day. Bas, she was here. That night."

"In her car? The one she ostensibly drove up to the lake? She was in it here in your fair city? When her spouse was breathing his last? That would certainly cancel her alibi."

"Yes."

Beault thought. "Hey, I know, the cops can look into gas purchases. If she drove up there to establish this alibi of hers and then drove back to shoot her mister and then drove back up to Tahoe and used a credit card for petrol, there'd be a record of that."

"See, you are a fair detective."

"Yes."

"More than fair, love."

"On some days," Beault nodded. "This means she likely had a hand in the thing," Beault said almost to himself.

"That crowd Byron ran with and her a part in it. She flaunts herself, Bas, like a cheap hooker. Anybody might have helped her if she pressed hard enough."

"She could have found an independent contractor to do it," Beault said.

"That what you tecs call them? Independent contractors?"

"Assassins, hired killers, hit men, yeah. I'm getting to know more about that. I'll have to tell you about my new friend, Mickey Truke."

"Well, I've told you what I saw," Miriam reiterated. "And I'm not mistaken. I also have to tell you that Donna-Ellie was not born with the depth to think it through by herself, to go out and hire a professional. She, if she is the one, would have turned her attractiveness to her advantage toward somebody who would fall for that. Somebody in that rap scene."

"Not a pretty picture."

"Any ideas yourself, Bas?"

"Funny you should ask." Beault described the mystery of the emerging assassination rings across the bridge that quickly jumped to take credit for the Byron Johnson killing. "There are doubts about those claims because there are doubts about the claimants."

"You on the case, Mr. Jaguar Beault?"

"Only on the sidelines, giving moral support to the real detectives. I got involved on a bike ride over in Lincoln Park."

Miriam asked him what that meant and he told her the story of Mickey Truke and Uncle Ben.

"You sure do run into the weirdest people, Basil," she said.

"Just lucky, I reckon."

"He planned to assassinate you, and now you're having cookies and coffee with him and asking him for help in a mystery. What are you, some kind of rehabilitation service?"

"Naw. I...we plan to use Mickey in a scheme to quash these assassin-pretenders. He'll fit right in."

Beault paid for the coffees and the two strolled back to Miriam's junk store.

"When are you going to tell your Lieutenant Blough about Donna-Ellie?" Miriam asked.

"As soon as I am back in my office. He'll want to move on this pretty fast. He can act the big city cop with your little seaside resort police force. Show off. Pose like a know-it-all. The peacock of the walk."

"Really?"

"No. He's more professional than that. He will, however, gloat a little."

"And you won't, Bas?"

"Me? Good lord no. No. Not a bit. Not my style. Professional. Low key. Civic minded. Pass the credit on to others."

They both laughed a little.

"Give us a kiss, Basil, and tell Nadine I return her hello. And be careful, you big lug. You are going to invite me to the wedding, aren't you?"

"Of course. I know you'll want to see Grenville."

"Oh yes, Grenville."

"Lieutenant Blough, please."

"He's not here."

"Do you know when he will be back?"

"No."

"Do you know where he is so I can reach him?"

"No."

"It's kind of important."

"That don't change my answer."

"Huh. Well...oh, is Sergeant Headley in?"

"Hey, Dick, line three." Beault quickly pulled the phone away from his ear as the shouting pounded in.

"Headley."

"Hi, Dick, it's Beault."

"What's up?"

"First, where'd you get that guy who answered the phone? He acted like he's five minutes away from retiring on a full pension."

"That's Sergeant Young. He's old. Not quite ready to hang up his shield and piece yet, but soon. He doesn't think it's his job to play phone operator."

"What's he do?"

"Nobody knows."

"Oh, I get it. He's bulletproof."

"Yeah, if he was a ballplayer, he'd have a long-term, no-trade contract." Headley heard Beault guffawing.

"Dick, I have a source who I trust who says that our poor Widow Johnson, who is in deep mourning over the sudden demise of her wealthy husband, was not up at Lake Tahoe when those two bullets pierced his head."

"And she was where? Or do I even have to ask?"

"You guessed it...Sausalito."

"Isn't that the scene of the crime?" Headley sniggered.

"I believe it is, but I would want to review the police report to be sure," Beault sniggered back.

"This source you trust, he describes how he knows the bereaved Mrs. Johnson was in the bayside resort at the time of her hubby's death?"

"She saw her. Also Mrs. Johnson was in the company of someone dressed like a hip-hopper."

"She, Beault? You got a she housed someplace across the bridge? I don't like the sound of this. I may have to tell Miss Berry."

"Miss Berry is well acquainted with my Sausalito past...emphasis on past, Sergeant."

"Okay, go on."

"The hot little Mrs. Johnson drives a big gas-guzzler. If some enterprising police investigator discovered a couple of tanks of gas purchases allowing the anti-ecological car to be driven down the I-80 from Lake Tahoe and be in Sausalito at the time of the killing and then return back up the I-80 to Tahoe to establish her alibi, that investigator might have some useful evidence. With a couple of credit card receipts, the enterprising investigator could bend Mrs. Johnson like a twig."

"They wouldn't need to resort to a rubber hose either. I think you are on to something," Headley agreed.

"There's more, Dick. The SFPD will look like the stellar and cooperative public safety organization we all know it to be when you and Joe report this, uh, this sighting to the police over in Sausalito. Brownie points for the good guys."

"Thanks for the tip. I'll tell Joe."

"Don't ask Sergeant Young to help you find the lieutenant. I doubt you'd get any assistance."

"I know."

"Rubber hose, Sergeant Headley?"

Click.

"This shooting troubles me," Beault said, "and I..."

"It troubles all of us," Nadine pointed out.

They were in the living room in their new home. There with them were Mickey Truke, Ben Franklin, and Grenville Protherington, Beault's brother.

"Well sure, I know it bothers you as well," Beault said. "What I'm getting at is that it clearly is not your run-of-the-mill whack job by street thugs. You got your elderly rich guy, no signs of robbery, in the quaint salt air of Sausalito, and claims from these weird callers just as we're forming a posse to chase assassins. Too close for comfort is what I say. Appearances aside, these two seeming buffoons or losers or whatever they are, one of them might be telling the truth. Okay, I agree the widow is holding ticket number one at the arraignment bench. But what if she's not the responsible party? That opens the door for this Los Menendez Banda or this Haight-Ashbury Wild Bunch to walk right through as the real shooter."

"Los Menendez Banda? Sounds Jamaican, doesn't it?" Mickey Truke speculated.

"Why Jamaican?" Nadine asked him.

"They have the reputation. Very tough. Ruthless. We had run-ins with the Jamaicans down south," Mickey offered. "Not in Beverly Hills, for heaven's sake, but in some of the grimier places around L.A. where they had a foothold." The others listened. "Two caps in the head of that guy in Sausalito with a small caliber. Used to be mob style, now the new guys in town are doing it the same way. Jamaicans."

Uncle Ben put down a coffee cup. "I've got some doubts about that. A lot has happened in the past few weeks. First, we got multiple rumblings about a new assassination organization. When I put the word out to people I know, funny reports came in. You know, funny, not ha-ha funny, but strange. Then this guy across the bridge is toast. Right away here comes Los Menendez Banda and," Ben giggled and then huffed and puffed and coughed to get his breath back, "and the Haight-Ashbury Wild Bunch comes out taking credit too. I don't think these dots will connect for us because, unless you have been on Jupiter for the past century, you gotta think that his precious little bride looks pretty good for his demise."

Grenville asked, "Shouldn't it be Las Menendez Banda?"

"What?" Beault snapped.

"Las. It should be feminine, I think, because the article, las, needs to agree with the feminine adjective, banda, modifying the noun, Menendez. Of course, it's been a while since I had high school Spanish."

"What difference does that make?" Beault asked his brother.

"Maybe nothing. Maybe something. Let's say I'm right. Wouldn't a real Latino gang know how to brand themselves? It's their language. They'd get it correct. But if a gang wanted to divert attention from their real identities, they would, well, take on a fake identity not knowing necessarily that they got it wrong. On the other hand, maybe they are Latino and were D students in Spanish and just don't know any better."

"Oh, that's ripe, Grenville. You know that was the year I had mono," Beault protested. "All my grades suffered."

"Si-si, mi hermano," Grenville laughed.

Uncle Ben broke in. "Sir, you may be on to something here. I can't help you with the Spanish grammar, but as I was saying earlier, I'm getting a different story. It's a bit skimpy on facts right now, only some feelings. Not mine, but an associate of mine in Chinatown. He owns businesses around the bay. Well, even beyond the bay," he smiled and huffed. "He tells me that he's getting reports from shopkeepers about a protection racket. You'd be shocked at how pathetic it is. This gal is running numbers and bags, and at the same time she's exacting protection money from the merchants. Not much, and without her knowing it, they're skimming the numbers take to make up the difference. She hasn't got a clue. The numbers gig in the community is all just innocent fun, small change for the folks picking numbers. It's one of their favored recreations. Nobody gets hurt. That aside, the woman is also dropping hints about how she knows how to solve other problems. Boasting like. It's all happening at the same time as this Los Menendez Banda thing."

"Could be a connection, Uncle Ben," Mickey offered.

"Could be. Try this on for size, though," Ben said. "The woman is a tall, blonde-haired, blue-eyed Brit, Australian or New Zealander or something like that with a funny accent. Not your typical Latin."

"See," Grenville answered, "diverting attention away from her real identity. I was right."

"Oh, look, Pastor Protherington, the clever detective," Beault interjected.

"Yeah, well, at least I had an idea about this," Grenville responded.

Nadine stared. "Are you two finished, or am I going to have to send you boys to your rooms? Without your dinner."

"Well he..."

"Enough," Nadine scolded. "We have serious business to discuss."

"So where do we go with this?" Truke pursued.

"To the sources. We need to get a look at these credit-takers," Beault said.

"Take a look? As in inviting them to tea and asking them to lay out their hit man credentials?" Grenville teased.

"Funny. No, we should do it the sneaky way. Find out if they are real, where they roost, who they are, find out if they have the fiber to pull off a killing of this magnitude. We'll go all sub-rosa on them. They..."

Grenville snickered and started to say, "Sub..." when Nadine gaveled him quiet with her pencil. "These are well-thought-out ideas, my turtle dove." Nadine stared at Grenville, but she was speaking to Beault, who tilted his head in acknowledgment of his perspicacity, "but isn't this the job for the Sausalito police? The killing was in their front yard, and they have heard the same claims as we have. Don't you suppose they're on to this as well?"

Beault looked around the table, then said, "Take all the fun out of it, why don't you. Yes, you are right, my precious." He waited. "But it doesn't mean we can't poke our nose under their tent." He looked at Grenville and raised his eyebrows but got no appreciation for his jest. "Besides, I think we all agree that Sausalito will be throwing all its assets at the woman. They'll look at these Banda and Wild Bunch claims as so much hokum. If they get their man, oops, I mean get their woman, it will still leave open the question of an assassination operation or two looking to set up shop. The Sausalito police are not going to think paid killers are looking for commercial space up there. It makes more sense that it would be down the peninsula or here in the city. That would be our target."

No one said anything for a few beats before Nadine spoke. "I can accept that."

Truke said, "We still don't know where to go from here."

"That it does," Grenville echoed.

"Oh, ye, of little faith. I may have an ace up my sleeve," Beault chuckled.

Grenville started to say something, but Nadine cut him off waving a finger in his face. Truke and his uncle shook their heads.

13

San Francisco's cool weather and sea of fog butted up against the window on Beault's office in the Outer Richmond, usually a haven from the damp it brings. Today he was troubled. His decision was made; he was going to make the call, although he had no clue where it might lead him. He sipped his coffee and put down the cup and held his breath. He dialed the phone. After more than a few rings, he felt it was not going to be..."

"Bodie."

"Oh. Hello, Ping, it's Jaguar Beault."

Silence.

"Ping, talk to me."

"Hello, Beault. You are the last person I thought I'd be hearing from." That old familiar raspy voice.

"Nonsense. We can always talk. Took me a while though. I tried your business number and found it disconnected. I'm glad I had your other number written down."

"There's no need for a business phone when there is no business."

"Sorry to hear that. Maybe my call will change that a little."

"What do you mean?" Bodie asked.

"I need some clever work done, and I thought it was something that is right up your alley. Think you'd be interested?"

"Depends on what it is."

"I'll tell you. I..."

"No, Beault, hold on a mo. I don't want anybody feeling sorry for me. I took the money you sent to me, and Ty did the same, because we knew you wouldn't let us give it back to you."

"You deserve it, Ping. Same with Ty. I could afford it."

"I didn't deserve anything. I let my world fall apart. I could have...I should have seen what was driving Leticia. I'm to blame."

"Now you hold on, Ping. Take some blame, okay, some. There are others who were there and didn't do...didn't see what she was going through and didn't or couldn't do something about it. I am one of them. Don't take this the wrong way, Ping, but Leticia – I keep wanting to call her Mrs. Smith – has to take full responsibility. Your daughter is the one who killed those three men."

"And shot you," Bodie added.

"Yes, she, not you, not anyone else. I can't put my feet in your shoes or even come close to feeling what you are feeling. Christ, this is your daughter. If it was me, Ping, I don't know how I could deal with it. I'd be going nuts."

"I'm not going nuts, Beault. It is just a huge load on me. I've tried to manage it. Miriam's tried to help me, and help Ty, too. She's been terrific and we've responded by not listening to her."

"You should not shut her out."

"Yeah, only it is so hard for me and Ty to look people in the eye and not think they know that we've been big failures."

"Ping, I repeat, I cannot imagine how you are feeling. This sure as hell is not where I wanted my call to go. I was hoping, planning, to get you involved in a pretty important case. Not a case, no. It's a matter that needs some good footwork and good brainwork. I thought of you."

"What is it?"

Beault recited the whole Sausalito shooting and the claims by Los Menendez Banda and the Haight-Ashbury Wild Bunch and the worrisome rumors of new assassination rings. Ping said he was up on some of that from the news coverage. When Beault told him about efforts to sink the would-be assassins, he said he needed outside help. He needed Ping Bodie.

"What do you want me to do?"

Beault let out a very quiet sigh and smiled. "Hit the street and find these Bandas and draw us a clear picture of them. Right now we don't know anything about them. We have just been guessing. Once we know who they are and where they are, we want to spring a trap on them so they can hang themselves. Will you do this for me?"

There was quiet at Bodie's end of the line. Beault waited. "All right. I owe you a favor...cripes, Beault, I owe you a lifetime of favors."

"I'm not asking you to do me a favor, Ping. I am asking a first-rate private eye to work the magic I know you can. What are your rates?"

"My rates? What for?" Bodie asked.

"So I can pay you. I'm hiring you. I need professional work."

"I'm not going to charge you. After all you've done for me and Ty and the fund you set up to care for Lavernia, how could I ask for more?"

"You ain't asking, Mr. Bodie. You are going to do valuable P.I. work, and you are going to present me with a bill once a week so you can be paid accordingly. That's the deal. What are your rates?'

Beault and Bodie got it settled. After the call, Beault reflected on Ping Bodie and his grandson, Ty Lavender, and the cruel hurt on their faces as they watched Ping's daughter and Ty's mother led away in handcuffs from Kezar Stadium on her way to jail for murder. Beault thought of Leticia's – Mrs. Smith's – bizarre plan to track down the mysterious Madagascar Pigeon statue hoping it would yield the legendary jewels and the potential fortune she wanted to use to pay for her daughter's institutionalization. The desire for the fortune was so gripping that Leticia resorted to three killings. The shot into Beault's chest and the bulletproof vest he was wearing was a crazed last gesture of surrender by Leticia. Beault saw Ping and Ty destroyed that day when their house of dreams crashed down around the woman and the family.

Beault dialed again.

"Berry."

"Hi."

"Bas, hi."

"Hi."

"Okay, what is it? Everything okay?"

"Yes. Sorry, I didn't mean to mislead you."

"So?"

"I need a hug."

"What a good idea. Is there a reason I should know about?"

Beault related his phone call with Ping Bodie and the agony Leticia's father was reliving.

"I see. Well, Mr. Private Investigator, the hug store is open and you don't need an appointment."

"I'll be home later. Let's you and me and the little one walk to Harris' Restaurant."

"Delicious idea. Alana can help you with your filet," Nadine said.

"And she can help you with your baked potato," Beault offered.

"Then we can hug. And more," she cooed.

Beault smiled, but Nadine could not see that. However, she was smiling too.

14

Beault could not shake the sympathies he was feeling for the numerous women and men who had called seeking a job in his office. They were not going to get any employment satisfaction from him. He could hire only one of them. And he had done that. Dagmar said she would start on the following Monday. "I know what I'll do," Beault said to his empty office, "I'll call each of them with the unhappy news and tell them how sorry..." That was about as far as he got on this telephone scheme when it bore in on him that he would be on the phone for weeks trying to apologize.

"What I will do," he kept talking, "I'll put a temporary message on my machine – Nadine can help, she knows about electronic toys – and I'll apologize for not calling and then I will explain that I have hired somebody. That way, if any of the callers called a second time they would get the message." Beault was about to congratulate himself when he considered, "Doesn't that sound a little cold? *'You're not hired and you have to learn about it on this recorded message'* does sound cold," he answered himself. I won't ask Nadine about that.

"I am beginning to wonder if this office assistant idea is really worth it," he said to no one. There was no one there to say it to. "Working up the job notice, dealing with the lengthy governmental mish-mash at the employment office, carefully noting all the names and numbers and work histories and qualifications of seemingly desperate job hopefuls." All this had Jaguar Beault talking to himself out loud.

Dagmar Davos's Monday, her first day on the job as office assistant to the famed San Francisco private eye, was greeted by fog outside courtesy of San Francisco and a half-dozen donuts inside courtesy of Basil Protherington. Dagmar is a small button of a woman, a bit over five feet tall, maybe sixty years old, and quite healthy looking. Her white – or gray – hair is sported proudly. She spoke softly but confidently in a very articulate way. Educated and well-read, Beault assumed.

No, she does not eat donuts, Beault was told...softly but confidently. She goes real low on the sugar intake. Also, she is a vegetarian. The phone call with Jaguar Beault on her hiring day had settled the work-day hours question, the hourly wage, the disappointing lack of health insurance coverage through the job; here she said that would be okay because she was perfectly happy to obtain her coverage through the country's relatively new affordable care insurance deal. She seemed to like calling it Obamacare. She did that more than a few times as if she was putting the onus of her health care on the man himself. "I'll be on Medicare in a few years," she explained to Beault.

Beault warned his new employee of the challenging parking situation in the streets around his building, saying, "It can be very frustrating, Mrs. Davos, and you should just try to bear with it."

"Oh, please, call me Dagmar," she said. In response to the excellent parking advice, Dagmar explained to Mr. Beault – "Oh, please, call me Bas," he reciprocated – that she uses public transport in the city. "Only a nutball would drive in San Francisco. Do you drive in the city, Bas?" she smiled. Beault grinned without answering.

Not including the donut misfire, Monday got off to a pretty good start. Beault gave her a tour of the office. "This is the office and the ladies room is across the hallway." The office tour took as long as it took Bas to say those words and do a full turnaround pointing at nothing in particular.

They sat for a while and Beault backgrounded his new employee on his recent history. The escape from an assassin, the need to squelch the other assassins they had heard about, that sort of thing. He wanted Dagmar to know about these unusual events so she wouldn't be shocked if and when they came up in the line of work. He decided to leave out the pigeon statue thing. Painful memories.

Beault added, "Now, if you need anything to do your job, just let me know."

Dagmar smiled again and said, "What is my job?"

An eerie calm settled over the silence that followed Dagmar's intelligent question. Time passed; it always does. Dagmar canted her head ever so slightly and smiled that smile Beault was getting accustomed to since her arrival this morning. Ultimately, he came up with the answer. "Office assistant."

That smile from Dagmar again. "I see a phone. Does the office assistant answer the phone?" she asked.

"I...yes, yes, that's a good idea."

"I see boxes over there on the floor. Is that your filing system?"

"I...yes, I guess it is. Haven't got around to..."

"I don't see a computer." Dagmar glanced around the office reception area.

"I, uh, I don't have a computer...not one here I mean. We have one at home. Only thing, Nadine uses it a lot more than I do."

"Nadine?"

"Nadine is my fiancée. We're going to be married."

"That's what fiancés often do," Dagmar joked.

Beault was treed by this obviously professional office assistant and felt like a helpless feline after her earlier question – "What is my job?" The fiancé comment raced right past him.

"A phone," Dagmar observed, "boxes for a file cabinet, no computer, donuts, though. Let me ask this, Bas, what is your job?"

The eerie calm paid a return engagement to the office along with silence in tribute to Dagmar's question. And her smile. Beault kicked the question around in his head, not the answer, just the question, until he happily spoke. "I'm the boss."

"Of course you are, Bas. Every office needs one," she said almost to herself. "Just what is it you do as a private investigator? Are you a Sherlock Holmes?"

"Ha-ha, no, I...I don't know. That's why I hired you."

"I am happy to hear that. Let's keep going. You were about to tell me what you do as a private investigator."

"I was?"

"Yes, you were."

"Well...I..."

"How about this, Bas, I will start with those boxes – I apologize, I mean your file system – and put them into good shape. You tell me what cases you are working on now. That way I can learn what you do as a private investigator and I can separate active clients from old cases." Dagmar smiled. "I am assuming," she went on, "that all of the old cases are solved cases."

"Oh, Dagmar, you have much to learn. Only in the private eye novels do the private eyes solve every case. I'm sure Mickey Spillane would not consider writing a mystery with the final sentence being, 'The case was not solved.' Readers would clamor for their money back. But here in the real world where private eyes go toe-to-toe with crime and criminals as well as more mundane investigating, there are instances when even the best shamuses can't get the gum off their shoes."

Dagmar smiled. "Bas, how long have you been waiting to say that, 'can't get the gum off their shoes'? A while I bet."

"Maybe a year or two."

"Cases, Bas, shall we start with the assassins you mentioned to me?"

"No paperwork on that, Dagmar. I don't have a client. It's the same as with the pigeon statue fracas."

"The what?"

Beault relented and told Dagmar the story, parts of it anyway, of the Madagascar Pigeon.

"See," he said when he thought he had shared enough of that, "no clients. Wait, yeah, I did have a client then...she...for a measly hundred bucks. That hardly counts as a client, though. Never did get the other fifty from that poor woman." Beault shook his head slowly.

"Only a fortune in jewels."

"A lot of people say I earned it."

"I'd say, too. Kidnapped, threatened, pistol-whipped."

"Walloped in my solar plexus...twice...by a girl. She and I had a history. It all evened out at the end, though. She was pretty helpful to me in that near-disaster."

"Don't be a sexist, Bas. Girls can fight just as well as men. I guess you found that out from your old playmate." Dagmar smiled. Beault rubbed his mid-section.

"Let's move on to my cases so I don't have to stand here and look like the guilty party in the docket," Beault said.

"You talk, Bas, I'll take notes."

Beault talked. He talked of background checks he was undertaking on three prospective employees at a prominent tech firm in Mountain View...no, not that one...assisting a lawyer who's trying to prevent a family from declaring their mother mentally unfit to handle her own affairs, meaning they want to get their hands on her money now and not have to wait until she dies...representing a neighborhood watch crowd on a cul-de-sac where vandalism of cars has escalated and the vandals are leaving notes saying they are messing only with the cars that drive too fast on the street. "They want me to find whoever is doing it, and I'm kind torn on this," Beault explained to Dagmar. "I get a little testy when I see driving like that. Not that I would resort to revenge...well..." Beault stopped and stared. Then he added, "I'm also snooping around a sports collector store where a client is sure they're faking autographs and selling them at outrageous prices." He stopped.

"I could go on," Beault told Dagmar, "but I think you'll be able to sort out which cases are hot and which are not. Now, Dagmar, as you can see, life in the private eye lane is not as gritty and grimy as people might think. You get a Madagascar Pigeon foofraw only once in a lifetime. The rest is boring and routine. Not much to get the old adrenaline squirting."

"Like escaping from an assassin's gun." Dagmar smiled.

"Okay, two in a lifetime," Beault blushed.

"And the rest is routine, boring," she said.

"Uh-huh," he answered. Dagmar smiled. "You smile a lot, Dagmar," Beault said. "Some of the time I think you are actually laughing at me."

"No, Bas, I'm not laughing. Smiling is my way of saying that I am a happy person and that I believe in the good of others and they should know it." She smiled and then narrowed her eyes and gruffed, "You got a problem with that, wise guy?"

Beault recognized the joke and laughed. "You told me you have sons. What are their names?"

"Devon, Deron, David, Douglas, and Petros."

"D, D, D, D, and then Petros. What happened, did you run out of D names?"

"Petros is my youngest. He was born a month before his father passed away. I named him for my husband, Petros."

"Petros Davos. Sounds...what is that, Scandinavian?"

"When his family came to America in the eighteen nineties, the authorities on Ellis Island did not like his name. It was Davosopopolous. Greek. So as with so many other immigrants, the name got changed. In Petros' family's case, it was merely shortened. The family thought it was unfair, but they also thought it was not worth arguing about when they got what they wanted, which was a new life in America."

"I hope to meet them soon. They live here in the Bay Area?"

"Yes, all five."

15

Eight chairs surrounded a table in a church in the Castro district whose interior displayed nothing of the grandeur of Grace Cathedral on San Francisco's historic Nob Hill. Likewise, the exterior did not say House of God in the way more traditional churches speak at first glance. It did have a new roof, something the tall minister proudly pointed out.

The eight chairs were occupied. Jaguar Beault and his future wife, Nadine Berry, sat in two. Mickey Truke was in another. Ben Franklin sat in a fourth. The tall minister, Beault's brother, Grenville, who had welcomed everyone to his church, was in one. Two strangers held the sixth and seventh. The eighth chair was for the toddler, Alana Berry. She was on it and off it depending on her undisclosed itinerary around the room.

Everyone at the table seemed to know who everyone else was except Mickey, who studied the two strangers. Introductions were bypassed even as Mickey nodded to the two men he did not know and said, "They look like cops to me."

Ben Franklin answered, "Now, Mickey, do you really think there'd be cops at this table? Discussing this subject? Right in their jurisdiction?"

Mickey thought about that, and then said, "Takes one to know one."

Six chairs lined one wall of the room. Six more were against another wall. Nine men and three women were seated on them. Nine healthy-looking alert men of varying ages and three thirty-ish looking and alert women. Relaxed, they said nothing, listening rather to the discussion at the table. Mickey determined they were not cops. They just didn't look the type to Mickey. Right. Unbeknownst to him, five of the twelve were on the job in three cities in the Bay Area, and two were retired

San Francisco deputy sheriffs. Congregants of the Congregation of Brotherly Love in the Name of Jesus Christ.

Mickey turned his attention to the table where he was hearing a rough outline of how he was going to fit into a scheme to unearth potential assassins. "So in your plan I just walk in there and tell them I want to join up with them in an illegal assassination ring. I doubt that they will find me that naïve. Nuts, maybe, but not naïve." Mickey was sounding very skeptical of the plan.

"You sound skeptical, Mickey," Nadine said.

"Skeptical, yeah," he agreed.

"You ever do any undercover down there in Beverly Hills?" Beault asked.

"No, no way," Mickey quickly protested. "I wore a uniform, I drove a patrol car, racked up my light bar's blues and reds – real patriotic, you know – blasted a siren. Pretty overt. No, I am not your man for going in like a mole."

"None of us here believes that this Los Menendez Banda outfit is responsible for the Sausalito shooting, Mickey," Beault said. "It just doesn't meet the smell test. However..."

"Likewise," one of the un-introduced strangers at the table butted in saying, "it does not add up that they are a real assassination organization. There's been no homicides to fit that profile until this guy got it over the bridge." Mickey stared at the man. "Until we learn different," the man continued, "and I don't think we will, we have to assume this is an empty threat from both of these callers." He looked around. "But like that man said...however. I think he means by however that we can't close the book on anything just yet."

Beault watched Truke staring at that description. Then he said, "Mickey, you go in there with a resume of assassinations. They'll buy into you because they'll want to demonstrate that they are your equal."

Mickey shook his head. "And who's going to tell me where to find these criminals? Am I supposed to walk the streets of Daly City..."

"South San Francisco, Mickey," his uncle corrected.

"...South San Francisco with a sandwich board over me asking for directions to the local assassin house?"

"I've been working on that. I have a resource that ought to pay off. We'll find them for you. You won't have to wear that sandwich board, Mickey." Beault said.

"Oh goody," Mickey sighed.

"After we have them on our radar," Beault said, "all we will need is a hook. We'll find one. So far the assassination idea is only a rumor. There's been no killings that could be called hired hits, even if we count the Sausalito shooting. That still looks too much like the lovely Mrs. Johnson." Beault shook his head and said, "Other than her, there is just the normal senseless murders by gangbangers."

"I hope to hell you're not going to send me into that scene," Truke asked excitedly.

"Of course not. They're police business," Beault answered. "They aren't the assassins we're looking for, just punks."

"Deadly punks," one of the strangers murmured. Several in the room nodded.

"Ben," Beault spoke up again, "you said you are looking further into the rumors coming from Chinatown. Do you think there's any chance this is a Chinese thing?"

"Doubt it. No. I would have heard if that was the case. There's a strange undercurrent to the rumors – like I told you before. Little hints being dropped here and there, but not by an Asian. By the white woman. When I find out more I'll let you know."

"Excellent," Beault said, "the more we can learn, the easier it will be to cuddle up to the plot. The easier it will be for Mickey to sell himself in on the scheme."

"So this is it, huh? This is what you want me to do? You want me to be the patsy?" Mickey scoffed. "Now I'm not skeptical anymore, I'm terrified."

"You'll be safe. We can pull the plug if we think we need to," Beault said.

"I'm not terrified of that," Mickey retorted. "I'm terrified of you people. I think you're out of your minds. I won't do it," he said, putting his hands palms down on the table and leaning back into his chair. The room fell silent. One of the two strangers at the table spoke.

"I'm no expert on this, you understand, but I think this gentleman is within his rights to refuse – well, to decline – to play a part in this plan. It sounds more like something an official agency would undertake, somebody like, well, the FBI or state cops, for example. They would have, oh I don't know, maybe a judge's order or something like that to authorize, what's it called, undercover ops." When he finished with that he turned to the other stranger who was sitting next to him and asked, "Does that make sense to you?" The other stranger didn't answer, he just nodded. "See?" the first stranger said, grateful that he was agreed with.

This made sense to Mickey, too, who sat up in his chair and pointed to the stranger and said, "You got that right, mister. It's not a job for me – for us – it's for the authorities. They should put together a task force – yeah, a task force – and solve the problem that way. Why, Uncle Ben, you and me, we'd cooperate, wouldn't we." Not a question, a statement. Uncle Ben answered anyway, "Mickey, Mickey, Mickey."

That was somewhat dumbfounding and Mickey did not seem to like what he heard. "Wha..." is what he got out before the stranger spoke again.

"A task force can be a good idea at times," the stranger said. "Then again they can be clumsy, what with overlapping jurisdictions and varying prosecutorial interests and, yes, probably, competing egos. I guess it could be the right framework...that is if the right people were involved. I'm still thinking out loud here. You don't mind if I say a little more, do you, Mr. Beault?" he asked. Beault smiled and shrugged. The man continued, "I'm still thinking that this plan does still need a central player, a player who would have the right resume to bring verisimilitude to the part. Someone like Mr. Truke here who has actually – that is if I am correctly informed about his recent past – been an assassin."

"He'll do it," Uncle Ben announced.

"No I won't," Mickey repeated.

"He's right, sir," the stranger said. "He cannot be forced into a role like this." He saw Mickey put a smile of relief on his face. "On the other hand, he is an admitted felon. Again, I am no expert on this, but I think that he would be facing some serious charges by local police bent on removing this kind of crime from the streets."

Nadine Berry could not contain herself and started laughing. Mickey Truke was ashen as he listened to this and looked around the table. Uncle Ben winked at him.

The stranger started again. "Oh, hold on. I just said I am not an expert on this. Now I think on that, I am."

Mickey gushed, "Who in hell are you?"

Beault interjected. "Sorry, I should have introduced these two gentlemen. That's San Francisco Police Captain Joseph Blough. His associate is Lieutenant Richard Headley. They run the Homicide Division over at the SFPD."

"You're Joe Blough," Mickey shouted. "You're the Joe Blough they've been talking about," he said, pointing at Beault and Berry. "Am I in some kind of twilight zone?"

Alana came running over to her mother and said, "What's a tilight zone, mommy?" Nadine picked her up and sat her on her lap. "That's a place where people learn more than they want to, hon." She kissed Alana on her cheek and looked at Truke with a big smile on her face.

"Captain? Lieutenant? When did this happen, Joe?" Grenville asked Blough.

"Actually, it's not public yet, Grenville. Probably be announced next week. Your brother has jumped the gun on our two promotions."

Mickey folded his arms on the table and put his head down. The tall minister got up and went to a door and talked briefly with someone on the other side. He came back and sat down. Mickey raised his head and turned. He looked at the dozen men and women seated against the walls. Beault saw Mickey's curiosity and said, "Oh them, they're some of Grenville's congregants. They, they are, they, well, Mickey, they like to help out in any way they can. You know, Good Samaritans." Mickey's head slumped to his arms again as the door opened and several people came in with sandwiches, salads, rolls, drinks, a plate of cookies, fixings for lunch.

Without looking at the food, Mickey spoke into the tabletop. "City cops here in this room are telling me they know I am, oh, I and Uncle Ben, we are, we were assassins. Well, sort of." He coughed back his anxiety. "How much trouble are we in, how much trouble are me and Uncle

Ben in? Are these co...policemen going to arrest us and toss us into a cell for the rest of our, oh my God, for the rest of our lives?" Ben, sitting next to his nephew turned his head to Captain Blough. He had the same question on his mind.

Blough considered. "Well, Mr. Truke, we have you dead to rights, don't we? The fact that you can't shoot straight, or whatever it was that left all your targets unkilled...is that the right thing to call it...shouldn't make a difference. However, Dick and I have heard your story...and Mr. Franklin's...from Beault and Nadine. We have been talked into the proposition that you can be more, uh, helpful here with us."

Truke had raised his head and was breathing easier.

"I've been known," Blough went on, "to make mistakes in judgment at times. If this is one of them, if you disappoint me and Dick and your other friends here...well, Mickey, Ben, you'd wish you'd never been born."

"I..." Mickey started.

Headley, who spoke rarely at meetings, said, "Joe means it, Mr. Franklin, Mr. Truke. We can't change your past, but we sure can change your future. You are going to be a part of this effort because Mr. Beault and Miss Berry and Captain Blough and I see you contributing. It may be unconventional, but what the hey, this is an unconventional mystery."

Mickey and Ben looked at one another. They bumped shoulders. Franklin huffed, "Thank you." Mickey was shaking slightly, but noticeably.

"Don't think we are just looking the other way," Headley added. "We are looking straight at both of you. We will be watching." His controlled voice filled the room.

Another voice from a chair against one of the conference room walls announced, "This is police procedure right out of the manual. I know, I've read it." That got a good laugh from almost everyone in the hall. Mickey and Ben confined themselves to deep sighs of relief.

The aroma of food followed the laughing and the attendees got up and helped themselves to lunch items. After the lull, Nadine said, "Is there anything on that Haight-Ashbury Wild Bunch, Captain?"

"Um...well, uh, no not yet."

"What's up with that, policeman, these ums and uhs?" Beault pressed. "What are you holding back?"

"I'm a senior policeman, just remember that, shamus, and I don't got to tell you nothing never, not now, not never," Blough camped. "But if you must know, and I will personally spike anyone on the pointy tip of the Transamerica pyramid downtown who lets this out of the room, we will have an ear into that crowd. Just a precaution, you understand. Not a flippin word about this to a soul. Understand?"

"Well there, somebody is making some progress," Beault said. "We still need more. We need action. Something to light a fire under the Banda or the Wild Bunch. What could it be I keep asking myself."

"You mean get them out in the open all exposed like," Blough offered.

"That's the idea, Joe," Beault said, "but if Mickey and me could...no, if you..." He stopped. He stood up and shouted, "I got it."

"Got what?" someone reacted.

Beault didn't hear. He slipped away from his chair and walked to the coffee urn and refreshed his cup with his back to the table. He drank a gulp and turned around. He looked at the others with a big grin across his face. He walked back.

"Uh-oh," said Grenville.

"Uh-freakin-oh," Beault responded. He stood behind his chair. "I got the hook. It just came to me. Told you we'd find it. We will kill someone," he announced.

The others didn't say anything, assuming Beault would continue. He didn't. So Nadine prompted her fiancé, "You better explain."

"I think we can discount the Wild Bunch for now," Beault said. "That name wants to make me gag. But the Banda. If we assume there's anything at all behind the rumors Ben brings to us, then we have to assume they are drawing up plans to become assassins. And we have to act accordingly."

"And," Nadine nudged.

"And we draw them out." He wrinkled his face. "No, we draw them in...to an offer they can't refuse." He smiled to himself.

"And?" Nadine again.

"We will hire them to shoot Jaguar Beault."

That quieted the room. When he stood unspeaking for a time, Grenville said, "It's about time we did something positive." No one laughed at his joke.

"Is any of this legal?" Mickey asked, looking all around the table. "Any of this?" There were a few muffled laughs.

Captain Blough decided to field Mickey's question. "Why, Mr. Truke, of course this is legal. All we are doing is enjoying ourselves at a lunch hosted by Minister Protherington. Nothing more than that. Nothing."

Mickey heaved a big sigh. "Oh man," he exhaled, "this kind of police work does not mesh with what I trained for down south."

"There are lots of different kinds of police work, Mr. Truke," the sergeant/lieutenant spoke. "You just have to grab the one that gets results."

"Chapter two in the police manual. Ends justify means," came another voice from one of the walls.

"Good lord," Mickey whispered.

Grenville said to Mickey, "Are you a religious man, Mr. Truke?"

"No," he answered, then he added, "maybe I oughta start. But I'm not so sure I would qualify for a church with this name."

Grenville laughed and said, "We accept all kinds in our church, Mickey. You'd be welcome any time."

16

In Chinatown at a restaurant near Grant and Clay, customers side-stepped along the buffet line deciding what they wanted for dinner. It was a nightly ritual, three hundred sixty-five days a year. Tourists tended to dine early, locals later. Sun Shin Wong noshed from a small plate of a few tidbits brought to him at a back table from the kitchen by a young woman sporting an apron and a hairnet. "Shay-shay," he thanked her.

She smiled and bowed slightly, responding, "English, grampapa, English. We must speak in English."

Mr. Sun waved her away dismissively, grunting, "Me no likee English." Then he added, "Please bring me another pot of tea and ask your lazy brother if he has made any plans to help on the serving line tonight."

"He is not lazy, grampapa, he is very busy with his school work," the young girl answered.

"Yes, I am sure he is" Sun admitted. "I like his devotion. Tea, my angel, please."

"I will, but you still owe two dollars for the first one," she laughed.

Sun Shin Wong was not a wealthy man. He was an extremely wealthy man. He was a textbook example of the difference. Yet he didn't show it off. He dressed conservatively, drove a nice car but not a luxurious one, wore only a wedding band for jewelry, and lived in a, well, in a really big house in the Marina. That was helpful because some of his extended family roomed with him and Mrs. Sun. There was also the practical consideration as many of his neighbors were prominent San Franciscans, including businessmen, financiers, artisans, and a bevy of political figures from the national, state and local levels. The proximity pleased Mr. Sun who enjoyed mixing with people. The convenience was more appreciated by his neighbors. Mr. Sun, they knew, was an extremely wealthy man. He tended to have influence.

Sun Shin Wong looked up from his teacup and saw Ben Franklin walking past diners toward his table. "Good evening, Mr. Sun," Ben said, sitting down.

"To what do I owe this visit, Ben," Mr. Sun said by greeting. "Your phone call about trouble brewing has intrigued me."

"A matter of mutual interest, my friend. There is mystery afoot that we need to talk about."

"So serious, Ben. Are we in danger?"

Ben laughed. "I am certain, Wong, that if danger were in your presence it would cower, turn tail and disappear."

"Such high esteem you pay me. Are you trying to curry favor with me?"

"Is that possible? No, never mind. First, how about a drink. I could use one."

"Ben, this is an unlicensed traditional Chinese restaurant, not a speakeasy. I'll have some tea brought out for you, yes? We want to honor the traditional ways."

"Tea. Traditional. Honor. Jesus, Wong, you own saloons all over the city, liquor stores everywhere, and now you are buying a famous vineyard up in Sonoma County. And I can't get a simple cocktail? Where is there any justice in that, I ask you? What has happened to your influence?"

"Justice is blind, Ben, but not deaf. I'll ask Elaine to bring you something from the kitchen. Those outlaws back there always have something hidden away."

Mr. Sun jingled a small bell he had on the table and Elaine stepped out from the kitchen. "Angel," he started and quietly gave her instructions. "A mystery, eh, Ben? What is going on and what role can I play?"

"We've already had a conversation about that woman who is running numbers and carrying a bag. The Britisher or the Kiwi or the Aussie or whatever the hell she is," Ben said.

"The one who thinks she is selling protection, yes," Sun agreed.

"Some of us think that she may be the one branching out into the more consequential matters we have heard about."

"A turf dispute with your own termination division? You are ready to get tough like in the movies?"

"No. It has come to my attention that it would be prudent of me to abandon that line of business."

"It has come to your attention?" Sun asked, smiling.

"Mickey and I had an instructive meeting with a prominent and well-placed member of the law enforcement community here in San Francisco. We negotiated a compromise. I would, and Mickey too, we would put our experience in that line of business at the disposal of the police department and some others by offering assistance in any way we can to help bring down any new assassination crowds trying to get a foothold."

Sun laughed. "A compromise, Ben. And what did you and Mickey get by way of offering your services?"

"We get to go on living outside of prison of a judge's choice here in the Golden State." Ben Franklin hung his head in what looked like deep thought...and undoubtedly was. "Mickey had some moments thinking about life in prison, I can assure you," he coughed.

"How is Mickey?"

"How is Mickey. If it wasn't for my sister, his mother, I'd...I still don't know how he became a cop. They must have had some pretty lax entrance requirements. What's more puzzling to me is how I could ask him to join me in my...my startup venture. He was hopeless. He would have fouled it up if I asked him to step on an ant. However, there is this silver lining. Since he didn't snuff anybody, we didn't have any blood on our hands and that was important during that negotiation we had with that cop."

"So you are done with that venture. You will remember, my friend, that I advised against it." Sun said.

"Oh, yes, yes, oh, for certain, we are done, no more of that. I should have listened to you. Boy, did I have some refunding to do over that."

Elaine stepped through the kitchen door and put a drink in front of Ben. "It's a Rob Roy, Mr. Franklin," she said.

"Thank you, Elaine, that's sweet." She stepped back into the kitchen.

"You got a full bar out there, Wong? A Rob Roy?"

"Outlaws, I'm telling you. That's all I can figure," Sun smiled. Then he said, "You mentioned a minute ago that some of you thought this woman was branching out. Who are these people you speak of?"

"I won't insult you by asking that you keep this to yourself, but it is a notable group. Besides, if we work together it is going to benefit everyone. Everyone meaning you and me."

"So, who are they?"

"Yes, who. Mickey is one and Nadine Berry of KSFG."

"Nadine Berry," Sun repeated. "That glamorous reporter. She may have got the job on looks, but she is a persistent, effective journalist. She was out front on that strange bird statue case, wasn't she?"

"Exactly."

"That private eye solved it. Funny name."

"Jaguar Beault."

"Beault? I thought it was pronounced beault," Sun said.

"He says it's Beault."

"You know him?"

"Of course. He's one of the group I mentioned. He is engaged to Nadine Berry."

"This gets more mysterious."

"Then there's a minister of a church in the Castro. Grenville Protherington. A resourceful man."

"A minister in the Castro. How's he involved?"

"He's Beault's brother."

"I am not going to be surprised if you tell me that Confucius himself is on the case."

"You might prefer him after I tell you who the other two are."

Sun stared at Ben. "Go ahead."

"Captain Joe Blough and Lieutenant Dick Headley."

Sun picked up his teacup and sipped, looking over the rim at Ben. He put the cup down and poured more tea from the pot. "Joe Blough and Dick Headley. Captain, you say. Lieutenant."

"It's a big promotion. It'll go public in a few days. Both of them. They told us about it, but asked us to keep it under wraps."

"Joe is a good man. He's a clever detective. He's fair. He can be ill-tempered at times. That probably works for him on the job. Tell me, though, why are Joe and Dick working this in this manner? It seems odd to me."

"Yes, why. Good question." Ben paused, then added, "They aren't. Not actively yet." Then he did the wink-wink thing.

"Ah."

"They're friends of Beault and Berry, if that helps any. I think they are involving themselves to make sure they are ahead of things if this mystery explodes in their jurisdiction. Right now, San Francisco doesn't have any skin in this game. But if it does..."

Sun thought. "Okay, Ben, that's the who. What is the what?"

Franklin said, "If this woman is telling people she can arrange it if anyone needs someone to disappear, Blough and Headley see the can of worms that would open for them."

"I read," Sun said, "that a claimant calling itself Los Menendez Banda took credit for that murder over in Sausalito. People are speculating it is Jamaican or Colombian or Dominican."

"That's right as far as it goes," Ben said. "We talked it over and we feel it is a diversion tactic. This name thing. We think the real gang may be this woman and her very Anglo family or friends trying to sound macho. God knows what else she is into or what else she wants to do. On the surface it appears that this Banda gang is the one you've been hearing the rumors on. The one in South City."

"Did your friends talk about this Haight-Ashbury Wild Bunch that also claims they did that shooting?" Sun asked.

"Yes. Sounds more like a prank or something. Copycatting the claim. It happens a lot when there's a sensational event. People want their moment in the sun, uh, Sun. I was hoping you might have some thoughts on them. Haight-Ashbury. You have interests there, do you not?"

Sun nodded and sat silent for a few moments. "I do have business interests in the Haight, and I did have some of my associates explore when the news reports came out about the claims for the Sausalito murder. A Haight connection was something we could not ignore. As a result, I am learning some things about this Wild Bunch. I fear that it will not add much to your intelligence, however. They appear to be quite pathetic." Sun told Ben what his inquiries into the Haight-Ashbury Wild Bunch had turned up.

Ben said, "My God, they do sound pathetic. And you are right, it doesn't add much. Well, whatever else you can tell us about them will be more than we have now."

Sun smiled. "I have already taken it upon myself to pass along what we have learned about this Wild Bunch to one of your friends. I should have mentioned this earlier."

"Who to?"

"Your Captain Blough."

Ben frowned. "And what did you take upon yourself to pass along, as you say?"

"The whereabouts of the Wild Bunch. They live in a building I own. It was the least I could do. Perhaps it is the most I could do since what we have discovered about them is so limited. It seemed that with assassination talk and credit-taking for a sad homicide in Sausalito, the police would welcome any new information. I do not know if it will be of value. That will be for the captain to determine."

Ben said, "It is my take that he will act on anything that comes his way. You said it right when you called him clever. Oh, and let me have that address. I can share it with Jaguar Beault."

Sun said, "You also said you and I might benefit by cooperating in this matter. I assume you mean the dissolution of this gang or, possibly, these gangs."

"Yes."

"And benefit how?"

"Importantly," Ben said. "As for me, the police will look the other way as I retire out of some of my, er, activities. Joe recognizes that an assassination outfit – especially one that actually works, unlike mine – cannot be tolerated in the area. He'll want to put a stop to it before it can get a foothold. He expects me to help."

"And for me?" Sun asked.

"You have business interests all over the Bay Area. The last thing you need is a murderous mob of upstarts going into the assassination business. I don't have to remind you of the olden days. Tong wars when nobody benefited except the ones with the most guns. Street gangs today are bad enough protecting drug and prostitution turf. But this?"

"Bad for business," Sun agreed.

17

Beault invited his brother to the gym. Grenville readily accepted. They are regulars. More regular now, that is, for Jaguar Beault since he no longer needs to avoid the place or hide the fact of his workout routines as when he was hiding a bird statue in his locker back in the day. That statue had changed his life in more ways than one. The changes came principally from a bullet to his chest and a subsequent financial windfall of significant measure. That very locker still had the combination lock hanging on the handle with the revealing series of numbers to open it...the numbers that reminded him of the unforgettable shape of his erstwhile college professor chick, Emily, the proficient applicator of solar plexus punishments. That was the relationship that had ended bumpily quite a while before Beault met Nadine Berry.

Grenville liked to accompany Basil to the gym because he would challenge his older brother on the free weights and nearly every workout machine they used. There were days when the mano-a-mano straining between the two drew other gym rats to watch. The older guys watched with recollections of their own younger days and longer-winded capabilities. The younger guys watched, glad that they didn't get called into the challenge. The women watched Grenville. Sure, they'd glance at Basil, too. For a long time as they were growing up, Grenville got all the glances, winning gold, while Basil settled for silver. Second place in the looks department.

If you came away from the reciting of *The Madagascar Pigeon* saga, you know that Jaguar Beault did not tell us what he looks like except that he is a tall man and probably in his early thirties. That's all you know since he was the one who dictated the statue story and he didn't see a need to boast on his appearance. That didn't satisfy everybody. Those would be you e-mailers and letter writers, texters and twitterers who badgered about Jaguar Beault's looks, like this is important. But readers want the goods on him.

All right. Basil, now Beault, stands about six feet three inches or a bit taller, between one and two inches shorter than Grenville. Where Grenville carried about two hundred fifteen or twenty pounds on his long frame, Beault went out at about two hundred, two hundred five. The work at the gym, a carryover from Beault's athletic younger days and a three-year watch in the Navy, built up his strength, toned his frame and left him with little body fat.

He wore his brown hair semi-long, framing green eyes. The women in his life saw him for a handsome man. Your author does not pretend to know how to limn the features of other men. Ain't gonna to try. He lets women do that. Nadine, for example, thinks her fiancé is pretty good looking.

There now, let's have no more messages saying what's he look like, please. Also, for that one pushy texter, no, the publisher will not add a photograph of him to these pages.

Okay, one more thing. Beault's wardrobe usually includes something loose fitting over his shoulders and arms to allow for freedom of movement to defend himself pugilistically, if that is ever called for, as it sometimes is in his chosen profession. And to conceal a holster with a gun in it.

Can we go on now? Yes. Good.

The Protheringtons always ended their gym visits with about five or ten minutes on the punching bags with quick, sure, on-target fists wrapped up with gloves against any chance of bruising or cutting. They also saved time for the same regimen with kicks. At six feet three or so and six feet five, both had long, strong legs. When there were crowds around for this, the men winced. The women dreamed. Some cursed. They were the ones aware that Grenville is gay.

Showered, re-hydrated, clothed, heart rates down to normal and hungry, the Protherington boys headed for an early lunch. "Where?" "I don't care...where?" "I don't care either." "Well, we can't just drive around the city streets wondering, the mayor will dispatch a squad of his Automobile Nazis to haul our butts in." "Wanna do Boudin up at the Wharf?" "Perfect. Soup and sourdough loaves." The decision was made. It was on to Fisherman's Wharf.

"You like it here, don't you?" Grenville said.

"Yeah. Boudin. Nadine thinks I'm an addict. Probably am. How can you say no to the best sourdough in the world?" He tore a roll in half and dunked it in his chowder.

"Tell me about your plan to get your sorry ass shot and killed," Grenville smiled.

"I really don't have a plan drawn. Not yet. It just seems to me that we need to do something to expose this Banda group as assassins, if that is what they really are. Showing their hand by shooting somebody would do the trick."

"Absolutely, and we can say how clever you were during your funeral."

"Well, please, the plan would include some clever *deus ex machina* to save my, what'd you call it, my sorry ass."

"How...what?"

"I'll be working on that. What I have so far is to insert Mickey somehow to be the shooter. That way we can have him miss and I can do my Oscar-winning death scene. If we can get him fixed up with the Banda, we'd have some control."

"Why you?"

"Why me? Why not? This way my name would be above the title of the movie. Jaguar Beault in 'The Famous Death Scene' at theaters now. I don't think it would be fair to ask anyone else because..."

"Quiet."

"What are you..."

"Quiet, I said." Grenville glared at Basil. His glare turned to amusement. He grinned at Beault and began nodding his head.

"What..."

"Quiet, I said." Grenville's gaze went off to the restaurant's outer reaches where there are about one million loaves of the best breads in the Milky Way, floor to ceiling. Beault decided to give him some time and space. Grenville came back and worked on his clam chowder. He buttered bread and ate it. He sipped on his iced tea. He ate more soup. He kept his eyes bouncing around the Boudin landscape. He put his soup spoon down.

"We do this," Grenville said with controlled excitement. "We get Mickey into contact with the Banda somehow like you said. Ben can give us some direction there. He already knows they might be down in South City. His contact – what's that all about I keep asking myself – says he hears rumors. Oh, and also you said you have another resource. I suppose you mean something about the Banda. Either way, once we have a picture of them, I do an end run and tell the Banda I need somebody offed. You. I hire them to off Jaguar Beault. In the meantime, Mickey tells them he's an assassin and is looking for work."

"How do you propose to make all that come together in a fool-proof scheme?"

"I don't know. You're the detective. You do it."

"I have to carry the water, eh?"

"What we would achieve here, as I think about this more, is a smoking gun, literally. The Banda, if they can be roped into this, would be the agent for murder. Attempted murder. That would put a quick stop to their assassination aspirations. Prosecutors might need to smooth out the edges of entrapment somehow, but we can leave that to them."

"Where'd this come from?" Beault asked.

"Don't laugh. It kinda flickered in my head while I was kicking your ass on the big bag at the gym..."

"No way were you..."

"And I was thinking about what you said about killing yourself. It just kinda started to form. A shooting. An assassin. We already have Mickey. We had a victim volunteer, you. All we needed was the ding-a-lings who want to be in the hit business. Los Menendez Banda."

"You will not be happy, Gren, until you have satisfied your barely concealed dream of becoming a private eye. Let me assure you, though, that our family already has one. One is enough."

Grenville picked up his spoon and continued on with his clam chowder, grinning between mouthfuls.

"Smug jerk," Basil called his brother.

18

A man dressed in tattered camo pants, old army field jacket, tennis shoes with his toes showing, a beard he obviously was not cultivating, and a watch cap pulled over his ears leaned against a wall observing people on Haight Street. He was not out of place here. The wall he was leaning on housed a medical marijuana dispensary, which, even in San Francisco, is not a euphemism. It's a legal and licensed business providing cannabis to the needy, providing the needy had a prescription written by a real doctor. There was a real doctor right inside. He had a prescription pad.

The man in camos had already been inside. Inside he told a receptionist he wanted cannabis to ease some pain he was experiencing. He was told he needed to see a doctor, have an examination, and, if warranted, get a prescription. He said he didn't have his own doctor. There's one right there, he was told. Oh. The doctor asked him what was bothering him. The man said he had a boil on his butt and it hurt when he sat down. The doctor, bored and underpaid, did not fall for the opportunity to answer the man's complaint by saying don't sit down. The doctor had no time for comedy. Instead, he diagnosed the medical issue and determined that the best course of treatment was cannabis. He wrote a prescription. The man took seven steps to where his prescription was filled. Even fans of Obamacare had to hold their noses over this health care delivery option.

Outside, the man leaned on the wall waiting. He did not partake of the medical prescription he had in one of his pockets. He was watching. Then he eyed two street people dressed a little better than he. He had been stalking them for a few days. The two tended to follow the same patterns that brought them past this spot. They were panhandling, and not very successfully at that. The man crossed Haight behind a passing double-decked sightseeing bus.

Approaching the two, he started talking like they were old friends. They weren't, they'd never met. "Did you see how easy it is to get weed over there? Just walk in and tell 'em you hurt somewhere and, pow, you score. Want some?"

"What?"

"Weed, you want any?"

"Uh, well, yeah."

"Here."

The three looked at each other. The one with the boil on his butt said, "Just got here to Frisco. Need a place to flop. Maybe take a shower." The other two stared. "I've got money to throw at somebody's rent," he tempted. "Don't want to be a parasite."

"A what?"

"A para...a scrounger."

"Oh, yeah."

"Know anybody with some space and who could use some help with the rent?"

"Maybe. You just got here, huh? Where from?"

"From somewhere else."

The two told the man to come with them to their pad. He was told it was not a first-class hotel or anything, but there was space.

"Cool," the man said.

It was an apartment on Clayton in the Haight-Ashbury, a district known widely for, well, for this and that. On the way up the stairs to the apartment, one of the two asked the man if he had a name. He answered yes. Not to be dismissed by this taciturn traveler, one of them said, what is it? The man answered, "Harold Wobber."

The Haight-Ashbury Wild Bunch got a new recruit. The man was not sworn in, he was not issued a uniform, there was no field-training manual, no secret handshake. Only, "You say you have some money to throw at our rent, right?" That sealed the deal.

19

Frank "Ping" Bodie had been a private eye in San Francisco for more than forty years when Beault hired him to track down Los Menendez Banda. As a young man, he had aspirations about becoming a policeman, but he also had strong objections to the Vietnam War. Three arrests in the nineteen sixties for protesting too recklessly were on his record, and the cop authorities at the time blackballed any interest they may have had in him. Doing cop-on-the-street work from a private office was what he had left open to him. He got very good at the job. He learned San Francisco at the bootstrap level where he found most of his cases. He learned the people. He could separate the law-abiding from those who didn't give a rip about laws.

It hit him hard when he was informed that his granddaughter was diagnosed as a paranoid schizophrenic. He berated himself, admitting he was unable to provide any help or answers to the medical tragedy. He muddled on only to see his family disintegrate because of his own daughter's irrational and murderous pursuit of the pigeon statute that promised, she hoped, riches to use for her daughter's hospitalization.

Bodie sat at a table against a wall in a sandwich shop on Grant near Columbus. This was his second hour on the second day into the rate structure he agreed to with Beault. On the first hour of the first day, Bodie had intercepted a tall, blonde woman doing business in a shop in Chinatown. Today, he dunked a donut into a cup of coffee and bit into it. About ten feet away, June Menzies exchanged envelopes with a man behind the counter. When June left, she was not alone. June did not know she was not alone. June was in the dark. Bodie could have been carrying June's purse for her and she still would not have known she was being tailed. And had been for the whole day before.

Bodie counted the stops June made today at thirteen before she headed out of the city south down the 101. In South San Francisco, June unknowingly revealed one of the Menzies residences to Bodie. Bodie began watching who was coming and who was going and determined that June had a big family.

Day-by-day, Ping attached himself to another Menzies or two and catalogued their work routines. There were the two boys who did early – real early – paper routes and that bold separating of other people's possessions from parked cars.

There were the big guys who went into North Beach and helped keep order at a few night spots. The limo driver went all over the peninsula, not once knowing he was followed. Two other family members, presumably parents, spent most of their time in their apartment.

Three women went together every late afternoon and went with cleaning materials to several buildings in San Mateo.

Two young women who looked amazingly like June catered to the breakfast and lunch throngs at buildings housing tech companies in Mountain View and Sunnyvale. Bodie even bought lunch from them one day. They were oblivious, confirming his conclusion that they were related to June.

Bodie set aside an hour each day to document all he was learning about the Menzies, aka Los Menendez Banda. He made thorough descriptions of the family members noting which ones went where and did what. He was pegging them through an experienced and keen eye for faces and figures and behaviors and work patterns.

Not once did Jaguar Beault call Ping Bodie and ask how he was doing.

20

The phone rang and Beault reached for it. Dagmar was closer to it and picked up the receiver. "Jaguar Beault Investigations," she said professionally, smiling at Beault. "May I tell him who is calling...will he know what this is about...are you a client...one moment please...this man says his name is Grenville."

"Ah-ha," Beault exploded, "yeah, I'll take it." Dagmar smiled.

"What's that all about? Who is that?" Grenville said.

"My new office assistant."

"Since when?"

"For a few days."

"What for?"

"I'm beginning to wonder."

"Were you going to keep it a secret?"

"Thought about it. But she's turning into a real plus." Beault smiled at Dagmar. She smiled back. "Actually, I think she's going to turn into the boss." Dagmar smiled again.

Beault said, "What do you need?"

"Want to have lunch today?"

"Lunch. Okay."

"Come on over and we'll walk up to the Haight. There's a deli there with killer falafel sandwiches."

"Falafel? That's vegetarian, isn't it?" Beault smiled at Dagmar. Dagmar smiled back.

"Can be if you make it that way. How about noon?"

"Okay, noon. Wait. Did you say walk? How far is that?"

"Eight or ten miles at least. Could take all afternoon." Dramatic pause by the younger brother. "It's only a mile or so, you wussy wimp."

"I am not. I..." Beault began to gripe, but Grenville had impolitely hung up.

"That was Grenville," Beault explained to Dagmar.

"I thought it might be when he told me his name is, um, Grenville."

"Yes. Oh I see. Grenville is my brother." Dagmar smiled. "He lives here in the city," Beault added. "I am going to go to lunch with him today."

"I got that impression."

Beault could not remember when, or if, he had ever tasted falafel. He wasn't sure what it was. But he was willing to give it a try if his brother was going to speak so highly of it. Can't be all bad, he thought. Besides, he could give it to Gren to eat if he didn't like it himself and then he would just order something conventional.

The walk to the Haight was a lot easier than Beault had worried over. Only about a mile one way. Can do. As the two turned up to Haight Street, Grenville questioned Beault about his new hire.

"She seems to smile all the time," Beault admitted.

"You hired her without even interviewing her?"

"Well, yeah, I sure wasn't going to interview seventy-nine people."

"Well, good luck with her. What's her name again?"

"It's Dagmar and she already has me thinking like a real office guy."

Before the Protherington brothers reached the deli, they were approaching seven middle-aged dropouts from the no-skills academy shuffling into their path, one of them bumping hard into Grenville.

Grenville said, "Sorry," in the reflexive way innocents often do in this encounter.

"Out of the way, stringbean," the bumper stared up, "and you better say sorry when you hit me."

"Not exactly what just occurred, sir. You hit me."

"You calling me a liar? Nobody calls me a liar." He squared around at Grenville. He was about fifty years old, just over six feet tall and over-weight. His big arms, tatted up and down, were exposed from a short-sleeve shirt. His friends were as unimpressive as he was. They came up behind their buddy trying to look fierce but failed at that.

"I didn't call you a liar," Grenville said. "I said you hit me. It wasn't the other way around. Why don't we just leave it at that?"

"I don't want to leave it at that. Me and my crew here don't like it when somebody calls me a liar."

Beault coughed. "Uh, excuse me, but does that happen to you a lot?"

"Huh? What?"

"People call you a liar a lot, do they?"

"Piss off. I'm talking to this shithead."

Grenville said, "Sir, this has gone way past where it should. I am a man of peace. I apologize to you. Let's call it over. It's quits, okay?"

"Big prick's gonna turn tail and sneak away," the man said over his shoulder to his buddies who thought that was a correct description of the encounter. "Good thing, too, because if you don't walk, I'd have to kick shit out of you. Second time today," he said, again turning to his buds with a smile on his face.

Grenville looked at his brother standing next to him. He mouthed, "Second?"

Beault said, "Who'd you kick shit out of already today?"

"I told you to piss off, don't you listen? Guess I'll have to kick some shit out of you after I do this asshole."

Grenville glared at the man. "Answer his question."

"Whater ya talkin about?"

"Who did you kick shit out of today already?"

"Somebody who called me a liar, just like you," he answered with a dopey smile aimed at his buddies again.

"Bust 'em one, Frankie," came a suggestion from one of his pals. "Yeah," said another, "drop the bean pole." Frankie considered it and then complied, swinging his right arm around and up toward Grenville's chin. It got just past half way when Grenville covered Frankie's fist with his own left hand and brought it in toward his jaw before bending it back down, twisting Frankie's wrist and releasing it. Frankie was shaking his arm.

Grenville looked back at Basil and said, "Is God going to forgive us for what we are about to do?"

Basil shrugged and said, "That is your province," as he threw a punch into the oversized belly of the man. Frankie bent over from the blow and took another shot to the forehead from Grenville's elbow. Frankie went down hard.

"Just like the old days, eh, Bas?" Grenville said, rubbing his elbow. "That hurts."

"Want to get some ice on it?" Beault asked.

"Ice for what?"

"For your elbow. You said it hurts."

"My elbow doesn't hurt."

"You just said it does."

"No, I said his head hurts. Look at him." Grenville pointed down at Frankie who was holding his head and groaning.

Beault grinned. Turning to the fallen foe's friends, he said, "Anybody else? One at a time or all six of you at once? How do you want to do this?"

It was immediately clear that none of them wanted to do it either way. They didn't move. Beault added, "I have to tell you gentlemen that it is your good fortune today that you did not make my brother angry. Because when he's angry he hits people."

"He just hit Frankie. You hit him too. What are you going to do about him?" one of the six asked, pointing at Frankie lying on the ground. "You just going to leave him there?"

"Oh yeah, right," Beault said. "Let's roll him into the gutter out of the way from folks using the sidewalk."

"You can't do that."

"You're right, sir, we can't do that. If we did that, dogs would come along here and use Frankie as a fire hydrant."

"Well, what then?" one of the six said.

"Your friend," Grenville said, "your problem."

The Protheringtons walked away toward the falafel-laden deli.

"This is pretty good, you know that?" Beault said through a full mouth from a falafel sandwich.

"Of course I know it. I've had it before," Grenville said. "It's why I wanted to come here. I like it. Figured you would, too, being the adventurous epicure you are."

"Do they make hamburgers here also?" Beault asked with a straight face.

"I hope not."

The Protherington brothers finished their falafel lunches and leaned back. Basil said, "I'm getting married" as if no one was listening.

"Married? How nice," Grenville said. "Who to?" Beault smiled at that. "Like I haven't talked about it with Nadine," Grenville added, grinning at his brother.

"I didn't think I ever would. I asked Miriam a couple of times and got the same answer each time. Now if you had asked Mir..." Beault said to Grenville who laughed out loud. "I didn't have the nerve to ask Emily," Beault said. Then he paused. "Whoa, can you imagine what that would have turned into if she had said yes? Married to Emily Birch-Aspen-Protherington? She would have socked the poop out of me once or twice a week." Grenville laughed out loud again. "And Nadine. I never thought that I had the slightest chance of marrying her," Beault said. "You and her and her secret. I was completely taken in by that. My dream, a lesbian."

"I would have told you sooner or later," Grenville said. "I, oh and Nadine would have too, we just needed the right time to tell you."

"Like after I got myself shot?" Beault laughed. "Well, all's well that ends well, right? Thank God and thank you and thank Nadine. By the way, we talked about the wedding and decided we want a small ceremony with just a few close friends. And we want it in your church and we want you to marry us. Nothing big, nothing fancy."

"That is a very nice idea. I'll be pleased as punch to perform the ceremony." Grenville looked at his brother. "Nadine is on board with this? What I mean is...small ceremony and just a few close friends? Most women, I'm guessing at this, see their weddings as more than small and few."

"No. After we talked it over, she said she agreed with me," Beault said.

"If you say so," Grenville raised his eyebrows. "When's this going to happen?"

"Well, yeah, that's the thing. We also thought we ought to wait until this assassination nonsense is settled. Don't need one of these things messing with the focus on the other. Planning a wedding, even a modest one, and trying to rid our favorite city of cornball opportunists at the same time...we thought that is not a good idea."

"Wow, my old brother and my favorite girl are showing some mighty powerful maturity. Oh, wait, you aren't getting cold feet, are you?" Grenville smiled.

Beault didn't answer that question, instead he said, "You know, I know you're a pretty good trash-talker. Keep it up and me and Nadine will run off to Vegas and get hitched down there so you won't have any part in it."

The cook walked over to the table and asked, "How was your lunch, gentlemen?"

"As good as always," Grenville said.

"You have a new fan in me," Beault told the cook.

When Grenville reached for his wallet, Beault said, "Allow me."

21

After Mickey Truke was jockeyed into a role in the plan to unearth assassins, another meeting came to order in the Castro church assembly hall where Grenville holds forth for his church-going crowd. Today's meeting was greeted by an alluring aroma from the kitchen. Mickey, Nadine, Beault, Grenville, and Uncle Ben sat at the familiar table. There was coffee, tea and fresh-baked chocolate chip cookies spread around.

They drank their drinks, nibbled at the treats and talked about what they knew and what they didn't know. There was more of the latter, of course. They agreed there had been no productive insights into Los Menendez Banda or the Haight-Ashbury Wild Bunch because the two gangs had only made claims. They had not gone public in any other way. What troubled most of them at today's table was that they did not have a means to touch either outfit.

Mickey said, "What we need is radar to pinpoint where these perps can be contacted, especially the Banda."

"I've got an iron in the fire for that," Beault said.

"An iron in the fire," Grenville said to Nadine. "Does he talk in these riddles at home or only when he has a wider audience?"

Nadine started to answer when Beault said over-politely, "Let the man have his rare moment of an attempt at a humorous put down. If we bear with him, he will run out of these sophomoric jokes and we can get back to serious sleuthing."

"Wanna step outside and settle this like men?" Grenville pointed at his brother. "That would give me another star on my crown."

Nadine leaned over toward Ben Franklin and gave him one of those stage whispers that everyone is supposed to hear. "I have to live with one of these children and host the other one on too many occasions." Ben laughed out loud. Mickey was giggling.

"Back to business," Nadine said when the snickering ended.

Grenville smiled. "What are you going to tell us about your iron in the fire?"

"Nothing right now. I want it to get real hot first."

"I hope you..." Grenville spoke quietly and slowly and then petered out. He laughed.

"Dang right," Beault said. After a pause, he snorted, "Haight-Ashbury Wild Bunch. I've been wondering about them. That can't be serious, can it? It's gotta be a scam. It sounds more like high school guys with nothing better to do than to pull a prank."

Ben said, "I agree with you because the name sounds so addle-brained. But my contact says we should take them seriously until we don't have to anymore. He's not saying they're capable of a shooting like this, he's only saying they are a little desperate for money and a lot short on smarts. If they didn't do this hit, they still may be thinking they could do something like that under the right circumstances. Course, they would need a lot of luck and a complete intellectual makeover. That is, my contact says they would."

Beault said, "How does your contact know about this outfit?"

"He owns the apartment building where they live. He didn't know them as the Wild Bunch per se, just as a, er, a bunch of misfits. He moved quickly – but carefully – after he heard their claim that they killed Mr. Johnson in Sausalito. He had some of his people, friends, you know, scour the Haight and it paid off."

"Your contact sounds like a man who has many sides," Beault said.

"Many," Franklin agreed.

"The Haight-Ashbury Wild Bunch," Beault repeated. "That cracks me up." He thought. "Let's play it safe. I'll call Joe Blough and tell him what we know from your contact, Ben."

"The captain already knows," Ben said. "He was told earlier."

"Oh, now I get it. That's how Blough knew to, how'd he call it, to put an ear into the Haight-Ashbury Wild Bunch. Ben, you are a man of untapped depths. I swear."

Ben sighed. "My untapped depths, as you describe them, are...that is...is a man who also has many sides and has his own ear to the ground in the city." Ben puffed and coughed and laughed again.

"Say," Mickey suddenly spoke, "where are those two Frisco cops?"

"Uh, Mickey, San Francisco," Beault corrected.

"Yeah, those two who were here last time."

"San Francisco cops."

"That's what I said."

"No, you said Frisco cops."

"What's the difference?"

Nadine answered. "In some parts of the city, the difference would be a full-court punch-up, leaving you with a new appreciation for the city's name. The acceptable name. San Francisco."

"Really?"

"Really."

"So where are they?"

"Who?"

"Those two Fr...uh, the captain and the lieutenant."

Beault smiled. "I don't know who you are talking about, Mr. Truke. There have been no San Francisco police detectives here from the homicide division unless they were attending Sunday services conducted by my brother. Maybe just stopping in for lunch and conversation."

"Yeah, but..."

"But what."

"Oh, I get it," Mickey said. "They weren't here."

"They weren't here," Grenville confirmed.

"You people don't do police work up here the way we did in Beverly Hills," Mickey said.

"No," Beault explained.

"You'll get used to it, Mickey, don't worry," Grenville said. "Hey, have you thought about coming to church here? I told you you're welcome anytime."

Truke looked up at Grenville and didn't say anything.

22

The last thing on Mickey's mind was to go to church. Except for the pressure he got from Beault, cops, Miss Berry, his Uncle Ben, and the irresistible baked goods, he would have scorned this particular church. But he knew better. His presence at this non-religious tete-a-tete was not voluntary, it was required. That being so, he decided to show he could stand on his own two feet at times. Therefore, pulling Beault aside before departing the Castro, he inquired, "Is it true you walked away with a fortune in jewels from that bird case?"

Beault gawked at Mickey. "Uh..."

"From that bird statue case I keep hearing about."

Reluctantly, Beault said, "Yes."

"How much was it, you know, if you don't mind me asking?"

"A lot."

"Uncle Ben said – now this was before he met you and got to know you better and kinda likes you and really doesn't mind that you took the money – Uncle Ben says you didn't...that it wasn't yours to take."

"Did he?"

"I heard you gave a lot of the money away. That true?"

"Yes," Beault admitted.

"Who to?"

"Different folks. Deserving folks."

"And you bought a house?"

"Yes."

"In San Francisco?"

"Yes."

"In Pacific Heights?"

"Yes."

"Where prices are insane?" Truke observed.

"The house is out on the edge of Pacific Heights where prices aren't insane," Beault defended himself.

"Oh right. You get a good deal?"

"We had cash and that seemed to have some influence."

"You Jew 'em down?"

"Mickey! Christ!"

"What? You got to negotiate these days. Jew 'em down to get a better price."

"Holy shit, Mickey, people don't do that anymore."

"Sure they do, all the time. Everybody negotiates."

"They don't call it that. Political correctness, Mickey. We don't say 'Jew 'em down' anymore. That's not nice."

"I've been saying that for ages. It's an old saw."

"But we've come a long way from the old days. We're more sensitive about ethnicities today. You shouldn't go around talking like that."

"No, it's okay."

"No, it is not okay. How would you feel if you said that in the presence of a Jewish person?"

"Are you Jewish, Beault?"

"No."

"I am," Mickey said.

Beault glared at Truke. "Is there any argument that would convince you that that phrase is just wrong?"

"I don't know. Everybody in my family has talked that way as long as I can remember. I never thought about it that way, that it was wrong."

"Maybe you should start thinking about it."

Mickey was thinking about something when he said, "Well, how much?"

"A lot of thought," Beault advised.

"Not that. How much did you make on the jewels? And don't say a lot."

Beault shook his head, but decided to answer anyway. "Grenville has a jeweler in his congregation who really knows his way around the precious stones world. He..."

"This church of your brother's. Is it really a church? It sure doesn't appear to be when I'm around it and Grenville's so-called churchgoers. People tell stories about it."

"Oh, it's a church. Grenville insists on that even though they conduct themselves in, let's see, how can I put this? In..."

"Non-church ways?"

Beault laughed. "Hmmm, yeah, that about says it."

"Okay, how much?"

"Right. The jeweler has been – there were nearly seventy stones in the statue – he's been dealing them to private collectors. Apparently, the jewels and stones are rare and exceptional. He's dealt almost all of them."

"How much?"

"Geez, Mickey, you are really nosey."

"I am that. How much?"

"Close to eight million...and climbing."

Mickey had nothing to say to that. A few minutes passed in silence when Mickey said, "With all that money, why are you still in the private eye business? I'd be on an island in the Caribbean under a sunhat and next to a pina colada and a half-dressed native who couldn't take her eyes off me."

"Sounds pretty nice, Mickey. Two things. Nadine is committed to the news business and intends to keep her job. I don't believe she would go to that island with me, even if the native girl wasn't a part of the deal. And I couldn't blame her. She gets a real rush from her job."

"What's the other thing?"

"Oh yeah, that. I like my job, too. Not everybody can say that. It's like if a guy's an assassin and he keeps getting hired to whack people. He gets a big payoff and thrill each time..."

Beault started laughing when Mickey broke in to say, "Funny, real funny. You don't have to keep bringing up my unproductive career in the hit business."

"And thank God for that, eh, Mickey?"

Mickey grunted. "Yeah." Then he said, "You bought a car, too."

"I did. It was heartbreaking to give up that old heap of mine. We were a couple. A love-hate relationship. I'll take the new one though because it works when I want it to, and it does not compress my spinal column like my old one when the shocks and suspension proved feisty. First time I've ever bought a new car."

"You Jew 'em down?"

23

The Haight-Ashbury has gone through changes since it was ground zero in the nineteen fifties for the Beatniks and the nineteen sixties for the hippie movement. But mostly what they are – these changes – are just different people playing the character roles of the past. Something that has not changed, however, is the lure the neighborhood has for those who are politely termed low-income. Just, you know, different people is all. You also know now, because I have told you, Haight-Ashbury is a district in San Francisco. Well, duh. San Francisco. Where rents are not happily copasetic with low-income citizens. And this leads us back to the Haight-Ashbury Wild Bunch and the apartment they live in almost on top of one another in a small two-bedroom unit that they can afford most months. Picture a rabbit warren.

"Hey, everybody, look what I, uh, found. It's a computer. Now we got a computer. Maybe it will tell us something about them Mexicans who mouthed off about Sausalito," the twenty-something announced proudly as he came through the door.

The new computer addition became the only modern device in the whole apartment of the Haight-Ashbury Wild Bunch. Two or three of the Wild Bunch stared at the laptop like it was a deity. "Cool," one of them said, "where'd you get it?"

"Uh, well, somebody musta been throwing it away. So I brung it here." He brung it here from the library branch over on Page Street when he came out of the men's room where he had taken a leak and saw it sitting idly near where a high school girl had just stepped over to reach for a reference book. When she got back to her chair, her laptop was missing. Her laptop was under this guy's arm outside on his way to the apartment.

"Know how to use it?"

"Me? No. You?"

"No."

One of them asked, "Anybody know how to use this thing?" Blank stares.

When nobody said he knew how to operate a computer, Wobber said, "Yeah, I can."

"Cool, now we're going places. Hey, where'd you learn to work one of these? You don't look like a nerd."

"When I did time," he said. "I had a choice, either work with these things or do grunt work. I don't like grunt work."

"You did time? What for?"

Wobber looked at the one who asked and did not say a word.

The forty-something leader of the Wild Bunch said, "How can this help us if we want to do some business? Can it do that? You know how?"

"Do you?" Wobber threw it back at him.

"No, that's why I'm asking you."

"Yeah, I know how to do that. Give me some time to fiddle with this thing. It's not the same kind I used when I was at...uh...before."

His Wild Bunch clubmates gazed at Wobber.

The leader pressed the issue. "What can you do? How will it work?"

"I guess the best thing to do is build a Facebook page. It..."

"What's a Facebook page?" one of the loungers asked.

"It's a place on the web that'll be all about the Haight-Ashbury Wild Bunch. We can say whatever we want. People talk to other people this way, too."

"Cool. How much does it cost?"

"Nothing. It's free."

"Way cool."

Wobber looked at the HAWB leader and said, "You can take credit on this for the Sausalito shooting, too. You know, besides the calls you made to the press. Other people will see it and give you more street creds."

"Why do that?" the leader asked.

"Why not?"

That stumped the leader. "Uh, I don't know," he admitted.

"Also," Webber gambled, "you got a gun in case somebody comes along looking for a hit man?"

"Yeah," the leader rose up, "yeah, I got a gun. Guns. I got that covered."

Wobber turned back to the laptop and didn't say anything.

Someone asked, "What else can this computer do?"

Wobber thought for a moment and said, "Well, there is one thing. It can help you figure out your income taxes." He looked around at the Wild Bunchers. "Makes it easy for you to file your taxes." That got a big laugh from everyone in the room.

"No, I'm serious. Income taxes," he repeated and laughed again.

Then, "What else? What else can this thing do?" the guy asked again.

"A whole lotta things. You just have to add the right kind of software stuff to it and then you can do other shit. Software isn't cheap though."

"Oh."

"We won't need more than the Facebook. That'll take care of what we want to do. That's all I'll have to do."

"Oh."

Wobber did not tell them that he could also add very helpful password-protected e-mail sites for useful – and covert – communications with people not known as Wild Bunchers. And he did just that. "Cool," he said to himself.

24

Beault and Truke chose a day to sneak around, you know, sub rosa, to see if they could learn anything about the Haight-Ashbury Wild Bunch. With a name like that it might just be a scary opponent, and that prospect meant it was advisable for the anti-assassin team to get a fix on what they were getting into.

Truke drove. He felt more confident behind the wheel. He had gone through urban driver training as part of his police career down south. At a red light, Mickey turned to Beault and said, "I did urban driving training down in L.A. The instructors never drove in this city, I can tell you that. Where do these drivers come from?" Beault tried to laugh but choked.

Not behind the wheel, Beault handled navigation since he was acquainted with the city's streets and how to avoid some of the pot-holes. Mickey found an unoccupied parking spot on Haight Street east of Stanyan. After depositing a fistful of coins in the meter, the two, dressed San Francisco-casual, began strolling on the streets in the famous old district.

It was just before noon on a weekday and, surprise-surprise, sunny. The tall Beault and the below average height of Truke might have drawn some glances, but this was Haight-Ashbury. Being glance-worthy was no big deal in this neighborhood. What might have separated them from their fellow pedestrians in one essential way, however, was their disdain of San Francisco's unwritten law about fitting in. They did not have a dog on a leash. Or dogs.

They knew the address of the Wild Bunch, but they felt they needed to tread cautiously and not spook anyone there or others who might have a connection with the HAWB. No, just wander around and carefully pick spots where they could drop innocent questions.

"Let's eat," Beault suggested. "I know a place that serves up killer falafel."

"No way," Truke protested. Beault started to object but stayed quiet.

Instead, they found a small sandwich joint and stepped in after slipping their guns from holsters on their belts at the small of their backs into their pockets. Easier to sit that way. They grabbed a table against the wall and ordered sandwiches and drinks from a skinny, bearded, twenty-something kid who came out from the back. They settled in.

"Haight-Ashbury," Beault said to Truke louder than needed since they were only three feet apart, "this is a cool place."

"Oh yeah," Mickey agreed.

"Lots of history, lots of color," Beault continued, "and some wild characters. A bunch of wild characters if you believe all the stories people tell about this place."

"What," Truke picked up, "a wild bunch here in Haight-Ashbury?"

Beault saw the kid look quickly down at them. "Uh, yeah, that's right. You're right. A wild bunch here in the Haight."

The kid brought over a coffee for Mickey and a diet soda for Beault. "Is that right," Beault asked the waiter, "a wild bunch here in the Haight? You look like you might live around here. That's what we've heard. The Haight, it's got a history. Like there's a wild bunch around. Think that's right?"

Beault was watching the kid who rubbed his bearded chin. "Whata you mean, mister, about a wild bunch?"

"Oh nothing. We just, you know, we hear things about Haight-Ashbury."

Truke smiled. "I've heard it too. But what I heard was...oh, never mind, it don't sound like it could be true."

The kid looked at Mickey and then glanced around the empty café to see if anyone might overhear him as he started to say something when "bing" went the bell on the chef's counter. The order was up. The kid didn't say anything as he put the two plates on the table and walked away. Beault and Truke went dutifully through their sandwiches and drinks. The kid stood watching with his back to the chef's counter. The chef did non-cooking chef things behind the kid. No orders to prepare. No customers except those two loud guys.

"You know what, Herman," Beault said to Mickey, "this Haight area, I don't think this is where you'd find a wild bunch. You know where I'd look for that?"

"Where?" Herman – Truke – asked.

"North Beach."

"Hmmm," Mickey digested the answer. "The North Beach Wild Bunch sounds more realistic."

Beault finished his soda and nodded at the waiter. "Check, please."

The kid went through the adding procedure slowly and brought the result over to the table. Beault looked at it and said, "You probably didn't hear us. We were talking about the history of the Haight and the people and all like that. But we decided that if there was a real wild bunch of locals, it was more likely to be over in North Beach. What do you think?" Beault was pulling out his wallet as he was talking. The wallet was in, you guessed it, his front pocket. No easy pickings for a pickpocket.

The waiter looked down at Beault and after hesitating said, "I think you'd be wrong."

"Well, there you are, Herman," Beault said to Mickey, "this fellow here says we'd be wrong. And he looks like he knows what he's talking about. Probably does live here in the Haight and gets around and, you know, knows stuff."

"Yeah," Mickey offered, "I think you're on to something there, um, Malcolm." Beault smiled. "But darn it," Mickey added, "I'm not convinced. Just look at this district. It just doesn't look like wild bunch turf the way North Beach does. No, I'm not convinced." Mickey looked up at the waiter and said, "Sorry, my friend, Haight-Ashbury and wild bunch, I don't see them two things connected."

The waiter was shifting from foot to foot showing a little impatience with these two non-believers. "What if I told you I happen to know there's a wild bunch here already?"

"A wild bunch? Here? In the Haight? Well I'll be a monkey's uncle," Beault admitted. "Right here in the Haight," he confirmed to Truke. "But that's, what, just a name, isn't it?" Beault went on. "They're not really wild like, are they? Just a name, right?"

"Keep your eyes open," the waiter said as he lowered his voice and looked around. "You'll see for yourselfs."

"Wow," Mickey said. "That's scary."

"Damn straight," the kid said. He looked back at the chef who was still doing a lot of non-cheffing what with an empty diner at the moment. He was also shaking his head as he overheard his waiter talk about the neighborhood. The chef was twice the waiter's age and did not look like he believed the kid.

The kid said, "I'm not saying nothing, but you heard of that dude who got hisself kilt over in Sauspalito?"

"No, what's that all about?"

"Well, I happen to..." the kid looked at the front door and then back at the chef who was still shaking his head..."I happen to know who done that."

"You do? A killing?" Beault said quietly, looking around the café.

"Yeah. It was in the news."

"Wait a second, it was in the news and," Beault whispered, "you are trying to tell us that this wild bunch in Haight-Ashbury killed someone?"

"I ain't saying nothing about anything, but yeah. Only thing is, if I was you, I wouldn't go around saying you don't think we..." the kid looked around again..."think the Wild Bunch isn't a tough bunch, if you know what I mean."

Mickey looked at Beault and said, "This fella sounds like he is on to something. You know what, Malcolm, I am one guy who is not going to be saying anything about this."

"Me, too," Beault said.

"Damn straight," the kid said.

"Well hell's bells," Beault looked up at the kid. "Say, you, uh, what I mean, are, um, are you one of...do you know who these people are? Are you..."

"I told ya, I ain't saying nothing about nothing, okay?"

Beault raised his hands in surrender and got up, tossing money down to cover the lunch and tip. "Come on, Malcolm, we'd better finish our business here and head back."

Mickey laughed and said, "Okay."

Sated with a sandwich and a coffee and soda, the two diners stepped outside into the unusual glare. They both put on sunglasses. Mickey said, "I'm Herman, you're Malcolm."

"What?"

"You called me Malcolm in there at the end."

"I did? Did I get that wrong?" Beault asked.

"Actually, I don't know, but I'm sure that it went right over Einstein's head. He was busy bragging on the Wild Bunch. Sure looks like he's one of them."

"I got that idea. If he is, well, God help them. He is not the smoothest billiard ball in the rack."

Truke looked down the block toward his car and uttered, "Uh-oh."

"What?"

"My car."

Beault looked. "Uh-oh."

They took their guns from their pockets and put them back in their holsters.

"How many?"

"I see five, six, seven. Seven I guess."

"Well, Malcolm, let's go."

"I'm Herman, aren't I?"

"Dunno anymore."

They began walking slowly toward the car. One said, "How many can you take?" "One," said the other. "Okay, I'll take six then." Laughing.

"Hold on," Beault stopped Mickey. "Look in here." They faced a shop window. "Are they watching us?"

Mickey glanced down. "No."

"Good, I'll cross the street and come around from behind."

"Okay."

"Mickey."

"What?"

"I know these guys. It was them who Grenville and I met up with last week. They are not as tough as they look."

"Bas, they look like clowns."

"Bozos. The fat one there on your hood is Frankie."

"Okay."

Beault crossed the street. Mickey waited a few moments before walking again. As he got to his car he saw Beault had crossed back to his side and was now a few car lengths away looking into a newspaper rack. Mickey counted again. Seven. He was right. All were older than he figured. Forties, maybe even fifties for a couple of them. Frankie was sitting on the hood of the car, another on the trunk. Two were leaning against the curbside doors. Three were just milling about.

Mickey stopped. "Hi," he said.

"This your car?" the paunchy fellow on his hood said.

"My car? Let me look." Mickey stared at the auto, looked at the front, and went along it to look at the trunk. He came back. "Yes, I believe this is my car."

"We've been watching it for you so nobody'd mess with it or steal it."

"Isn't that just the nicest thing," Mickey said to him. "That's real neighborly."

"Neighborly, yeah, but not that much. It's going to cost you."

"Cost me? Like I pay you to watch it out here in public view where it's pretty safe anyway?"

The attention of the six pals of the paunchy Frankie was on Frankie and Truke. They hadn't seen Beault slide in behind them. Looking on.

"Yeah," the hood sitter said.

"How much? How much does it..." Mickey started but then stopped. He cast his eyes over the seven. Unformidable, middle-aged and obviously not among the more prominent citizens of San Francisco, he easily deduced. Bozos. "Hey, I know you guys, don't I? You are the famous Haight-Ashbury Wild Bunch, aren't you?"

Frankie laughed out loud. "Them shits. No fucking way. Them pussy assholes are, well, they're pussy assholes. Dumb as dirt."

"How do you know that? How'd you figure that out?"

"I don't need to do no figuring out. I know."

"What I mean is, you look like you couldn't figure out, oh, let's see, how to clap hands."

"Hey, shorty, watch your fucking mouth. I got a need to beat somebody's ass today and yours is just right for that."

"You are pretty tough looking, that's for sure. Like that big knot on your forehead. And that ugly color. How'd you get that, you run into a bus, knock it off its route somewhere?"

Frankie rubbed his forehead. "That's nothing."

"It sure doesn't look like nothing. It looks like it hurt like hell. Did it hurt? Looks like somebody might have clocked you a good one there. That's what it looks like."

"Eat shit."

"Not today. Let's get back to the Wild Bunch. I heard that they were a box of donut holes and you guys look just right for that."

"Hey, prick, you heard wrong."

"I guess I heard wrong then if you say so," Mickey said. Then he looked at the parking meter. Only a few minutes of legal time left. "Why don't you get off my car now. I have to leave."

"You ain't paid me yet."

"Oh yeah, that. How much again, how much is it?"

"How much you got on you?"

"Whoa, you want all of it?"

"You want your car back, don't ya?"

"Yes. Yes, I do. I guess that makes sense. But first get off my car."

"Pay up and then I'll get off."

Mickey looked around at the other six guys. He eyed Beault who nodded. Both hands were behind him. Back to the hood sitter, Mickey said, "Frankie, you noxious germ, I am going to count to three and if you are not off my car by the time I reach three, I will rip your heart out."

"Ooooh, I am so...how'd you know my name?"

"Three!" Mickey dictated, ignoring one and two, as he grabbed Frankie's ankles and pulled him off the hood, his head banging down the side of the car and to the sidewalk. The six bystanders gasped and started to advance. "Don't do that," Beault belted out. They all turned and recognized the tall man standing there. Holding a gun.

Mickey helped Frankie up to his feet then hit him in his ample stomach. Oooof. Then Mickey hit him in the mouth, crying "ouch" from the blow as he shook his hand. "Oh hell," Mickey gulped. Then he hit Frankie's stomach once more, putting him onto the sidewalk again where blood was splattered from his mouth and nose.

Mickey stood over the fallen guy. "Should I hit him again, Malcolm?"

"I'm Herman, aren't I?" Beault laughed. Then, "Gentlemen, pick up this trash and get him out of here. I know you know how to do that. Experienced at it, aren't you?" he winked, but nobody saw that. "I'm going to count to three and if you haven't..."

"Three!" shouted Mickey, who was shaking his sore hand and blowing on it.

The six non-combatants hustled the bleeding Frankie up Haight Street passing three women walking down the street with five dogs on leashes. "What is going on here?" one of the ladies inquired when they reached Beault and Truke. "Was there a fight? That man was bleeding all over his snout."

Beault looked at Mickey. They looked at the women. "Oh," Beault recovered, "no, no, ma'am, not a fight." He hesitated. "We're making a movie."

"A movie? Where are the cameras? There are no cameras," the woman declared.

Beault paused. Mickey butted in. "Cameras? Where are the cameras? They're, uh, they're up on top of those buildings. Upstairs, ma'am."

The women turned around to look. Beault said, "Yeah, they're hidden. Uh, it's a, you know, a special technique. The director is a brilliant young film maker from Iceland. He makes all his movies from above the actors. Realism, you know."

The women looked at Beault and Truke as though they needed psychiatric supervision. One of the ladies said, "This is horse puckey. These weirdos are full of it. An Iceland director on a roof. Realism... to hell with this crap. That's a movie I sure as shit will not go see. Come on, girls, let's get moving. Princess here hasn't taken her dump yet today.

Let's get to the park. I don't want to have to wipe her poop off the sidewalk. That's so messy." The women walked off, the five leashes getting entangled around the legs of Beault and Truke after two of the dogs urinated on Mickey's tires.

As the women headed along Haight Street, Mickey turned to Beault, "Do they make movies in Iceland?"

Beault said he had no idea.

25

The phone rang every little while as Beault was confusing Dagmar with more descriptions of private investigation work in yet another attempt to answer her question – "What do you do?" Dagmar picked up the phone each time it rang and in nearly every case had to declare the office assistant job at Jaguar Beault Investigations was filled. Someone had been hired, she informed everyone in a warm and sympathetic manner, adding "I'm sorry," while passing that smile to Bas. The new office assistant on the job.

"I am hearing you say, Bas, that being a private investigator is not an easy profession to define." Beault's face reddened slightly. "You seem, Bas, to bend with whatever the wind may blow your way." She smiled. "I expect, too, that there are dangers associated with your job. I say that only because I enjoy watching mysteries on television where there is always intrigue and violence. On the TV, all the characters have guns. Are you allowed to have a gun?"

"I…"

"Wait," Dagmar stopped Beault. "I have wanted to say this for the longest time." She stretched up to her five-foot-two-or-three height and said, "Do you pack heat?" Her smile turned to a giggle.

Beault broke out laughing before he said, "Dagmar, you are as lovely as a flower. Yes, I pack heat. I'm not a big gun rights guy who says everybody should carry one. I am very big about having bad people prevented from carrying them. Then again, that takes us on a slippery slope of a political and private rights debate where I prefer not to go. On the other hand, I carry a gun because it often comes in very useful when I am, you know, investigating."

Dagmar smiled. "Have you ever shot anyone?"

"Only once, when I was in the Navy and...I was an SP – Shore Patrol, or Navy cop – and we had to break up a fight. I was in San Diego and we'd just come home from a four-month deployment at sea. The guys were drinking and, surprise, it got out of hand. Some guy tried to take my weapon from me. He didn't get it. I pulled it free and it went off. Got him right in his sit-downs. I think I was more embarrassed than he was."

Dagmar smiled. "Have you ever been shot?" she asked.

Beault nodded.

"Where?"

"Right here in good old San Francisco."

"What I meant was," Dagmar smiled, "where on you were you shot? In your, er, your sit-downs?"

"No, right here," Beault answered, pointing at his chest.

Dagmar recoiled slightly, which led Beault to recount the big climax at Kezar Stadium at the park and the bullet he took from Mrs. Smith into a bulletproof vest he was wearing. She listened intently until Beault finished.

"You did not tell me that part when you were giving me your history."

"I like to forget it."

"It must have scared you," she said.

"Hmm. Know what? It happened so out of the blue that I didn't have time to get scared. It knocked me on my butt, and I got pretty disoriented for a bit before I realized I wasn't dead. That bulletproof vest stopped the bullet but not the craziness. People came to my aid."

"You couldn't shoot back?"

"I was flat on my back. Wasn't armed anyway. Not that day."

"But most of the time?" she asked.

"I pick and choose. Depends on where I am, where I'm going, who I'm going to see, where there might be...you know, a threat. I'm licensed thankfully. Almost everybody is not and I like it that way. I could give you a long list of reasons why that's the case."

Dagmar pulled a gun from her purse.

Beault recoiled and not so slightly. His heart rate went off like a surface-to-air missile. Not again, he worried.

Dagmar saw Beault's instinctive reaction and uttered, "Ooh, sorry." Then she showed the gun to him, careful not to point it.

Beault got his bearings back some. "You carry a gun?"

"Why certainly. I feel so much safer with this."

"Is it...are you...is it registered?" Beault's heart rate was dropping back toward normal.

"I suppose so. I really don't know. My son gave this to me years ago. It's cute, isn't it?"

"Dagmar, it's a gun. Cute is not one of the ways guns are usually described. Have you shot it?"

"Oh yes. My sons and I go to a range and practice."

"I am overwhelmed."

"Whatever for?"

"Your gun, that's whatever for. I would have never guessed." Beault gaped at Dagmar. "They have given you a gun to carry concealed against the law, they have taught you how to shoot it, and now they keep you in shooting shape with target practice sessions." Beault said, "That is why I am overwhelmed."

"It's quite all right, Bas, really. They have taught me well. I'm pretty good at it, by the way."

"Again, Dagmar, that is not the point...to become good at it. It can be very dangerous. Do you know how many accidents happen to people with guns? The statistics are staggering."

Dagmar smiled. "I am very careful. Besides, I'm probably better with mine than you are with yours anyway." She smiled again. "Perhaps you would show me how you shoot. No," she got excited, "we should have a shoot-off. You and me. Last man, no, last woman standing."

"Are you challenging me to a contest with our guns?" Beault sneered. "Okay, toots, you're on," Beault accepted.

Dagmar beamed.

26

They were at Harris' Restaurant for dinner. Beault, Nadine, Alana, Grenville, and Dagmar. Dagmar was meeting Basil's family and soon-to-be family for the first time. As the five were led to a table in the "Library" by Harris' elegant hostess, Elise, they passed along the bar where Beault said "hi" to Robert, Freddie and Dave who were mixing drinks. "Pepsi or Coca-Cola tonight, Bas?" Dave called to him. Beault laughed. Nice to know your bartender remembers your "usual," he mused.

"Dagmar challenged me to a shoot-off," Beault told the table after they ordered drinks. "Dagmar packs heat and...oooh, don't you think about bringing it out in here and showing it off, Mrs. Davos. This is a class joint." Dagmar smiled.

"Why do you carry a gun?" Nadine asked.

"I don't want to be a victim. I figure nobody is going to fool with me if I have a gun pointed at them."

"There is logic in that, Dagmar," Grenville said. "I hope it doesn't come to a confrontation."

"I'll be ready."

"I have told her," Beault said to the others, "how dangerous it can be. How the tables are often turned on people who think they are protected by having a gun."

"I believe you, Bas," Dagmar agreed, "and you should know, shouldn't you, about gun slinging since you are the one who has been shot before." She smiled. Beault coughed and rubbed his chest.

"A shoot-off?" Nadine said. "How's that going to work?"

"Just shooting at targets. I'm pretty good at it," Dagmar bragged. "In point of fact, I am very good at it."

Beault said, "We'll see."

When Dagmar ordered Steak Diane, Beault chirped, "Hey, I thought you said you are a vegetarian."

"I am, but sometimes I cheat."

"Do you cheat at gunplay too?" Beault asked.

Dagmar looked at him. No answer, no smile, just a wink.

The adults talked about Grenville's church work, Nadine's news job, Alana's pre-school, Dagmar's sons, San Francisco's fog, Harris' delicious filets, and a little about assassins.

Dagmar finished off her meat dish after the others had mopped up their own filets. She said, "Thank you so much for this dinner and this opportunity to get to know Nadine and the beautiful Alana and Grenville. Now I know what you are talking about, Bas, how your brother is way handsomer than you are. No wonder everybody..."

"Enough," Beault stopped her. "I..." That's all he got out when he began laughing along with the others at the table.

27

After more than a week of watching the goings and comings of the Menzies, aka Los Menendez Banda, Ping Bodie had a report ready to hand over to Beault. The call came into the Outer Richmond office. Dagmar said, "This man says he is Ping Bodie." Beault said he would take it.

"Hi, Ping."

Bodie rasped, "Got it."

"Great," Beault replied.

"Want me to mail it?"

"Oh no, I want you to come to a meeting and bring it with. You can make the report yourself. The people at the meeting are the ones who will want to hear it."

"Just let me know when and where," Bodie said.

"Tomorrow. I'll pick you up and take you there."

"You're the boss," Bodie said.

When Beault hung up, Dagmar said, "That man sounds like he has smoked his entire life."

"No. He told me he's never had a cigarette."

"I can admire that, but that voice," Dagmar said. "Who is he?"

"Remember the pigeon statue story? Well, Ping is the father of the woman who shot me."

"Good heavens."

"He's a private eye himself and is one of the top ones in the city. That day at Kezar tore him up real bad. I had to talk hard to get him to help me on this matter. He's a plus. Oh, you'll meet him tomorrow."

"Will I?"

"Yes, I want you at that meeting."

Beault arrived ten minutes late to that meeting in the Castro at Grenville's church and the convenience of the assembly hall. He was late on purpose because he wanted to get a rise out of the people already there. He wanted to show Frank "Ping" Bodie that he was not only welcome, but also he was supported by Grenville and Nadine who remembered him from that day at Kezar when Bodie's life sank after his daughter shot Beault. They also remembered him for his exuberance with a shotgun at the Top of the Bottom drinking hole when Beault retrieved Pablo Pedro Perez, the bail jumper.

Bodie got a hearty greeting from Grenville and a hug from Nadine. Ping responded warmly when Beault said, "This is my office assistant, Dagmar Davos. I invited her to be here because I think she should hear your report, too. She's my new strong right arm." Bodie smiled at Dagmar, who, naturally, smiled back. He shook Truke's hand when introduced. He winked at Ben Franklin who said, "I shoulda known I'd run into you again some day, Ping."

"You know each other?" Mickey asked.

"There were times in my past," Ben said, "when Mr. Bodie here might have sawed me off at the knees. He didn't. Instead, he showed me why some of my business operations were overreaching."

Bodie took over and said, "Mr. Franklin has a sensible sense of right and wrong," he rasped. "He saw that it was right to listen to me and some others and wrong to, well, not to. Most of Ben's peccadilloes here in the city aren't any different than other businesses operating on the shady side of San Francisco's streets, so certain heads looked the other way when Ben was, well, operating. This arrangement worked for me," Bodie added, "because I got a backstage pass behind the curtain at San Francisco's theater of the absurd, where Ben and others were known to, yes, operate." He rasped his raspy laugh. "Ben thought it was sensible to cooperate in that sensible way of his." Another raspy chuckle.

Bodie stared at Ben Franklin. "Ben, how in God's name did you turn so mighty stupid and choose to kill people for money? Don't even try to answer that. There is no excuse, no rationale, no explanation that will justify that, again I say, mighty unenlightened choice. Do you know how lucky you are that you don't have blood on your hands?"

"Yes," Ben said looking at his nephew.

"Beault tells me he thinks he and Miss Berry have talked you out of that unenlightened idea. Is that true?"

"Yes."

"Then they are better than I am."

"Yes," Ben nodded and sighed. "Yes, I'm done with that. Their friend Joe Blough hinted" – and here he stopped and thought – "well, more than hinted that he too thinks that it was ignorant. He said quite clearly that it would be suicidal if I brought it up again...and then he easily got me to throw my weight into plans to axe these other upstarts at the assassination game. Ping, I'm a different guy now."

"Thought that might be the case," rasped Bodie.

"Who is this guy?" Mickey blurted. "Another cop?"

"Let's all sit down," Beault said.

"Grab some coffee and sandwiches," Grenville invited.

The table in Grenville's assembly hall slowly got populated with the small group spreading lunches in front of themselves. They began to eat.

"Well?" Mickey again.

Beault looked up from a sandwich. "Oh yes, Mickey's question, who is he?"

Grenville began laughing and nodding. "Mickey, this is Basil's iron in his fire, that's who he is. Am I right about that?"

"You are right about that," Beault said to Grenville. "Mickey, Mr. Bodie is a private investigator. He has been one for what, forty or fifty years, Ping?" Bodie shrugged. "People around our line of work know Ping for two things, one, he is one of the best at what he does, and, two, he doesn't crow about it. He doesn't need to be known for doing his job. Two things that set him apart from the rest of us."

"Three things now, Beault," Bodie said quietly.

"What else?" Mickey asked.

"Nothing worth mentioning," Beault answered for Bodie.

"Okay, if that's the way...oh, the pigeon statue thing and all that," Mickey recognized. "Oh, I see. Sorry, I'll shut up."

"No need to apologize, Mr. Truke. It's mostly over now. I'm living with it."

Beault said, "Ping is here to let us in on some critical findings in this assassination crapola." Beault described how he had persuaded Bodie to accept an assignment to track down members of Los Menendez Banda, to see if there was a soft spot to get an inside look at what they do. The others ate and drank. "What he has brought back is going to give us real momentum in our scheme to decapitate them. Wanna let 'em know, Ping?"

Bodie looked around the table. "Mr. Beault told me there was a tip that a woman was making mysterious rounds throughout the city. It was easy to find her. Her name is June, by the way."

Bodie went on. "June led me around to shops and businesses and stores. She drops into these places, talks quietly for a few moments, takes an envelop from the shop owner, puts it in her classy little briefcase and walks out like she has just stolen the Mona Lisa. At some of the stops, she hands over an envelope of her own. Many of the shops are owned by Asians, mostly Chinese it seems." Bodie looked around. "You would be amused at how the shopkeepers laugh at June once she is out their door."

Bodie continued. "After some days of this, June led me to her family. It's a big troop of people who live in a few rental places down in South City. I followed one or two of them at a time for a while and learned their habits. Just like I learned about June. More useful to all you folks, I profiled them. June is in a zone all her own and should be easy to scam. Two of the boys do that newspaper-tossing thing, steal gizmos from parked cars, and sleep the rest of the day, I'd guess. The limo driver I would steer clear of. He's a jittery guy. He's got issues about something."

Bodie coughed. "It's the other two girls, the ones who run the lunch truck. I thought they were twins, but no, they're part of triplets with

June. These two others, one's named April and one's named May, strike me as being as vulnerable as June is. My recommendation, um, suggestion, is to work the three girls. There are others in the family or commune or whatever the heck that pack of people is. I would give them all a pass for now. The three women look like the best access."

"That's good work," Mickey said.

"Thanks. I've written down all this for you. I've identified two or three of June's stops as the best places to intercept her. That's what I understand one of you is going to do, right?"

"Yeah, me," Mickey answered.

"I have the locations for the lunch truck where April and May run it. They're out front at one of those tech giants in Sunnyvale where the two girls arrive about ten-thirty. They're busy for about three hours. They do a two-hour breakfast gig in Mountain View, but the Sunnyvale spot looks like the ideal place to rope them in."

"That would be me," Grenville said, "and thanks for the solid work."

Dagmar was smiling throughout the whole description by Bodie. Beault noticed that.

Nadine said, "Did you see anything or any evidence that they are building an assassination business?"

"Not specifically. June likes to act as if she can do anything, get anything done, but that's just bluster, if you ask me. If she's offering anything like that, there's been no takers while I've been watching."

"Any real evidence is going to have to come from our scheme," Beault helped answer. "That is if it's true what we suspect about them."

"Like if we can believe their claim for the Sausalito killing," Grenville offered.

"Yeah, that," Mickey seconded.

28

South San Francisco huddled under a low ceiling of cold, wet, familiar, but damnable fog, mist, drizzle and, here in the Menzies apartment, an unwelcome apprehension.

"Bruchie, it sounds like you are going to bring up some sad and negative story again. Don't..." Zelda tried to hush her oldest boy.

"Now, mother, wait a tick. I've got something very important to ask." The family living room was crowded with Menzies of one kind and another. "The ball is rolling and we think we are in the assassination business," Bruce continued. "The ball is rolling and we have even claimed we have actually done one."

"What's your question, Bruschie?" Zelda again. She was drinking.

"Who is going to be our assassin when someone tries to hire us? Which one of us is going to pull the trigger?" Some feet shuffled on the floor and some asses squirmed in some chairs. "Anyone? Anyone with an answer? Any volunteers?" Bruce looked at everyone.

One of the B-rts said everyone could take a turn. Go in round robin. Bruce scoffed. Others involuntarily shook their heads.

"Anyone here every fired a gun?" Bruce asked.

Bryce said he had when he was about eleven or twelve and one of his friends sneaked his dad's rifle out of the house and the two of them decided to shoot birds but quit right away when Bryce pulled the trigger accidentally and blew out a window on a neighbor's house. They ran like hell, Bryce was confessing...and laughing.

"That hardly counts," Bruce said. "I doubt you were pointing that gun at another person, one you aimed to kill." Bryce shook his head. "Didn't think so," Bruce Said.

"Do we have to use a gun?" April or May asked. "Is there another way to assassinate someone?"

"Poison," May or April offered. "I've seen that in the cinema."

"No," Scott said, "all things taken together the answer is a gun."

"Which," Bruce said somewhat acidly, "we do not have."

"Oh, Brutshie, there you go again, you dingo," Zelda slurred. "This is America. We could have a gun in no time."

"I've said my say," Bruce said, "and I don't like the way things are looking. I think we have to make a different plan. One where we aren't exposed."

Scott said he understood Bruce's concerns. "We have some things to figure out," he added.

29

"Bas." Nothing.
"Bas." Nothing.
"BAS."
"Hmm? What?"
"You're mumbling," Dagmar advised him.
"I am?"
"Yes."
"Sorry."
"What's the matter?" she asked.
"Crystal," Beault sighed.
"Oh yes, your little Lolita."
"Crap...oops...crud no, not that. What happened is I told her never to call me again and if she did I would call her dad and..."
"And you would tell on her?" Dagmar smiled.
"Sort of. But I had good intentions," Beault reasoned.
"Now she has called and you are perplexed."
"Yeah, perplexed. Now what do I do? What would you do, Dagmar?"
"Bas, I had four brothers and no sisters, and I have five sons and no daughters. I grew up in a male world. I'm not the one you should ask."
"Right. I feel like I have to do something. I have to get her to quit calling me. Something. Maybe a good swift kick on her behind. Not a real one, just a scare to make her grow up. I thought I'd done that when I talked to her on that call that one time. Apparently not."
"What does Ro say? Have you asked her?"
"Yes. She's already told me to do nothing. Teenage hormones...it'll pass. The psychologist who knows about this stuff."

Dagmar smiled. "So what are you going to do?"

"I'll go see if Ro, the good Doc Willingham, has changed her mind. Or if I can change it for her." Beault got off his chair and went out the door and down the hall to his head doctor floormate.

Dagmar fussed around the office with an eye on how things really ought to be if she was going to help this unorganized private investigator.

Beault came back to the office and shrugged as he told Dagmar that Doc Ro decided it was up to Beault himself whether to call or not. He picked up the phone and dialed the number he had from Crystal.

Then he hung up. Beault said, "Gotta find out something first."

Beault called Grenville.

"Hi, Bas, what's up?"

"Yeah, hi. When does Vaughan open his Good Morning Joe café on Sundays?"

"I don't know. Early though, I believe."

"By eight?"

"Yeah, probably, for the early crowd. Bicycles, dog-walkers, you know. Remember, it's Sunday mornings and I'm busy. I preach, so I don't keep track of his hours. What's going on?"

Beault explained.

"That will cut things pretty close," Grenville said after he stopped laughing. "I get there by eight, have some coffee and a roll, help you deliver the Crystal message, inform her old man, get her to agree to grow up, hustle back to my church to change, and hold services by ten. Yeah, I can do that. Who do you want there?" Grenville asked.

Beault made suggestions.

"The A-team. This will be fun," Grenville mocked.

Dagmar listened and smiled.

Beault dialed again and felt relieved when he heard "Hello." That was not Crystal. It had to be her father. I'm off to a good start, Beault believed.

"Hi, are you Crystal's father?"

"Who wants to know?"

"My name is Jaguar Beault. I need to..."

"Beault? Are you the one's been leading my daughter along? I got a good mind to take you to the cleaners."

"No, no. You got that wrong. I..."

"I don't got nothing wrong. That name – Jaguar Beault – that's all the little hussy goes on about. Jaguar Beault this, Jaguar Beault that. I have to smack her to have her close that fat mouth of hers. You better leave her alone or I'll..."

"Shut up!" Beault yelled into the phone. "Shut up and listen to me. I don't even know your daughter. She called here by mistake one time and it all started. I told her not to call me. I told her if she did I'd tell you. I think..."

"I don't care what you think, shit-for-brains," Beault heard the man say. "What you need is a good pound-down."

Beault looked at Dagmar and grinned. Then back to the phone he said, "You do good pound-downs?"

"Oh, yeah, buster, just ask anybody."

"When?"

"When what?"

"When do you want to give me a good pound-down? Cuz we have to meet so I can get you to have Crystal stop calling me. Then after that you can give me that pound-down."

"Anytime, anyplace."

Beault grinned at Dagmar again. "Super. We'll meet somewhere and I can explain about Crystal and what she's done and maybe you and her mom can get her to act, well, act more grown up. Then you can give me that pound-down. I need one anyway."

"You're really a prick, Beault. I'm looking forward to this."

"Alrighty then. There's a café on Market Street about a block east of Castro. I think it's called Good Morning Joe. Get it? Joe as in coffee?"

"When?"

"When. Good. How's about next Sunday morning about eight. That'll give me all day to recover from that pound-down you're going to give me."

"Sunday at eight. Where's it at?"

"I told you, on Market a block east of Castro."

"That's over in Fairyville."

"Fairyville? No, it's in the city," Beault corrected.

"Fairyville. Where all them homos live."

"Oh, I see. Yes, the Castro. Well, it's easy to get to anyway. Eight in the morning so nobody'll bother you while you're pounding me down."

"You got that straight, Beault-fuck."

"Ouch." The line went dead. Dagmar smiled. Beault grinned.

"You need a good pound-down, Bas?"

"Probably."

"Ever anybody ever give you a pound-down? I'd find that hard to believe."

"Grenville."

"Grenville," Dagmar considered, "yes, Grenville, that I can believe." Beault laughed at that. Dagmar said, "So, Bas, after this individual gives you a good pound-down, are you going to try to lay the blame on Ro who gave you the go-ahead to call Crystal's father?"

"Ha to that. The good Doctor Rowena Willingham will deny all, I am sure. I think she thinks my profession is...well, silly."

"She's a psychologist, Bas, she reads people's minds." Beault stared out the window.

30

Beault walked around the corner from Balboa to the street where he keeps office space to do his detecting business. He was solidified with a blueberry scone and his first coffee. His second coffee was in a cup in his hand. His eyes went down the street to his building, outside of which was parked a delivery truck. From the delivery truck went a sizable file cabinet on a dolly pushed by someone he could not see.

The scene was just the reverse of that time when Jason Bevalaqua, his tax man floormate, and the building's horse's ass, moved out of this very building those months ago. Bevalaqua? The name thundered in Beault's head. Bevalaqua? Can it be? His step picked up as he hurried ahead to face the music. The dolly and the cabinet went through his building's front door.

"Oh no," he grumbled. Beault moved faster, holding the coffee away from his coat for fear of spilling on himself. Beault went through the same front door and saw the cabinet and dolly reach the top of the stairway and turn to roll down the hallway.

"Oh no!" Beault froze. "Bevalaqua!" he shouted. There was no response. "Bevalaqua," he repeated, "is that you?" He raced up the stairs.

The dolly stopped and tilted from its delivery angle to upright. Around the side came a face. It was not Jason Bevalaqua's face. "Need something, mister?" the face asked.

"Whose cab...where's it...are you...is that..."

"You okay, mister, you sound confused."

"Who's that cabinet for?" Beault gurgled out.

The face said, "Hold on." The man pulled out a piece of paper and began reading. Beault waited breathlessly. Eventually, the face said, "It says here this here is for someone on this floor. Goes by the name..." he started chuckling "...by the name of Jag Beault."

Beault blinked. "Jag Beault? But why?"

"Don't know, pal. All I do is deliver 'em. I don't try to explain 'em."

Dagmar showed up behind the dolly and cabinet and deliveryman. "What is all this shouting about? Oh, hello, Bas, good morning." Beault was licking coffee off his fingers and hand. It was hot, but it didn't burn. "Your new filing cabinet is here, Bas. Like it?"

"My new...uh, yes, I guess I do." His shoulders dropped in relief.

Dagmar said, "Come on in and I'll tell you about some changes in your office." The changes amounted to a redecoration of the Jaguar Beault realm. "I'm talented in this area, Bas, and I thought if we spiffed things up and got some useful furniture and a computer and some other items, we could improve our efficiency and productivity. Then I remembered that you could afford it. I took it upon myself to act. That's okay, I hope," she smiled.

"Yes, certainly, yes, of course" he mumbled. "You're doing the right thing, that's for sure. I am also sure you have figured out that I could not have done it alone." He tried to laugh, but it was too on target.

"Let's start here in the reception area, my domain," Dagmar said. "I plan to put the file cabinet against that wall behind the door. I have a nice bookcase on order and a computer station will go next to my desk here. Your office doesn't have much right now. You're going to be so tickled when you see the beautiful antique desk I found for you. It has a matching credenza."

Beault's head was spinning. "Dagmar, you have been busy. Where do you find this kind of thing?"

"I grew up not poor, Bas, but my family did need to be careful with money. That has stuck with me all these years. I shop for bargains. You find great things on the Internet, for example. I also love going to garage sales on weekends. Do you? No, I don't suppose you do, Mr. Moneybags." Beault laughed. "I have found some nice, but practical, office items," Dagmar admitted. "In a few days, we will have everything we need to do the business of Jaguar Beault Investigations. In style."

Beault glanced around the half-filled space then at Dagmar. "Am I even going to be needed around here, Mrs. Davos, or are you going to take over the shamus role as well?"

"Oh, Bas, that is so funny." She smiled. "Do not worry about that. I will do the office assistant part and you will do the detective part."

"I guess I'm still employed here then," Beault laughed.

"Yes," Dagmar allowed. "Now...who is Bevalaqua?"

Beault gritted his teeth and told his new office assistant about the tax man who once occupied this very office space where they stood. "I moved from down the hall when I didn't need a place to live," he explained. "He was gone and this office was more practical." Beault used the term "horse's ass" only a few times in describing his old floor-mate. Dagmar, not surprisingly, smiled throughout.

31

Mickey Truke, Grenville Protherington, Ben Franklin, Nadine Berry, Jaguar Beault and Alana Berry were in conference at the church in the Castro. The location was still the most popular destination, not least because there was free parking. And those baked goodies.

Grenville described his part of the plan, how he would hire Los Menendez Banda to assassinate Jaguar Beault who he would accuse of forming a Political Action Committee in support of neo-conservative ideologies as well as support for anti-progressive campaign financing networks aimed at defeating wrong-minded office holders. "I'll tell them California doesn't abide people who don't think like the rest of us. They'll conclude I'm a fruitcake. Then I'll tell them I want the guy who did the Sausalito shooting to do it. They'll be indignant that I think they were not the ones who killed the old guy even though they are taking credit. I'll tell them I want that killer, a guy who got things done and got away."

Mickey took over saying he would intercept June on one of her money drops and tell her he was ready to become the triggerman for the Los Menendez Banda because he knows they need one. He'd tell June that he did the Sausalito kill...not the Banda as they claimed.

Ben allowed as how Sun Shin Wong would make sure his extended business empire would give free rein to June so she wouldn't get wind of any funny business. "Mr. Sun believes June will be easy to deceive. Mr. Sun believes June is a moron."

Nadine said the plan sounded solid. And, to be polite, fluid.

Beault said why'd he have to be the target – again – when there were others who might want a turn to take a bullet for the cause. He laughed at his little joke.

Mickey said, "This time maybe I won't miss." He laughed, too.

"Okay, Mickey," Beault countered, "this time maybe I'll be on my bike again. How's that strike you?"

"Ouch," Mickey recalled.

Alana ate cookies and drank milk. As the room was emptying, Beault said, "Stay a minute, won't you, Mickey." Mickey stayed. It was just Beault and Nadine and Alana and Grenville.

"So, Mickey, tell us about your career," Beault asked innocently.

"Not much to tell. Rolling around in a police unit where there's little crime was..."

"Not that. Not your police career. Your five fail...your five missed opportunities. Before me that is."

"No."

"Yes."

"You don't make my life very easy, know that? These damn things are burned in my memory, and it has been my plan to keep them buried there. It's bad enough to fu...screw up a job, but five? And now you, six. You can't imagine what that is like. I hope my cop buddies down in BH don't ever hear about this."

"They certainly won't hear it from us, Mickey," Beault said. "It's not like we have a megaphone to shout out your past history. Oh, oops, that doesn't count Nadine and her television station."

"Oh God, you wouldn't, would you?" he pleaded to Nadine.

"No, Mickey, I will not report your, your, what did you call it, Bas, his past history?"

Mickey slumped and said softy, "Well, okay. I'll tell. First was a woman up in St. Helena. Her and her husband own a winery. She was stepping out on him and he found out. So he gets us involved. Don't they know about divorce or marriage counseling? Anyway, I'm up there to take her out when some guy – her lover I guess – sees me lurking around. Doesn't recognize me as belonging there and I tell him to bugger off. He pulls out a gun bigger than Dirty Harry's. He runs me off the property."

Mickey looked closely at Beault. "Don't tell Uncle Ben I'm telling you this. It really makes him mad." Mickey was breathing heavy.

"Let's see, the second one is this guy in Alameda who drives a tug-boat in the Bay. He's guiding some scrap dealer and this old barge the guy's hauling his metal shit around in. This one time the old barge goes onto a sandbar in the Bay and lists. He loses a bunch of his load and makes a mess. He's ordered to clean it up and pay, pay big. He blames the tug captain who shows different and how the old barge was hardly seaworthy. All the barge's fault, not the tug. Doesn't matter. The barge owner wants to whack the tug pilot. I sneak on board and start climbing this ladder up to the tugboat's wheelhouse. My foot slips on a wet step. I go down, hitting my chin on another step, fall sideways, slip over the edge and go right into the water."

Truke stopped, stared into space and dropped his head. Beault and Berry and Grenville were chuckling. Even Alana laughed at that one.

"The third one is this teacher at Cal, a professor, I guess you call him. He teaches political science. He's about sixty and he's around young co-eds all day. What a putz. He makes these gauche plays for them – so I was told – never getting anywhere. They can't fire him. Tenure, you know. So this other prof, a woman in the same department, says to him to retire or resign or just get the hell out of Cal or else she'll expose him in a real serious way. Being a bright, highly educated, professional man, yeah, he hires us to kill the woman. So I decide to cut her brake lines on this Lexus she drives. She lives up in the Oakland hills and has a lot of steep grades getting in and out of her neighborhood. She'd go right over a cliff into a canyon. I'm under her car with a hacksaw when she comes out, gets in the car and pulls out of the garage. Right over me," Mickey sighed. "Right over me."

Alana looked up at her mother and said, "Mommy, did a car drive over this man? Was he on his bicycle this time, too?" Truke turned red. Nadine and Beault confined their laughter to little titters. Grenville nearly choked.

Mickey stared at the toddler and decided to move ahead. "The fourth one. There's this restaurant down in Santa Cruz. It's owned by two sisters. They hate each other. Fight all the time. So they work it out that one is on duty when the other isn't. Still, they find ways to fight. One of 'em finally has it. We get involved. I go after the sister. I'm outside the restaurant out back knowing the sister who is supposed to get it comes out that way from time to time. She comes out. I fire. It's really dark. I miss. She starts yelling and swearing at me. I run. She was the one who hired us."

Then Mickey told them about Svetlana, Ms. Seakrit and the Marine colonel. How he went to Svetlana's house, wasn't sure at the time only to learn later that it was her house, didn't find her there but did stumble onto a burglary. Over that ill-placed dog. "Uncle Ben didn't even tell me why we targeted her. By then I think he was beginning to question my qualifications." Beault sat open-mouthed, Nadine the same. Grenville too. Mickey said, "You were number six, Beault. How's that for a career? Happy now?"

32

In a bar up the street on Kearny just around the corner from Sacramento, Mickey sat nursing a beer. Most of the lunch crowd was gone, leaving Mickey alone with maybe half a dozen thirsty patrons. The place had a maritime name and the drinking-industry-favored low lighting that enabled customers to hide in. Soon enough June arrived, walking past Mickey to where the bartender stood watching. That is why Mickey was there. To see June. She is tall, he noticed, and blonde and pretty like the way she had been described by Bodie. June went about her business with little said and subtle swapping of envelopes. The job done, June turned and headed toward the door. When she was near to Mickey, he said, "Hi, June."

Grenville was in Sunnyvale inside the circle of mystique of world-renowned Silicon Valley tech companies where if you weren't a billionaire you were just a millionaire still working out of your garage. Grenville was in his gray suit, powder blue shirt, and cardinal red tie. This outfit was accompanied by his Hollywood-handsome good looks and a smile that could melt a girl's heart. Those attributes were not lost on April and May as they welcomed him to their lunch wagon with covetous smiles.

"I'd like a tuna melt," he ordered in a very friendly manner.

"You could make this whole truck melt, handsome," one of the sisters answered.

"Well, aren't you just the sweetest thing. Are you April or May?"

"She's April, I'm May. You know who we are. We haven't seen you at this location before. And we would remember," May winked. "Are you new in one of these brainy companies?"

"No."

"Just hungry then?"

"No."

"But..."

"I'm going to eat my sandwich over there on that bench," Grenville pointed. "When I'm finished, business will be slow for you. One of you pop over. We'll talk."

"What are we going to talk for?"

"Oh, for about five minutes. It won't take longer than that for me to explain what I need."

"I don't understand."

"That's because we haven't talked yet. Oh, and I'll take a bottle of water with my tuna melt."

June stopped and looked at Mickey. "How do you know my name?" she asked.

"Word gets around, June, and I keep my ear to the ground. That has a way of paying off."

"Have we met?"

"I'm called Mickey. Now we've met."

"I have to go," June told Mickey.

"In a minute. I won't keep you long. Then you can get back to your rounds."

June's face fell. "I'm just..." she began.

Mickey stopped her with a smile. "Let's go over to a booth, shall we? We can have a nice visit." He slipped off the bar stool and pointed toward the back of the saloon. June stepped ahead of him where he noticed she was easily four inches taller than he was. Then he noticed about two of those inches were in the heels of her sensible work shoes. June's job kept her on her feet a good part of each day.

"What's this all about?" June whispered as she scooted into the booth.

"Business," Mickey said to her.

"What kind of business?"

"The kind you are in, June."

"Say, hold on. I'm...wait. Are you a copper or something?"

"Or something. Was a copper. No more."

"You were a copper?" June said aloud. Mickey patted her hand and shushed her, looking at the bar's customers who showed no interest in their surroundings, even including the hot dame and the lucky shrimp picking her up.

"Shhh," Mickey repeated. "I was a policeman. Not anymore. Now I'm into new things."

"Oh, like what?"

"Things that pay more than being a cop for starters. Things like you and your, uh, your family do for pay."

"You're not making any sense, mister, and I have to go," June said nervously. She started to slide out of the booth.

"Los Menendez Banda," Mickey intoned. "Did I pronounce that right?"

June edged back into the booth.

May sat down on the bench next to Grenville and eyed him. "You're kind of a mysterious guy," she said.

"Me? Oh no, not at all. Pretty average really."

"Why are you here acting mysterious then?"

"I'm sorry you see it that way. What we have to talk about is better said here than over in front of your lunch service and your customers."

"So say it."

"Good. Straight to business. I like that, April."

"I'm May."

"Oh, identical twins, are you?"

"Actually, we're identical triplets."

"Triplets. That would be June, right?"

"Yes, how did you know her name?"

"Lucky guess, I guess."

"Just what is it you want, mister?"

"First, a little background," Grenville said. Then he described someone up in the city who was planning to tap the megadollars in Silicon Valley to start a PAC to raise money to promulgate conservative issues, "You know, discredited issues." He said this individual – "He's over the cliff with old-fashioned ideas, if you know what I mean" – ignores the enlightened voting public in California which unflinchingly elects and re-elects right-thinking public servants to do the people's business. "Well, left-thinking anyway, and here's the kicker," Grenville said, "he will no doubt put himself in a position to profit personally from this. Know what else? This guy tries to pass himself off as a P.I. A private investigator. He thinks he's some kind of hero. Bah!"

May looked at Grenville. "I am new to American politics. But it appears to me that you are really around the bend about this, mister. It sounds to me like you have a real problem with him. What difference does it make?"

"Come to your senses, May. The future of our country is at stake. You'll learn soon enough that it is California that is the bellwether when it comes to the direction America takes." Grenville sipped his water. "You have a very pretty accent. Australian, isn't it?"

"Aye."

"Do you allow conservatives in Australia?"

"I don't know, I guess so. Australia is a free country."

"Oh, May, May, May. You want Australia to remain a free country, I am sure. So do we in America...want America to remain a free country."

May gazed at Grenville. "What does this all have to do with April and me?"

"Back to business, good," Grenville said. "I want you to help me put a stop to this."

"Me? Us? How? I don't get it."

"By putting a stop to this fellow organizing things."

"I...we have no...there's nothing we can do," May admitted.

"Sure there is."

"What?"

Grenville looked left and right to see if anyone was nearby, lowered his voice, and said, "Kill him."

May shot up off the bench. "What on earth?" she gasped.

"Los Menendez Banda," Grenville said quietly to her.

May sat back down.

"By the way," Grenville added, "shouldn't that be Las Menendez Banda, you know, feminine agreement between the article, las, and the adjective, banda?"

May stared at Grenville with a blank look on her face.

"Los Menendez Banda," Mickey said to June. "My Spanish ain't so good, but I think I said that right."

"I don't know what you are talking about," June persisted.

"Oh come now, June, let's not beat around the Australian bush," Mickey laughed.

June braced.

"Uh-oh," Mickey blushed. "I didn't mean anything anatomical, only geographical, you know, the Australian bush or outback." He smiled at June. "Let me be direct." He lowered his voice. "My new occupation ought to interest you. I do very special contract work. Much like you say you do as Los Menendez Banda. But when I do it, I actually do it, not like you when you say you did it and you didn't do it."

"Huh?" June offered.

Mickey explained about the dead guy on the boat dock in Sausalito and how it was reported that some outfit called Los Menendez Banda claimed responsibility. How that just didn't conform to the facts.

June was turning a little pale. Who is this guy, she wondered. What does he want? She decided to get tough. "You should be careful what you say about the Banda," she said to Mickey. "You could find yourself in deep manure."

"Manure is my middle name, Miss June, and...no, actually it's not. Urban is my middle name, but manure is what I slog around in these days. My new occupation, you see. So don't try to frighten me or threaten me. I know you and your Banda did not do the hit on that guy."

"Just how would you know that? I'm not saying you are right, but just how would you know?"

Mickey didn't speak for a stretch. Then he smiled at June and said, "Because I did it."

"You did it?" June gurgled out. "You?"

"Me."

Grenville heard a noise and looked over to see April closing up the lunch truck. She stepped down from the door and walked over. She saw amazement all over May and said, "What is wrong, what is the matter?" She looked at Grenville and asked, "What was so important to talk about?"

May looked up at April. "He...he wants...he said we..." April plopped down next to her sister. Grenville told her he hadn't meant to trouble May. He just needed something done and wanted May – and April, too, if that's how things worked – to kill someone.

April blanched. "Kill someone. What do you mean?"

"Los Menendez Banda," Grenville said by way of explanation.

"Oh," April said.

For the next few minutes the three of them did the yada-yada-yada thing, discussing the who, what, when, where, how, and how much things. When they got to the how much question, Grenville asked April and May what the fee was for that hit over in Sausalito they claimed they did. The women looked at one another. May said they didn't think it would be a good idea to reveal information like that, information about other contract work they were involved in. Grenville allowed as how that seemed reasonable, prudent even.

Grenville asked who would do the actual...the...he failed to come up with the right word. "You know what I mean." The women once again looked to each other and May, again, said that too was not something they ought to reveal. The fact was they could not reveal it because their new Los Menendez Banda had not killed the man in Sausalito or anyone else or anywhere else if the whole story were to be known. Grenville agreed that this also was reasonable on their part. But he did offer, "I'll feel good if it was the same man who was responsible for the assassination in Sausalito. Or woman, if that were the case. It looks as if he or she did you guys a good job." Then he said, "It was a man, wasn't it, not one of you?"

April and May had no response to that. Grenville let it slide. He said, "Well, we're good then. I believe I'll be on my way."

June was confounded. "You were a copper and now you're a paid killer?" she said to Mickey.

"Yes, and paid good."

June said she needed a drink. Mickey asked what she wanted. June told him. Mickey went over to the bartender and placed the order. June said what did Mickey want with her. Mickey told June he wanted to be the gun for Los Menendez Banda. That since they went out claiming hits they did not really do, the Banda was a sorry bunch that needed a steel spine. He liked the idea of a willing organization fronting for any kills. That would leave the easy stuff to Mickey. He wouldn't have a need to go out prospecting for assignments. He confessed he wasn't a good salesman, but he was a hell of a shot. His sharpshooting marksmanship was paid for by the taxpayers of Los Angeles County when he did his police training, he gulped. He tried to make it a scoff, but it came out a cough and a laugh.

"I don't know," June said.

"You'll be in here again Friday. I'll be here. You bring your family's okay to me then. I don't expect there to be a different response other than okay. Okay?"

June didn't say anything. Mickey said, "Good. I'll take that as a yes. I think it's time for me to be on my way."

33

Nadine Berry came through her front door at a few minutes past midnight, turned and set the deadbolt, flipped on the lights in the living room, then turned them off quickly when she saw the sudden brightness had awakened Beault who was sprawled on the sofa. "Sorry," she apologized. "Mmmm," he muttered. Nadine went to a table and turned on a low-wattage lamp.

"Better," Beault said. Nadine fell into a chair. "Long night," Beault observed.

"Yes," which gave the reporter a chance to explain what her long night entailed. It entailed murder. Murders. She and her film crew, monitoring the police frequencies on their way back from another news assignment – quite innocent by comparison – got to the first crime scene in Golden Gate Park shortly after Captain Blough and Lieutenant Headley were there.

Beault sat up. "Blough? Headley?"

"Yeah. Joe was called because the beat cops had called in the name of the victim. Jeremiah Witherspoon, the famous entertainment impresario."

"Jesus," Beault testified.

"No, Jeremiah," Nadine said with the lame humor people try when they are fatigued. Witherspoon, she told her beau, was found in his car slumped over the steering wheel with two small-caliber bullet holes in the back of his head.

"Uh-oh," Beault said.

"Right." She continued. When the police captain got a call on his cell and yelled urgently at Headley that they were going to leave the scene, Nadine and her crew cleverly followed the two homicide detectives south down Great Highway to the entrance to the San Francisco Zoo. The gates were closed and only a few lights helped. A couple of cruisers had their spotlights shining on a car that was out of place there. The body in this case was slumped across the front seat. Two bullet holes, Nadine described, etcetera, etcetera, etcetera.

"Holy crud," Beault underscored the moment.

"That's only a small part of the story," Nadine was saying.

"Oh no," he said, "who?"

The name of this dead body, Nadine revealed, was Uriah Murchison.

"Who's he?"

"Dee Doo Dad, the rap artist."

It was fairly clear that the two deceased had no legitimate business being where they were when their lights went out. Probably lured there with reason. Blough and Headley weren't sharing any information beyond the basics to the several groups of news people now flitting around the edges of these homicides. Nadine, like others, had filed stories and news was spreading, even interrupting regular shows during prime time.

At the zoo, Blough was talking to one of the medical examiners when he took another call on his cell, Nadine was telling Beault. This time Blough motioned Headley over. He whispered something and Headley went to get his car. Blough winked at Berry who nodded in surprise and gathered her film crew into the TV van. Blough got in the police car and it slowly pulled away. The KSFG crew was behind by about half a minute. They caught up with Headley and Blough on Great Highway heading back north and they both sped up.

"Oh no," Beault was confined to saying.

This time the police detectives and the TV van arrived at one of the old shuttered World War II artillery battery emplacements on the coast side of the Presidio above Baker Beach. Another police patrol car, another private car, another brain invaded by a brace of small-caliber bullets, and another name not unfamiliar to everyone.

"Who?"

"Ruby Davis."

"Never heard of..."

Her more familiar name, Nadine told him, was Hawt Chaw.

"Oh no," he said.

In defense of Jaguar Beault and his recognition of that name, he has no rap tracks on his iPod featuring the dead woman's hip-hop talents. Rather, he was acquainted with the name only because our intrepid private eye does read the entertainment portion of his local paper where clever rap artist names show up a whole, whole lot. Now this name – and those of the other corpses – will also show up on the obit page of that paper after it spends time on page one. And since dead is dead, Beault felt something was in the air. He is, remember, a qualified detective.

34

Some of the Menzies rolled out of bed in South San Francisco with yawns and stretches and trips to the toilet and gawkings into refrigerators and, in one case, mixing a highball. Somebody in one of the apartments they occupied turned on a television. "Cripes, will you look at this. Three blokes shot and killed last night. What is the world coming to?"

Another Menzies said, "Who were they?"

"Dunno. Let's watch."

In another apartment, Scott Menzies also had a TV set glowing. "It's a bloomin tidal wave, all these..." He jumped out of a chair and ran to his desk and grabbed a sheet of paper. He looked quickly at a list of phone numbers and began making calls. When he was finished, he sat down and breathed easily.

"What did you do?" Zelda asked after setting her drink down on a table. "You were on the phone for a long time."

"I just told the press that we, that Los Menendez Banda, done those shootings last night. Some of those snotty reporters laughed at me. Well, we'll show them when it's our turn to pull a trigger."

Zelda took a sip and stared at her husband. "Sorry, what? What did you say?" Scott did not respond.

All but one of the Haight-Ashbury Wild Bunch were asleep in their apartment during the same moments that Scott Menzies was lying to the media. The awake one was getting ready to go to his deli where he waited table for the local breakfast and lunch crowd. He couldn't find his shoes. As an alternative, he turned on the old TV set in the room. The set warmed up and then a picture came into focus. A newsreader was recapping the shooting deaths last night of three entertainment moguls. "What in hell is a mogu?" the Wild Buncher asked himself.

Another Wild Buncher, awakened by the TV noise, griped, "Whatya makin so much freakin noise for? Can't ya see we're tryin to get some shut-eye?" The wide-awake Buncher grabbed his groin in that bite-me attitude. "Hey," the just-awakened guy said, "what'd they just say on TV?"

"Oh, just some dudes got theyselfs killed. Last night it sounds like."

From "it sounds like" the guy said until about an hour later, the Wild Bunch talked it out as others woke up. Despite the valuable input from each of the ones present on this particular morning, the talking ended with more questions than answers. Harold Wobber had sat on a mattress on the floor with his back comfortable against a pillow carved into a corner. He watched and listened and held his tongue, even when asked to join in. He did not laugh at anyone. As the end of that excruciating hour came near, Wobber got up and got a drink of water. "We gonna call the newsdicks and tell 'em the Haight-Ashbury Wild Bunch did those killings? Isn't that where you all are trying to get to with all this bullshit talking?" He sat back down.

"Hey, yeah," someone said. "We could do that." So they did that. It took almost an hour for the forty-something leader to make calls to five television stations and describe who his gang was and what they done… did. After five, he got tired. Wobber shook his head.

"Any of you guys seen my shoes?" the table-waiter Wild Buncher inquired. Another Buncher pulled a shoe from under his mattress and threw it at the unshod guy who asked, "Seen another one anywhere?"

At noon later that day while emotional reports of three dead entertainment superstars washed over the Bay Area and reports said that two unknown groups were laying doubtful claim to the murders, another conclave was coming to order in the Castro. At Grenville's church.

Because it was convenient. And important. And don't forget the parking. When coffee was poured, Mickey Truke indelicately wondered aloud why there were no cookies. Uncle Ben snapped, "Of all the sappy things to say!"

Grenville laughed at the two of them and apologized, then added, "Brownies today, Mickey," who uttered, "Oooh."

Berry and Beault were at the table. Alana was at her grandmother's in another part of the city. Captain Blough and Lieutenant Headley attended. In fact, it was Blough's idea – his order – that they all would meet. He spoke first when the conclave conclaved.

"Le merde hit le fan last night, boys and girls, and I want assurances right now that I can go about my chores knowing that nobody in this room is stupid enough to either do these stupid things or knows who is responsible for these stupid things and think they can get away being stupid and not telling me. You first, Mickey."

"Not me." He looked directly at Blough. "Ex-cop to cop. Don't know a thing."

"Ben."

"Don't know, Joe, really," Ben huffed. "The scary thing to me is that it is maybe a new push by somebody we haven't heard from before. Those killings are pure pro style."

"Opinions."

Grenville asked, "Is it okay if I weigh in?"

"Sure."

"I think Mr. Franklin is right. After my visit with April and May, I would guess that the Los Menendez Banda people are not involved even if they're out there saying they are responsible."

"Why?"

"Because they strike me as amateurs."

Mickey seconded Grenville's response by describing his meeting with June in the bar. "Amateurs, rank amateurs," he said. Then he added softly, "I should know."

"Well bully for the bad crowd. Now the lieutenant and I have a crime wave to stop. There's maybe a new shooter in town." Joe Blough was pissed.

Truke said, "We don't know anything about that Wild Bunch crowd except they look to be pretty worthless. Leastwise that's what Bas and I figured after we saw one of the guys who might be a part of them. A real zero, that one. Anyway, do you think they might be more involved? They're out there again bragging like they did this, these shootings."

Blough hesitated and then said cryptically, "We're working that."

Everyone was quiet for a moment when Nadine cleared her throat. "What!" Blough challenged. She glared back at him. "Sorry," Blough shrugged, "I'm tired. I was up most of the night."

Nadine said, "You saw it for yourself last night, Captain. All three victims from the hip-hop scene. All three alone in deserted spots when they are shot. Someone they trusted – or feared for other reasons – got them to show up. Expecting something. Not two bullets to their heads, that's for sure. It has all the earmarks of an inside job. Somebody's grabbing for power or position. There's loads of money in the rap scene." She paused a moment and then said, "And all this on the heels of the shooting in Sausalito of another rap scene impresario."

"Of course you are right and that's where we're heading with this," Blough agreed. "But goldarnit, I still don't like the coincidence of Ben's, uh, shithead decision to go into the hit business or the emergence of these other shithead organizations, Los Menendez Banda and the Wild Bunch. I just don't like it." After a pause, he said, "Dammit!"

Beault, just listening, had been watching them, sipping some coffee, picking at a brownie. "What about you, Private Detective?" Blough aimed at Beault. "Haven't heard from you yet."

"A real conundrum. You real detectives are going to earn your measly pay on this one," Beault told him. "I do have a question," Beault said. "Anyone here ever take a bullet? Anyone? No? Good for you. I did. The sergeant here, oops, pardon me, the lieutenant here saved my life. Dick Headley put me in a bulletproof vest when we faced down that mob of lunatics chasing the Madagascar Pigeon. That shot knocked me for a loop, but the vest did its job. I was thinking about that because I volunteered to be the target in this plan we're devising to take out these jerkoff assassin wanna-bes. I don't know if we still have to go ahead with that idea with the possibility that there's new shooters...ones who can shoot straight. I don't like it to have to put on another Kevlar shirt."

Blough said, "My hands are full looking for real murderers. Yeah, we all want to stop these other ass...a-holes..." he glanced at Nadine and shrugged an apology..."but have you bright people come up with any ideas to pull it off?" He stopped and got a strange look on his face. "They're innocent, you know, until they're proved guilty." He tried to look serious but broke into a sick laugh. "God, I'm tired." He went on, "We sure as hell don't want to see you take another bullet, Mr. Private Detective, so I am sure that all of you are crafting just the right kind of trap to suck these people out of their gopher holes." Blough got amused stares from around the table. "I told you I was tired. Anyway, what have you got going?"

Beault explained how Grenville has a congregant who is a computer wizard. They thought they had an idea to entice the Wild Bunch and the Banda to do something incriminating.

"Why am I not surprised at that?" Blough said to no one in particular. To Grenville he said, "Computer wizard, eh, a congregant. Do you trust him?"

"Do I trust him? What do you mean?"

"Do you trust him?" Blough asked with a gleam in his eye.

Grenville said, "You're leading to something, Joe, so I'll say no, I don't trust him." Blough didn't react. Grenville went on. "I don't play poker with him. I don't know anybody who does anymore. I won't let him drive my car, it's the only one I have. He cheats at golf. Ha, he's not alone at that, is he?"

Blough was smiling, Grenville smiling back. "But with computers and helping us here if he's needed, yeah, he is completely trustworthy. Do you need him?"

"Yes, to tell him something I think he needs to know."

"About computers?"

"Sort of."

"Sort of, huh? Is it something I can pass along to him? He might be nervous talking about his work and computer lifestyle with a cop."

Blough thought. Blough decided. "Okay, it's like this." He told Grenville about his undercover policeman who was now a part of the HAWB. More important, the cop had slipped himself into the job of computer geek for the losers. That was easy enough to do since the other part of the Wild Bunch were included in the one in a million in the population who didn't know the first thing about computers. He outlined how Grenville's computer wizard should make contact with the undercover cop and figure out how the two could set up a secret mechanism to work together. When he was finished, Blough threatened, "I've told you this because you said he's trustworthy." Blough looked up at Grenville. "Don't do anything to blow my guy's cover. His name is Harold Wobber."

Grenville said he would inform his computer guy. "You can trust him, Joe," Grenville added.

"I will. But just don't do anything to blow my guy's cover," the captain repeated seriously.

The room absorbed that.

"One more thing," Beault said to Blough. "I was wondering if there's anything new on the chap who got ventilated in Sausalito. Any leads? You hear things?" Beault grinned.

Blough grinned back. "Yeah, we hear things, you know. We hear the capable police department over there has, yeah, a lead." He kept smiling.

"I trust that they have some clues to lead to the big finish," Beault grinned. Blough grinned back. They were grinning at the thought of Mrs. Johnson and her not-so-clever road trip to her home in Sausalito from Lake Tahoe on the night her husband was eliminated and her drive back to Lake Tahoe that same night to cement her alibi. And those damning gasoline purchases with her own credit card for her big ride on the night of the killing, if, you know, that is what the darling girl had done. Just police leads at this time.

"What is all of this supposed to mean?" Truke asked. "You guys are acting like grade school kids."

Beault said, "That Johnson couple was well-known up there, him for his role in the hip-hop scene and his money and her for her curvaceous ways." He was talking to the table. "Apparently, and probably convincingly believed by everyone who knows her, she's a slut. What's more, I'm told that poor Mrs. Johnson may not have the gray cells sufficient to pull this off on her own. You know, a blank page. She would have had to talk somebody in to help, someone who would pull the trigger for her. Like I said, her curvaceous ways. Also, she maybe left a clue for the capable Sausalito Police Department to, you know, investigate."

"You're talking in circles. That doesn't strike me as real police work and evidence-sifting," Truke responded. "I would be a little more circumspect and want something hard to go on. Am I right, Captain?"

"Yes, Mister Truke, you know, cop to ex-cop," Blough laughed. So did Headley.

"Hey, it's just what I learned down south. Come in with hard evidence."

"Well, if you must...yeah, that's how the Sausalito police learned to do their job, too. They're working it. Wouldn't surprise me if they had some answers soon."

Blough rose and Headley stood up. "The lieutenant and I are going back to our place of business where we are going to be busy. We have experts on the job right now trying to discover what the motive was to send these three people in our city to their graves. Almost certainly it is money. Like who stood to gain. All that is clear, but, damn it, now we may have a for-hire shooter out there. Somebody who pulls the trigger, like our Jaguar Beault just accused. If that's so, we need to catch that guy. Even if it is our Sausalito slut."

Blough looked at everyone. "Ben," he said, "I suggest you do that thing of yours when you talk to people in the city. Find out what you can. There may be scuttlebutt my people haven't heard that might point to something new." Ben nodded. Then the captain and the lieutenant left without another word, which was easy for Richard Headley who hadn't said much all day anyway.

35

In an update on the overnight spate of murders of the three entertainment industry notables, the San Francisco police chief told reporters that the dead guy who was discovered on a boat dock in Sausalito just recently – Mr. Byron Johnson – known as a behind-the-scenes mover and shaker in the hip-hop world, was the half-brother of Jeremiah Witherspoon, one of the three dead notables previously referred to. The chief hated face time on television. He is a cop, not a talking head, but he knew his job included a big-time public relations responsibility and he did it, right up to the minimum.

Today he added little to the three new killings except to say the department was cooperating with Sausalito authorities and looking into whether there was a connection between the death of Byron Johnson and the murders of the others. The more experienced crime reporters scratched their heads over this and then lost their tempers when the chief refused to take questions.

As the chief left the podium and headed back inside, some of the media shouted out asking whether the morning claims by Los Menendez Banda and the Haight-Ashbury Wild Bunch that they were the killers had any merit. The chief ignored those questions. Television reporters spun quickly around to urgently describe what little news there was, one of whom stared into a camera belonging to another station. The camera guy slowly panned his camera up and down and back and forth as the harried newswoman tried to keep pace with the belligerent lens while relating her dramatic report to a camera that was not turned on. When she signed off and saw how hard the cameraman was laughing, she looked around, came to the shame of recognition, and shouted, "You pig!" He answered, "Oink."

Ben Franklin listened on the radio in his car as the police chief was announcing the new developments on the death of the man in Sausalito and three new sensational killings. Ben was driving to Chinatown to see Sun Shin Wong, who, as it turned out, had watched the news on TV and said so when Ben sat down in the booth at the rear of the restaurant.

"Tell me, Mr. Ben Franklin, is this how rap artists settle their musical differences?" Mr. Sun asked Ben.

"It would appear so," Ben answered, "and good riddance, I say, but I'm old-fashioned when it comes to music and cannot see any value in that crap."

"That is a hard-hearted opinion."

"Is it? Yes, I suppose so."

"This puts a new light on the killings," Wong said. "It seems to be confined to an internal dispute. Many parts of our community may feel it is of no consequence any longer just so long as these deadbeats kill one another and let it go at that."

"And that is not a hard-hearted opinion?" Ben laughed.

Wong said nothing.

Ben said, "You are certainly right about many parts of your community, but not the police. They intend to see this to an end."

"Which is what brings you here today, am I right?"

"It has been suggested to me," Ben Franklin answered, "that I try to learn what I can about mob-style shooters in our fair city."

"A suggestion? You get a lot of those from your friends in the police department, it would seem."

"Well, what can I say, it was presented as such, but I could see it was not an either-or. So I decided to act on the suggestion. Which, as you say, is what brings me here today."

Mr. Sun said, "I am told that your nephew had a quiet conversation with our blonde friend, June, at one of the cafes."

"At one of your bars, yes," Ben said. "Mickey offered his services to this Los Menendez Banda crowd to do their shootings. Claimed he was responsible for the Sausalito offing, the one they themselves said they did. Put June between a rock and a hard place. She knows her crowd didn't do the shoot. And here's a guy who said he did do the shoot. She can't say he's lying. Now the Sausalito one clearly becomes connected to the other three because every dead body was associated with the hip-hop scene."

"What do you hope to achieve by making Mickey the Banda's shooter, as you call it?"

"Control. It is part of the plan Beault devised before the bodies started to stack up. Parallel to this, one of our group, Beault's brother as it happens, is posing as someone who needs someone else killed. He said he heard that the Banda people took credit for the Sausalito hit and wanted their expertise. Even said he would feel better if the gunman who did the Sausalito gig took the job. He approached June's sisters, April and May, who could not deny the shooting they'd boasted on, nor could they not see why it wouldn't be the smart thing to use the real killer. Also, if we have a plant inside who says he can do the shootings, well then, there won't be any shootings, will there?"

"You and your schemers, you have been busy, my friend," Wong told Ben. "Do you need me? Perhaps not."

"On the contrary. Our team is of the opinion that Los Menendez Banda, perhaps scraping by on little felonies and misdemeanors, is flat-out clueless when it comes to assassinations. Clueless. Not to mention the Haight-Ashbury Wild Bunch. More cluelessness there. And if anybody can afford to say that, I can, based on my own dismal performance in that game."

"Mickey did have an unusual record."

"Lucky for him," Ben said.

"And for you."

"And for me, yes, Wong. Today, for that, I am very grateful. But all this said, we still have to get to know them so that we can step in front of them if they decide to follow through on their egotistical chest-thumping."

"You want me to keep my ear to the ground and…"

"Yes. If any of the rumors are true, or more important, if there is a new someone out there doing real assassin work, it could cause real problems for a lot of folks and over a long time. We need to discover who and where. Otherwise…"

"Bad for business?"

Ben Franklin smiled. "Yes, very bad."

Friday came and Mickey Truke sat in the bar on Kearny and listened as June said her family agreed to meet with him.

"As I suspected," he countered.

June gave Mickey a place and a time. "South San Francisco? Where is that, up in Marin County?" Mickey tried to joke.

June said no, it is just down one of the freeways toward the airport. She was actually pointing.

Mickey held his laughter in and did not say more.

Dressed in jeans, a worn sweatshirt, old running shoes, dark glasses and an Oakland A's ball cap, Grenville ordered a tuna melt "just like last time" at which April's and May's heads snapped up. "Hi," Grenville said gaily. Later they talked on the same bench. "You ready to do that for me? With the guy we discussed? All I need to hear is yes and yes. Yes?"

"Yes," from April.

"And yes," from May.

That was settled. Then they talked money. "Half now, half after," Grenville offered.

"All now," one of the triplets said.

"Right. Makes sense," Grenville agreed. "Only this. Hold on to it until Beault is dead. If something doesn't go right, I'll be expecting it all back." Grenville handed May an envelope containing eight hundred seventy-five dollars. He barely held his composure.

36

A Boeing 747 loaded with about one hundred eighty tons of aviation fuel, about three hundred fifty passengers and crew members and about ten tons of personal luggage and commercial cargo, not to mention the airframe's own three hundred ninety thousand pounds of empty weight totaling in all about eight hundred fifty thousand pounds of engineering amazement responded beautifully to the throttle pressure applied by the airline pilot as she climbed through a ceiling of fog at about two thousand feet after her five bogies carrying eighteen wheels ceded contact with the long runway at San Francisco International Airport on its way somewhere else. This was only one in many of these acts per hour in the symphony that airplane jockeys believed they conducted with every takeoff – the Romance of Flying they liked to call it. Nearly all the scores of passengers on the big jetliner gripped their armrests and tried to reassure themselves in the deep backrest they were pressing into in response to the gentle, but unappreciated, shaking of the aluminum phenomenon as it won the battle with gravity in defiance of those passengers' lack of belief in the possibility of powered flight.

"We're all gonna die," the less-stoic and seat-bound fliers told themselves in the mantra repeated by at least a quarter of the passengers on every commercial airplane takeoff. They didn't. The passengers didn't die. What they did – well, not them, what the plane did – was to interrupt a conversation just below them on the ground in South San Francisco because of the noise delivered by more than sixty thousand pounds of thrust from each of four Pratt & Whitney engines attached under the wings of the jet and the tooth-rattling vibrations sent down to the ground as the 747 plowed through the air giving each building below a taste of a little earthquake.

"That's kinda loud," Mickey Truke observed when the shaking subsided in the living room of Scott and Zelda Menzies.

"You get used to it," Scott said.

"Does this happen a lot?"

"Yes. The airport's right over there," Zelda pointed. "Planes are taking off all day."

"There's more?" Mickey said.

"Aye. What, maybe a few hundred times every day?"

"A day? And you say you get used to it? I'd go bats. My God," Mickey shook his head.

"The noise is loud and the shaking is disturbing," Zelda said, "but the soot that comes down over our apartment and on cars and the streets and sidewalks...that's kinda messy."

"South San Francisco," Mickey thought.

Mickey Truke was in the living quarters of the Menzies seniors because it was time to reveal his qualifications as the gunsel for Los Menendez Banda as he had orchestrated with June. Scott and Zelda Menzies were in the room and June, of course, because she was primary go-between with the admitted assassin. April and May had a lunch truck schedule to attend to. Bruce was absent, but Bryce and B-rt and B-rt sat nearby. A few other family members divided attention between the assassin in their home and the refrigerator in the kitchen where there was a stock of Foster's.

Scott said, "Junie tells us you were a copper before you became a...a..."

"Independent contractor," Mickey clarified.

"Assassin," one of the B-rts further clarified. He got a long glare from his mother.

"You say tomato and I say tomato," Mickey smiled at B-rt.

"Why did you make such a strange change of...uh...jobs?" Scott asked.

"I like money. And the short hours."

"How much do you charge for these...when you..." the other B-rt chimed in.

"This one will be for free as I told you. When we get our next client, I'll show you my, uh, my fee schedule."

"Yes, but..." A small noise turned into a louder one and then a really loud one in a matter of around five to ten seconds as the airport disgorged another behemoth into the sky right over the Menzies building. Not a –47, maybe a –67 or one of those obnoxious French-built Airbus competitors. The room was silent of talk until the noise subsided.

"How did you do...how...you know, over in Sausalito?" Bryce looked at Mickey.

"It's okay to ask how I terminated that old man. It's my job. I love to talk shop. I used a Ruger six-shooter. Two .22 caliber caps in the back of the head. No mess that way. A bigger gun tends to leave a lot of bone and brain and hair and blood to clean up." Several of the Menzies troop displayed some queasiness at this. "What's the good in that, I ask, when two twenty-twos do the task just fine?"

"Mister, you are a cold son of a kangaroo, I must say that," one of the former Australian Rules footballers said from the kitchen door where he was on his second Foster's.

"It's just good old American capitalism at work. Supply and demand," Mickey answered. "My part is the supply. It's you Los Menendez Banda members who go marketing for the demand. I don't see much difference. Why doesn't that make you folks sons of kangaroos, as you say?" No answer from the big footballer, just a long pull on his can of Foster's.

"We're in a marketplace," Mickey started. Outside, a loud siren from a fire truck or paramedic ambulance screamed by. Mickey halted so he could be heard after the siren quieted. "You operate a termination business in this marketplace. Obviously, you haven't staffed it as competently as you tried to claim. Telling the world you did that old man in Sausalito when you did not even have a triggerman under hire was pretty cheeky. So let's not do any more name-calling. We're professionals, or at least I am." Mickey looked around.

"What if you get caught?" someone ventured.

"Caught doing what?"

"Caught doing what you do."

"I won't."

"Well that may be easy for you to say now. People who go out killing people end up in your jails over here, am I right?" This from Bryce.

"Lots of people get caught at it, yes, you are right. There's one big difference though."

"What's that?" Scott asked.

"They're not me," Mickey said as he looked at each of the Menzies clan one by one.

Zelda said, "What is it with this private eye that's got you so boiled up that you're going to do this for us without charging? What did he do to you? Something bad?"

"Jaguar Beault," Mickey intoned. "How did he get a name like that? It's a bullshit name. Maybe you know he suckered a whole flock of people out of a statue that proved to be real valuable. It didn't belong to him, but that didn't stop him from leading all those people down a primrose path and then at the end fabricating a charge sheet of bullshit crimes which landed them all in the pokey. Then he runs off with the statue, and now he has a big new house and a new car and, oh, and some dame who probably helped him pull off the whole thing. I would have been one of the ones in the slammer now, only I'm good at what I do. I whacked that first guy. You may have heard about the boat captain, the one who was carrying the bird statue."

"No."

"No? Well, they didn't catch me, but here's the thing. I was this close to grabbing the statue until this Jag-u-ar Beault shows up and bollixes the whole deal for me. All that money, wow."

Another big jet airliner rumbled over the building forcing a break in Mickey's completely fabricated reason for wanting Beault dead...for free.

"Now's my chance to even the score," Mickey said when there was only an echo of the passing plane. "I'm looking for a way to get that money from him. Him and his lady have loads of it. Offing him is a start."

"Tell us how you will do this," June said tentatively.

"Do what, dear?"

"Well, you know, what you are going to do to this man."

"Can't say it, can you? How I am going to kill Jaguar Beault. See? That's why you people need me as the shooter for Los Menendez Banda. No ifs ands or buts with me on the job. No tip-toeing around the words that seem to turn you good folks off."

"This is new for us, Mr. Truke," Zelda confessed. "We are still trying to get used to it."

"If you say so," Mickey scoffed.

"Well how?" June persisted. "How are you going to...to kill this Jaguar Beault?"

"Like this. I walk up to him and invite him to turn sideways so that I am looking at the side of his head." Mickey is glaring from face to face. "Then I ask him to kneel down and lower his head to where I can put the muzzle of my silencer behind his ear. Then I tell him how he screwed me out of all the jewels he stole and he starts whining like a baby and maybe he's crying or peeing his pants and I..."

Boom, boom, boom lumbered another jumbo jet overhead. When the noise and trembling stopped, Mickey was laughing.

"What's so funny, Mr. Truke?" Bryce inquired a little angrily.

"First, do you really want to know how I plan to do my job? And second, if you do, do you really think I am going to tell you?"

"But..." someone said.

"I'm a pro. You aren't. Let me do my job. Your job as a matter of fact. That reminds me. Who's buying this kill?"

Scott related April's and May's description of a man's interest in stopping this Beault character from doing something up in the city. The elder Menzies filled in details of how the client was angry that Beault wanted to set up ways to underwrite political action to subvert California's long-honored progressive philosophies. "Somehow he'll probably try to profit personally from it," Scott added.

"Sounds like the bastard," Mickey said. "Another good reason to put him down."

"When will you do it?" Scott asked.

"I don't work on a schedule. I plan. I cover my ass. I look for perfection. If it takes ten minutes, okay. If it takes a month, that's okay too. I plan then I execute."

"You are a cold..." the footballer started to say. He was interrupted by the fire engine or ambulance outside coming back in the opposite direction, siren blaring.

"It's noisy around here," Mickey observed again.

"You get used to it," someone answered again.

Mickey took his leave. Outside, sitting in his car, he laughed out loud.

37

Alana sat on Beault's shoulders as they walked into the church in the Castro with Nadine. Mickey and Ben were a minute or two behind them. Captain Blough and Lieutenant Headley were already seated, talking to Grenville. Mickey watched as the group swelled with men and women who were similar to the ones who had attended the first meeting in this very room. Mickey was mesmerized and asked, "I don't get it. Who in heck are...wait, what's that I smell?" Grenville smiled and described an oatmeal and raisin cookie with a hint of mint. Alana scampered around the room jumping into laps, hugging a stuffed bear and begging for bites of cookies.

The captain spoke first. "I am here unofficially," he said as he looked slowly around the room at everyone there. "In fact, I am not even here. Dick Headley there, he's not here either. Are we here, Lieutenant?" Headley shook his head. "Must be true then," Blough said. "Now talk freely. Well, not entirely freely. Don't confess to any capital crimes," he laughed. "We already have enough elsewhere to investigate. What do we have?"

Grenville told about his encounter with the two Menzies women, how he'd set up the hit on Beault, how he'd maneuvered Mickey Truke, the self-admitted Sausalito hit man, into the preferred slot as killer.

Mickey confirmed he had met with the Menzies – "a pod of dim bulbs" – and got the job to whack Beault. "I told them I'd do this first one for free, you know, to show my qualifications." Ben dropped his head as his shoulders slumped. Mickey swallowed and went on. "I also told them I had issues with this private detective and was happy to have the chance to waste him."

When Mickey said he would find just the right place and time to pull off the fake assassination of Jaguar Beault, Nadine volunteered she would make sure a KSFG mobile TV van was nearby to report the death of a prominent – and handsome – local private investigator.

Beault said, "You are making me blush." Everybody thought that was cute. "You want my report, too? My part is to fall down when I hear gunshots." Everybody thought that was funny.

Blough looked around the table. "Ben? Got anything?"

Ben drew something out of a briefcase and passed it to Blough who opened an envelope, pulled out a sheet of paper and read. Ben said this was from his associate in Chinatown who wanted to be helpful.

Blough said, "Tell him thanks. This fits with what Dick and I have been hearing." He pushed the note over to Grenville who read it. Grenville looked at a congregant seated against a wall and nodded at him. "I guess the meeting is adjourned," the captain declared.

Mickey stood up to leave. "Can I take some cookies?"

"Help yourself, Mickey," Grenville said. "Take all you want. We can make more."

Mickey stopped. He said, "Is this really a church? I mean, all these things going on here. All these, well, them," he said pointing at the men and women heading out.

"Oh, yes, Mickey, we are the Congregation of Brotherly Love in the Name of Jesus Christ. We try to do God's work where it's needed. We are God-fearing."

Mickey thought about that, looked at the crowd, and replied, "Only of God, am I right? Afraid of him only?" Grenville laughed. So did the others who overheard.

The room was mostly empty. Left were Grenville, Beault, Nadine, Alana and a man Grenville introduced as James Gedmon. "James knows his way around computers, way around." Grenville handed him the sheet of paper from Ben Franklin. "This enough?" Grenville asked.

James read the note. "Haight-Ashbury Wild Bunch? Whyn't they just take out ads telling people how mindless they are? Do they really think people will believe they shot that man in Sausalito and now these others? I don't think low profile is in their vocabulary. I'll get back to you, G.P."

"There are some things you need to know, Jim," Grenville said, telling Gedmon about the undercover police plant in the Wild Bunch and the computer connection.

"Oh good," Gedmon said. "That should make my job a lot easier. And fun. And mysterious. I'll be like a double-o-seven."

"Don't get all spy-like on us. Let's maintain some perspective," Grenville said.

"Perspective. Okay, if you insist. Let me puzzle over what I've learned here today and see how I can contribute. I will, however, need one of those mechanical pencils that shoot out a poison dart. All of us..."

"Get the hell out of here, James," Grenville said as he pushed Gedmon toward the door. When Gedmon was gone, Grenville told his brother and Nadine, "James is an ex-FBI cyber forensics expert. Now he's working for a tech company down the peninsula building counter-terrorism systems. He must get paid a pile of money because he's really generous to me and the church."

Nadine asked Grenville, "Are you going to tell us what is in that note?"

"Are you asking as a future sister-in-law or as a needy television reporter on the heels of a story who is willing to watch people violate their confidences and turn a blind eye to their moral duties?"

"Just tell me, you big yo-yo."

"Okay, if you are going to be so personable about it. Ben got some more dope on the Wild Bunch from his friend over in Chinatown. They live in one of his rentals, and since they are making noises about how they are in the assassination business, we'll have to pay attention. They made that lame claim about Sausalito and now the hip-hop murders. James will look further into them if there's anything on the Internet. I expect he will also devise some way to get a good connection with the undercover policeman working from the inside."

As Beault and Berry were heading out of the door to Grenville's church, they heard the minister ask after them, "Yo-yo?"

38

Beault told Truke they should touch a man he knows, someone who knows things. A local.

Truke said, "Detecting work, right? You private guys skulk into the dark alleys of the city and turn up clues and leads and murderers and missing persons and suitcases of ill-gotten cash and..."

"Yes, Mickey, but only once in a thousand tries. The downside is I drink a lot of soda this way."

Mickey drove, Beault pointing the way. "Where?" Mickey asked as they moved west down Geary.

"There." The there is a drinking establishment on this very Geary in the Richmond District whose big neon come-on sign above the entrance reveals its name. It does not light up completely. It hasn't worked for years as good-deed customers are told who draw this defect to the attention of the on-duty barkeeper. The place is Trad'R Sam, a classic San Francisco dive bar.

After ten minutes looking for a legal place to park and walking the blocks to the saloon, Beault and Truke straddled a couple of stools over near the ladies room where Beault "helloed" Fred behind the bar. Fred turned his back for a moment and then came back with a glass filled with ice and a diet cola. "Fred, Mickey. Mickey, Fred," Beault said. Fred reached over and shook hands with Mickey. "Mickey, Fred is the guy I told you who knows things. He's been a great source for me."

Mickey ordered a cola with ice. Fred plopped it down and said, "Going straight as usual, Mr. B. The sleuth must be on the trail. You a shamus, too?" he asked Mickey.

Beault answered for Truke. "No, he's an assassin."

"Right," Fred assented, "they come in here all the time." Fred went to attend to another drinker. The place isn't just a dive, it's a neighborhood dive, an urban Grange meeting place where first names are all that are needed. Newcomers are dutifully instructed about first names. And used, though sometimes slurred. Beault likes the place because he is treated neighborly despite his reputation over the Madagascar Pigeon thing when he got so much news coverage. Nobody in this place was going to let him get away with a big head just because his name was in headlines and his face was splashed all over the television after that case he solved.

Plus, Fred knew stuff. "What's new, Fred?" Beault asked.

"Not a thing. Been quiet. What are you working?" Mickey jerked his head at Beault with a look that said, "Not a thing? That from the guy who knows stuff? Not a thing?"

Beault saw Mickey's reaction and smiled. Then he answered Fred. "A little dust-up over those hip-hop killings."

"Oh yeah, that sweetheart of a young thing had her sugar daddy done in. I thought that was settled."

"Could be...probably...that's the look of things, but there is some fallout from it about some scum who are trying to get into the assassination business."

Fred looked at Truke. "Like him?"

"No, some other scum," Beault said. Mickey laughed, but not real heartily. "So nothing, Fred?"

"Not about assassins, no. Just what I saw on TV about those two outfits. I don't think we'd be the place where gun pros would stop for a drink. We get a different class of people. People like you and this assassin here. Say, how's Nadine?"

"She's doing fine, thanks. Busy with the news. My special angel whose simple presence alone reminds me every day how lucky I am."

"You must be in love."

"I am," Beault answered Fred, who shouted above the jukebox, "Hey, everybody, this guy's in love."

"Who with?" someone shouted back. Beault and Fred laughed. Mickey shook his head and was about to say something about the dive and the people there when he grabbed Beault's arm on the bar and shrunk back.

"I don't believe it. I do not believe it," Mickey whispered to Beault as a man and woman stepped into the bar and glanced around for a place to sit. A table against a wall on the opposite side from Beault and Truke was free. The couple took it. The man went to the bar and ordered. He casually surveyed the bar as he waited for Fred to mix two drinks. As his eyes passed slowly by Beault and Truke, he hesitated, looked a little sharper, and then kept going. He took his drinks to the table and leaned into the woman to say something.

Beault waited as Mickey squirmed. "What's up?"

"That couple who just came in."

"Yeah?"

"It's the colonel and Vickie Seakrit."

"From your fail...your hit?"

"Yes. The burglars."

"You sure?"

"Oh yeah."

Fred was passing by. "Dude," Beault called quietly, "don't make a thing out of it, but look over there and see if you know those two."

Fred went to the cash register and fiddled. He refilled someone's beer order then stepped near Beault. "No. Must be first timers. She's a doll. You gonna try to make Nadine jealous?"

"No, but we may have to cause some commotion."

"Basil, does trouble follow you everywhere?"

"Not me, him," Beault nodded toward Mickey. Fred looked at Truke. Beault said, "Fred, wait about two minutes then go in the back and call the police. Tell them you need two units here ASAP. Tell them one should be a female officer and no sirens. Okay?"

"Okay."

Beault said to Mickey, "I'm going over to the men's room. It's just past their table. When I come out, I'll be sure I have 'em covered. Then you wander over."

"Got it."

Beault headed around the bar and stopped at an older man sitting on a stool. He joked with him for a minute before moving on to the restroom.

"Leave your hands above the table," Beault told the fake colonel and Ms. Seakrit when he came out of the toilet and stopped in front of the two. Their expressions told Beault that they felt something was wrong. Beault's one hand was inside his jacket.

"Who are you?" the man asked.

"Name's Basil, what's yours?"

"What do you want?"

"I want you to leave your hands above the table."

"What for?" the man asked.

"So that I won't have to shoot you because I was afraid you would be reaching for a gun."

"Mister, I don't know what it is you are thinking, but I want you to back off and go away."

Mickey showed up. "Evening, Ms. Seakrit, Colonel. Nice to see you again."

"That man is a killer," Ms. Seakrit accused. "He should be in jail. I think we should call the police."

"I just did," Beault told them. "I anticipated the need."

"Why?" the man said.

"You are burglars. High-end ones, I'll wager."

"No, sir, you are mistaken. You have us confused with someone else."

Beault said to Truke, "Are we confused?"

"No," Mickey said.

The fake colonel suddenly gripped the table and turned it up fast toward Beault and Truke. A second later, Ms. Seakrit reached for her purse to bring out a gun. Mickey saw that action as he sidestepped the table and raised his arm holding a gun into her face and said coolly, "Freeze or die." She froze. "Drop the gun." She dropped it. In the second or two that elapsed, the man edged off his seat and headed at Beault who was dodging the table. Beault saw that the man was not armed and let go of the gun in his pocket and began to defend himself against the tumbling table that rammed into him. Ouch.

It was over quickly. Beault dabbed a napkin on a trickle of blood from his nose and rubbed his stomach. The attacker was on the floor looking to be out cold. "I coulda handled it, Fred," Beault said.

Fred, holding a blackjack, scowled and said, "Holy moley, Basil, if you are going to get into a bar fight, always be sure to pick on somebody you know you can handle."

"I will remember to do that next time."

A policeman came through the door. He took the measure of the place and called out, "What do you got, Fred?"

"It's over, Tom, come on in. Two other officers trailed Tom in, another male and a female.

"A bar fight, Fred," Tom laughed. "Isn't this a bit much for us?"

"It's more than that, officer," Beault said, licking more blood from his upper lip. "You maybe have stopped a big-time burglary ring."

Calls went out to the station for some detective help and an ambulance. The female officer, Mary, a cool, efficient African-American, took Ms. Seakrit into custody and to jail. The fake Marine was transported in the ambulance so that the huge welt on the side of his head could be examined by a doctor. Truke filled in the detectives about the couple, skirting the issue of how he knew from first hand observation that the colonel and the lady were, in fact, burglars. As a former police officer, even one from Beverly Hills where such things were rendered rare because there was so little crime to document, Mickey knew how to fudge a police report.

Statements being made and written down and signed by Beault and Truke and Fred and some other witnesses meant that the police presence could head away. In their wake, a regular drinking at the bar said, "Put the damn game on the TV, Fred."

Back home, Beault admitted what happened. "You were in a bar fight?" Nadine said, smiling.

"I didn't start it."

"And you lost a bar fight," Nadine said, now laughing.

"Well, Fred didn't give me a chance to show my stuff."

"You know I love you, Basil, but you do vex me."

"I coulda took the guy, honest, I coulda, babe, really, I coulda if I'da had the chance, honest, babe."

Nadine gave Beault a wry smile. "I believe you. Come upstairs with me and I will try to comfort you and your ego."

39

An unusual high-pressure ridge for this time of the year extending out over the Pacific Ocean cleared the skies and warmed the city. Beault put the good weather to use after dinner on a bike ride with Alana in the child seat. The ride took the two to an ice cream shop, a sweet moment Alana did not think was strange. She had been there on other bike rides with her "daddy."

"Mommy," Alana cried out when she rushed through the front door, "we bought ice cream."

"Good, honey, now go wash your hands and your mouth. There's my good girl."

Beault watched, and then said, "Something is the matter."

"Something is. Something has happened to Dagmar. One of her sons just called here. Call him. He is...he'll need your help, I fear. Here's the phone number. Call him."

Beault went into a room the family uses as an office. He punched in the number.

"Yeah?"

"Hello, this is Basil Protherington. I'm calling about Dagmar."

"Mr. Beault, thanks for calling. Mom is...she's in bad shape."

"Who is this?"

"Oh, sorry, I'm Devon. I'm the oldest."

"Devon, tell me what has happened."

"She was attacked."

"Oh God."

"They beat her up kinda rough."

"What's her condition?"

"In and out. Asleep, sedated, awake but unawares of things around her. The sedation, you know."

"Where is she?"

"UC San Francisco Medical Center. They took her to the ER there."

"When did this happen? Where?"

"On the bus. Tonight. She..."

"On a bus? What does that mean?"

"She was on her way home from...well, from your office, her work. She doesn't drive in the city. Two kids came on board to rob everybody, the passengers, you know. One of them had a baseball bat."

"Oh my God."

"Yeah, but that's not what got mom. She wouldn't give up her purse and one of them hit her a bunch and then got the purse. When he found the gun in there he laughed. Then the son of a bitch..."

"Oh God no," Beault yelled.

"No, no, he didn't shoot her, he hit her across her jaw with it."

"Oh hell."

"Right. Well, then the two punks grabbed all they could from the passengers and ran off."

"Police?"

"Not in time, it went down real fast, the other passengers said. Fortunately, one of them knows mom and got in touch with me. Mom lost all her stuff and ID when the son of a bitch stole her purse. I went over to the bus right away. My brother, Petros, is with mom at the hospital."

"Your other brothers. They live here, too, don't they?"

"Deron, David and Doug. They're out now looking for the two bastards."

"Are you serious?"

"Sure, we..."

"Devon, no. That is...can you reach them? Call them. Tell them to quit looking right now. If they find the two guys, they would...God knows what they would do. Whatever they did, Jesus, they'd be in so much trouble. And it won't help your mom. Oh Christ. I already know you Davos boys are into guns. This won't do. Please believe me. I know you want revenge. Hell, now I do, too, but doing it your way is not the right way. Please, please, believe me. Call them off. Then tomorrow or the next day we all can talk and see how we can help the cops. This will get the full attention of the police. An attack on a public bus will draw big attention. Please believe me."

"I'll call them, but I don't know if it will do any good. They're in a rage."

"Devon, that is exactly why they cannot be out there. They will not be thinking clearly. They could do something that would put them away forever. Call them. Then let me know what they are going to do."

"Okay."

"Can your mom take visitors tonight?"

"No, the doctor said nobody but family. It might be a day or two."

"I want to see her as soon as she's ready for me. God, I am so sorry for her and for you and your brothers."

"Thanks, Mr. Beault."

"Bas, it's Bas for Basil."

"Okay, Bas."

"Call your brothers. Tell them to go home or to the hospital. We'll get this taken care of, Devon, but we will do it smart and not make a bigger mess of it than it already is."

"Okay."

Both shut down their phones. Nadine was standing in the doorway. "This is horrible," she said.

Beault nodded. "Three of her sons are out looking for the robbers. Can you imagine what they would do to those guys if they found them?"

"I heard you. Do you think Devon can convince them to stop looking?"

Beault crossed his fingers and showed Nadine. "Hope so."

"When can we go see Dagmar?"

"Don't know. Only family right now. A day or two," Beault said.

An hour later, Devon called Beault and said his brothers were at the hospital. "They're going to want to do that meet-up with you to see what we can do about those pricks who beat up mom."

"Your mom comes first, Devon, her recovery. But we will get together and talk and see what we can do about those guys. We can do it Sunday afternoon. I've got a lecture to give in the morning and then I'll be free."

40

Nadine watched as Basil dressed for his Sunday morning meet-and-greet with Crystal's father. "You aren't going to lose another bar fight, are you?"

"I did not lose a bar fight. How many times do I have to tell you? Fred did not give me a chance to strut my stuff. I coulda took the guy if Fred hadna coshed him. I was just about ready to..."

"Yes, uh, Rocky."

"Funny. And this isn't a bar this morning. It's Arky Vaughan's Good Morning Joe café."

"Arky?"

"He's from Arkansas. You know him."

"Yes I do," Nadine blinked.

"You are really having your way with me," Bas griped. Nadine smiled. Beault shifted gears, "Wanna come with? Cup of joe, say hi to some friends."

"Watch you get your nose bloodied."

"You have so little faith in your hero right now, I don't know."

"Tell Gren he's welcome to dinner tonight if he doesn't have other plans," Nadine said.

"Okay, kiss-kiss."

"Wait," Nadine called. "I want a real kiss." They kissed real. "You're going to see the Davos boys today, right?" she said. "Well, I hope you can calm them down."

"Yes, but really what I want to do is keep them off the streets looking. That'll go nowhere and would be a disaster if they had any luck.

No, I just need to calm them down like you say." Nadine smiled back at Bas. "You are always right, Miss Berry. Now good-bye, I have to go get a cup of joe."

Good Morning Joe sat forty people when the fire marshal limit was observed. This Sunday morning it was half full. Half of that half comprised congregants from Beault's brother's nearby church. Grenville sat at a window table with two others. Beault was alone on a bench seat farther away, his back to a wall. He was facing the door. It was eight o'clock and Crystal's dad was a no-show. Five minutes passed, ten and then at eight-fifteen, a mid-heighted, broad-beamed, pugnacious-looking ape came through the door. A step behind was a teenager, shortish, plain, overweight and glum. The man looked around. The girl pointed and said something to the man who followed her finger to Beault. The man studied Beault without moving. He looked around the café more, and then walked slowly to Beault's table.

"You Beault?"

Beault nodded, looked at the girl and said, "Are you Crystal?"

Before she could answer, the man said, "You leave her outta this. She's only here so's she can see you get your face smashed in."

"My pound-down."

"Yeah."

"Okay, but let's do that later. We got talking to do first. Sit down." The man did as he looked at the others in the café and lowered his voice. "I betcha some of these guys in here, I'll betcha they're fairies," he sneered.

Beault held his noncommittal expression and said, "You think? Let me look." He made a theatrical move scoping out all the patrons, looking this way and that. "No...what did you call them, fairies...no, none in here."

"How do you know that?"

"Just look. Nobody in here is wearing a Peter Pan pin."

"A what?"

"Peter Pan pin. If you are a homosexual, you have to wear one. Nobody here has one on."

"That's horseshit. That's not true."

"It isn't? Dang. Let me find out." Beault glanced around the room, spied Crystal briefly and saw she was trying not to laugh at her dad, and then called to a coffee drinker. "Say, mister."

No response. "Hey, mister," a little louder.

Grenville slowly turned his head toward the noise.

"Are you talking to me?" Grenville answered back.

"Yes, you. Isn't it true that if you are a homosexual you have to wear a Peter Pan pin?"

"No."

"No what?"

"No it's not true that if you are a homosexual you have to wear a Peter Pan pin."

"But that's what I've heard. My friend here says it ain't true."

"You heard wrong and your friend is right."

"That's strange. I'm sure I heard that somewhere," Beault said.

"Did you also hear that if you are an idiot you have to wear a dunce cap?" Grenville asked.

Picking up on the joke he thought was going to be aimed at Crystal's father, Beault said, "Yeah, I think I have heard that."

Grenville waited a beat or two then said, "Where's yours?"

"That's not funny, mister," Beault called back to his brother.

"Who said it's funny?" Grenville grunted.

The customers in Good Morning Joe must have thought it was funny because most of them were howling.

Beault looked around, glowered at Grenville, turned to Crystal's father and said, "You are...wait. What's your name? I know Crystal's here, but I don't know yours."

"You don't need to know my name. We ain't gonna be buddies."

"I'm sorry to hear that," Beault said and paused as he looked back at Grenville. "Well," he said to Crystal's dad, "I'll just call you, um, uh, I know, I'll call you Gus," Beault smiled. "Today you'll be Gus."

"Whatever. Say what you are going to say and get it over quick. I got things I want to do."

"Excellent. Crystal here called me for a while and I thought it was inappropriate."

Crystal broke in to say, "But I..."

Her father said sharply, "Close your trap."

"Dad, let me tell you..." Her father said shut up and added a back-handed slap to her cheek. The coffee shop quieted a little.

Beault wavered and then went on. "When I finally did talk to Crystal, I told her she had to stop telephoning me or else I would call you and I didn't think she would want that. I..."

"Damn right about that," Gus said, turning to Crystal and saying, "You and your slutty ways." He smacked her again.

Behind Gus, Grenville stood up and nine other men did the same. Grenville walked a few steps over to Beault's table. He said, "Look at this watch, will you, I have to be on my way. I may miss this big pound-down if it starts any later."

The nine other men surrounded the table. Gus looked around at all of them. "What the hell is this?" he asked with reasonable concern. "What's going on?"

Beault looked at Crystal who was wiping tears. "Does he hit your mother, too?"

Crystal looked at her dad who growled, "Keep your fucking mouth closed."

Beault looked at Gus and said, "You just answered my question. You're a tough guy," Beault smiled. "Hey, Arky," he called, "is there room in the back where we can take this tough guy and beat some manners into him? You know, for maybe a half hour?"

Arky said, "Sure. Give me a couple of minutes to wipe the blood off the floor from last night."

Gus's head was swiveling. "Before we do that," Beault said to Gus, "I want you to hear this. Hear it good. You shouldn't hit women and girls. There's something just all wrong with that. I hate that more than about anything. I got the idea on our phone call that you were going to disappoint me. But this? An abusive husband, an abusive father. That won't

198

fly. So here is what you are going to do. You are going to stop hitting your missus and Crystal. Or anyone else in your family."

Beault glared at Gus. "If you do hit any of them, Crystal is going to call me. Then you are going to go to jail. How do I know that? Because that San Francisco deputy sheriff standing here" – a man nodded and flashed his shield – "will arrest you and everyone in this café will swear out statements that you are a battering man."

Gus's eyes were darting from face to face. "I..." he started.

"Stand up, Gus," Beault commanded. Gus stood. "Turn around." Gus turned. "Is that guy bigger than you?" Gus tilted his head back and looked up at Grenville. "Well, is he?" Gus nodded. "Do you think you could give this guy one of your famous pound-downs, Gus?" No answer. "I'll take that silence for a no."

Beault looked at Crystal who was sniffing and tearing. "Have we learned anything today?" Crystal began crying and shaking. In between, she nodded. Beault was now standing and towering over Gus. He said, "Gus, there's always someone who's tougher than we are. Today, you met one," he said looking at Grenville. "In reality, you met about ten. Makes you think, doesn't it?"

Gus looked at the faces of the men standing around him.

"If Crystal calls me and says you hit her or her mother again or if I hear some other way you've done that," Beault said, "you won't like what happens. You will actually wish for these guys to take you into the back room here and work you over for a while. That's what you will wish for. A better choice than going through the system as a felon. A wife beater. A child molester. Cons love it when you types come through the big prison gates."

Gus turned pale. "Git," Beault said to him. "Goodbye, Crystal," he added.

Gus and Crystal disappeared through the front door. Beault thanked everyone and handed three hundred dollar bills to Arky. Then he told Grenville he was welcome to come to dinner if he didn't have other plans.

"You cooking or is it Nadine?" Grenville asked.

"You're hilarious."

41

Beault and Nadine stood outside Dagmar's hospital room listening to the doctor say that her vital signs were splendid throughout the whole ordeal, sedation was called for mostly because of the shock of the attack, "but she's a strong woman and she's coming along fine now. Her jaw should have been broken from the description of the attack I heard, but no. Just bruised. And I have to guess as a medical man, very painful. She's still on painkillers. Go on in and spend some time with her. She'll like that."

Dagmar, propped up in bed, saw them enter. "Don't you dare cry, the two of you," she said through clenched teeth when she saw Bas and Nadine wiping their eyes. "I'm the one got clobbered," she smiled slowly. Bas and Nadine wiped more tears. "Oooh, the hard-bitten private eye. Bas, you're spoiling all those fantasies I've built up about shamuses. And you, Miss Berry of television fame, I thought you were tougher than this." That smile again. Beault and Nadine leaned in for careful kisses and hugs to the patient. Then they sat down for a visit. Dagmar told her story.

"That's all I can tell you, Bas. I told the police the same things once my head cleared. I'm sure the other passengers told them the same. Two of them. Eighteen, nineteen years old, average height, thin, dressed in workout clothes. Nothing really stands out about them except they seemed so angry while they were robbing us."

Dagmar took a sip of her apple juice through a straw. "The strange thing is that when I first saw them standing at the bus stop, I didn't take any notice of them as potential thugs. One of them, the one who brought on the baseball bat, was jumping up and down like he was shooting a basketball. Just kids, Bas, Nadine, just kids who turned out to be monsters."

"They'll get caught, Dagmar, sooner or later. Jerks like them always do," Beault told her.

"I want them caught before my boys find them, Bas. I don't want to think what they would do to those kids."

"That's settled. We had a good talking about that. This is police work, not for your boys to get involved. I finally talked them out of any free-lancing. It wasn't easy, but they got it into their heads that things would go worse for them and for you if they took the matter into their own hands. They're intelligent boys, er, men."

"Thank you, Bas. Devon says you have been real supportive."

"Now it's your turn, Dagmar. When are you coming back to work, tomorrow?"

Nadine grabbed Beault by the arm. "Bas!"

Beault looked at Nadine. "Hon, we have all those heavy boxes to alphabetize into the new file cabinet I am paying for. You want me lifting those things? I could strain my back."

Nadine laughed. Dagmar sipped more apple juice. "I'm feeling better than I look," Dagmar said. "I want to get back real soon. I like the work. My boss is a real drag, but I'll have him changed in no time."

Nadine said, "You change him, you get a big bonus, darling."

Beault and Nadine visited for a while then stood. They gave another kiss and hug to Dagmar and were about to turn around and leave when there was a knock-knock on the door frame. Ping Bodie put his head around into the room. In his raspy voice, he said, "I thought I'd visit for a while if it's approved." Dagmar smiled and raised her hand in greeting.

Beault and Nadine looked at Bodie and at Dagmar, tried not to act like giggling eighth graders as they took in the surprise visit, and went out the door after quick ta-ta's.

The famous private eye and the oft-honored investigative journalist asked each other at the same time, "What's that about?" Neither had an answer.

42

Mickey was on the scent. Driving around the city eyeing promising places to shoot Jaguar Beault. Planning was his ace in the hole, he bragged to himself. If he could just pull things off. The Jackal pulled things off, he told himself nostalgically. Well, anyway, this time it would be a feather in his cap, which was a different matter now. Now was now and it was Mickey's aim to find just the right venue to do what he had not done in Lincoln Park: shoot Jaguar Beault. Okay, not really, but it had to look real and be someplace to get publicity.

"Where? Not Lincoln Park," Mickey began explaining to himself. "Not enough witnesses, no easy way to carry off the 'deceased' and there were those embarrassing memories of his calamitous introduction to Beault's racing bike.

"Ooh, I know, how about on the bridge. Loads of people, easy escape into Marin County or back into the city through the dormant toll booths. Wait. No. Could not guarantee controlling the motor traffic. If the escape car didn't arrive just as the shots were fired, it could be a real bust. No, we won't do the bridge even though Beault has this unhealthy love affair with it.

"Over in Marin? No, it's gotta be in San Francisco. Ghirardelli Square could do. At noon when there are plenty of witnesses with all those tourists milling around. Beault would be standing near a chocolate counter and I would come around from…" Mickey slapped the steering wheel. "Too many stairs to get up there and that meant no easy escape. Not to mention the deadly traffic and brain-abused drivers rubbernecking the sights."

More exploring. "A cable car? One of the true iconic symbols of Frisco, er, San Francisco? I could be passing by and he's hanging out the side and I blast away real loud and he falls off and...and he gets run over by one of the city's distracted drivers. Sorry about that, Jaguar Beault." He grimaced at the image.

"Union Square? He's on one side of the ice rink and I'm on the other. Our stand-by Good Samaritans from Grenville's church are right there near him when I shoot and he goes down and they pick him up and carry him off. Nope. Their car is too far away and somebody may interfere even if they are trying to help. Damn," he thought.

"Hell, this is not easy," Mickey was saying, starting to doubt his ace in the hole...planning. "City Hall? No, there'd be cops all over the terrain around there." Cops, ugh.

"How about a shopping mall? Westfield, right there at the Powell Street BART station or over at the Stonestown Galleria out by San Francisco State. Stonestown, yes. Plenty of roadways conveniently in and out, plenty of witnesses spread out, no big police presence. Oh no. A mall shooting? There's been enough of those. The cops would shut the place tight as a drum for hours while they combed through every square inch of the place. America has had enough of that," he thought.

"But where? Awk! I got it. A brilliant place with some local color added in. Jaguar Beault would come out of AT&T Park at the end of the seventh inning onto Willie Mays Plaza on King Street when the Giants returned to San Francisco for an upcoming home stand. Crowds out there would be thin, maybe only a few stragglers or passersby before the game was over. Giants' fans stay in their seats to the last out. Not like those disinterested pseudo-fans down at Dodger Stadium in La-La land, heading for the exits starting about the fifth inning to beat the freeway traffic."

Mickey was on it. He would be tuned to the Giants game on the car radio and when the seventh inning ended he would cruise by, firing twice with loud pops from his .45 caliber pistol loaded with blanks. Beault would go down, grabbing his chest exploding fake blood vials across his Tim Lincecum jersey. Associates of the good Pastor

Protherington would be situated strategically nearby to do the Good Samaritan transporting to a hospital. Beault, of course, would not need a hospital because he would not be shot. Blanks. Mickey cleverly called the mission, *The Night of the Living Dead*. He did not see the cruel irony in the fact that on the very night he chose for this "living dead" theater of Beault's killing, the San Francisco Giants were hosting the never-achieving dead-end Chicago Cubs.

Jaguar Beault did not own a Tim Lincecum Giants jersey. If he did, it would contrast mightily with the conservative – nay, undistinguished – wardrobe he invested in on those rare days he went clothes shopping by himself. Shopping with Nadine, however, was an entirely different experience. But if it meant he was going to bring down these budding criminal elements in San Francisco, he would sacrifice his usual humbling ways and go out and buy one of those orange and black telltale baseball tops. Thinking about a baseball uniform, he was carried back to those days at Cal when he was starring on the Bears' diamond. He remembered fondly how good he was and how, if things broke right and he kept pounding the ball the way he did those two years and if the family tragedies...well, it did not work out.

He was behind his new desk in the Outer Richmond where he looked around his spiffed-up office thanks to Dagmar. He was not a major league baseball player. Now he was a private investigator with new and important matters that defined him as a workingman. Masquerading as a Giants' mound ace in the Lincecum jersey, for even just a few innings on the night he was gonna get his butt shot, might be a little redemption for not becoming a star on the major league scene. Again with the reminiscences of what might have been.

Beault was testing himself. "How are we going to get the Banda and the Bunch out in the open where they will demonstrate just how guilty... and half-witted...they certainly are? Gedmon and Blough's undercover cop can talk, but what will they do or say to get these two gangs performing something culpable, something impeachable, somewhere to be seen with their hands in a cookie jar?" he wondered.

When he remembered those climactic days, that climactic day, at Kezar when he corralled the gun-totin lice trying to grab the Madagascar Pigeon, Beault pounded the top of his desk.

"Holy fu...fudge," he screamed. Then he grabbed his hand and blew on it and put it in his mouth and tried to make the real bad hurt go away. He shook it and put it into his armpit and sat on it and shook it and blew on it. "Damn," he reproved himself.

"When you have finished this very entertaining pantomime, Bas," Dagmar said from the doorway into Beault's office where she was standing and watching, "you let me know if I need to go find some ice for your pinkies." She smiled. Beault turned red.

"I should not have done that, is that what you want me to say?"

Dagmar said, "You can do what you want here, Mr. Beault, you are the boss. Have you been acting like this while I was away enjoying myself in the hospital?" She smiled again. Her smile was not the full one she sported often before she was smashed across her mouth by the buttface on the bus. Dagmar was regaining more movement with her jaw.

"It's just that I got an idea. An idea that just may be the ticket home on this assassination tomfoolery. I..."

"Tomfoolery, eh? And you went to Cal?" She did not smile. Beault got red again.

"I like the word."

"Of course you do."

"Anyway. We bring the Banda deadheads and the Wild Bunch deadheads to the field over at Kezar, and we get them confronting one another somehow, I don't know, I'll figure out how, and then we have Blough and Headley and their troops there to pinch them."

"On what charge, Bas, what crimes?"

"Oh, uh, shoot, you're right. How about murder, tax evasion, arson, high treason, jaywalking, kidnapping, low treason? We'll have to figure that out, too."

Dagmar said, "You will be a busy boy, Bas. All this figuring. But that's your job, isn't it? Detecting. Grappling with murderers, kidnappers, traitors, jaywalkers, arsonists."

"Yup, that's me. You know, that kidnapping idea, that might work. They could try to kidnap me. Then we all..."

"Bas, if I understand correctly from the plans you people have already put together, you will be dead. You will be lying in a pile of fake blood in your pretty little baseball blouse."

"Ah cra...ah crud. You are right."

"Kidnap somebody else," Dagmar suggested. "Grenville, Nadine, Mickey Truke..."

Beault snapped to. "Alana!"

"Alana?"

"Alana, yes. They would think they would have a big advantage snatching a child. They'd want the money they believe Nadine and I have. They'd see Nadine doing whatever it costs to get her little girl back. Yes, if we could get them tied up with a kidnapping, they'd go down for a long, long time. There's your crime, there's your charges."

"Kidnap Alana. You should consult with Nadine."

"I will," Beault agreed. Then he added, "Dagmar, they are not called blouses in the big leagues. They are jerseys."

"How charming," Dagmar smiled. "How many jerseys do you own?"

"Oh heck, I don't own any. I have to go buy one so Mickey can blast away at me in one."

"Where do you buy jerseys?"

"There's places all over the city where you can buy Giants' goodies," Beault revealed.

"Can I?" Dagmar smiled.

"You are teasing with me, Dagmar, I can tell. Do I detect that you are not a baseball fan?"

"My boys played soccer."

"Do they wear blouses in soccer?" Beault teased back.

"Touché, Mr. Beault," Dagmar nodded.

43

Beault had changed his end of day schedule so that he would leave his office about a quarter of an hour before Dagmar's usual departure time. Dagmar's boys traded off every day to bring her to work and pick her up and take her home so she would avoid the tension of stepping onto the bus. She was still skittish over the attack – her boys even more so – despite the friendly feel of a gun in her purse, a replacement from her sons. The two attackers had not been found.

Each day on Beault's new schedule he drove down to near the ocean's edge at La Playa and Cabrillo where the bus would start its eastward journey on the Balboa route. Eastward himself, he drove just under the speed limit with an eye on the roadway and the sidewalks. On the fifth night of this, he saw them at 25th Street, hanging at the bus stop. Two eighteen, nineteen-year-old kids, average height, thin, dressed in workout clothes. One of them was shooting imaginary jump shots. There was a baseball bat leaning on the bus stop.

Beault thought, "Aha, gotcha, you pieces of shit. You are demonstrating your eagerness to make another score from bus passengers who would prove to be defenseless. In addition, you are revealing yourselves to be dumber than dirt. Do you think that nobody will recognize you, that nobody described the two bus robber culprits?"

He said these things to himself as he hung an illegal U-turn and raced like hell back to 32nd Street where he parked illegally and ran to the corner as a bus was approaching. This was the bus stop just before the one at 25th. He was wearing his pistol under his left arm. Beault is right-handed. Ready for action, he put his wallet into a back pocket.

Right on schedule, the big vehicle rolled up and stopped, disgorging an older couple and taking on a tall, resolute, neatly groomed man. Beault followed that fellow onto the bus. It was about half full of passengers. "How much?" Beault asked the bus driver.

"How far ya goin?" she asked back.

"Oh, just a few stops." He dropped in a pile of coins for what she said ought to be enough. He took an aisle seat on the port side four rows into the bus, sat down and collected his breath. Nobody next to him on the seat. "This is convenient," he told himself.

The long articulated bus signaled its intention to re-enter the flow of traffic and pulled away. Only two cars had to change lanes abruptly to allow the behemoth to merge. The driver dutifully motored the bus to the stop at 25th and slowed to make its next pickup with open doors. She gasped when she too late recognized the robbers from the descriptions circulating out to all her brother and sister drivers.

"Oh no," the driver expelled as the two teens jumped aboard and began shouting for everybody to hand over their money. The first one in waved his gun, one that looked very much like the one Dagmar had shown to Beault. The bat-carrying kid was behind him making sure the driver stayed right where she was.

"Get your money and you purses out and your wallets and your phones and your watches out," the gun was hollering. He grabbed a purse from a lady across from Beault and a wallet from a man sitting in front of the private eye.

The teen got to Beault and shouted, "Where's your wallet, motherfucker?" pointing the gun.

"Right here," Beault said, turning into the aisle to bring it out of his back pocket.

"Hurry up, hurry up," the kid yelled. Beault brought out his wallet and handed it toward the kid but let it fall – "oops, sorry" – to the floor.

"Pick it up, asshole," the gun shouted. Beault reached down with his left hand to get the wallet while reaching into his holster with his right hand where the kid could not see. Beault's left hand came up with his wallet and the right with his gun. The left hand and wallet didn't stop but pushed Dagmar's gun upward toward the roof of the bus while the right hand, loaded for bear – Beault's gun – drove hard into the kid's groin.

"You better not move a muscle, not anything, no moves," Beault advised calmly as he got to his feet, bringing the muzzle of the gun up along the kid's torso into his neck and then between his eyes. Beault was also reaching up to take Dagmar's gun out of the teen's hand. The kid's eyes crossed so he could see the gun there, then they went up into Beault's eyes. Beault smiled down. The kid's eyes opened big. "This is not going good for you, is it?" Beault said.

"What's up?" the bat-carrying kid shouted.

"Your buddy here," Beault said evenly, "is going to die if you don't hand that bat to the nice driver real, real slow. Then you lie down on the floor."

"A.J., what's he talking about?"

"Just fuckin do what he said, Izzy," A.J. answered. Beault turned A.J.'s head sideways so Izzy could see the situation better. There was a gun pointed at his friend's brain.

"Oh fuck me," Izzy gulped.

"You haven't done what I said, Izzy," Beault said. "Now I have to shoot A.J. Then I can shoot you, too. And, Izzy, I don't miss." Izzy complied with the bat and with the floor.

"Now it's your turn to hit the deck, A.J." A.J. went to the floor too.

Beault returned the stolen items to their owners, getting lots of thanks from the bus riders. Five of them had their phones out and dialing 9-1-1.

"Man, what's going to happen to us?" A.J. croaked from the floor.

"Nothing you are going to like, A.J. I can tell you, though, as bad as it's going to be, it will be a whole world better than what would have happened to you if that woman's five sons had found you."

"What woman?"

"The one you smashed in the mouth with this gun last week."

"How'd you know about that?"

"Jesus, A.J., shut your goddam mouth," Izzy counseled A.J.

Beault laughed. The bus riders cheered.

44

The plans were laid. Roles were assigned. Communications carefully defined. Everything was set. The Giants were home at AT&T Park where they split a series with the Cincinnati Reds, took two of three from the Pirates, and were now facing the Chicago Cubs in a night game. The moment for the Jaguar Beault assassination had arrived.

Mickey Truke was parked in a dark alley a couple of blocks from the ball park eating a Happy Meal he ordered at a drive-thru window. He had the Giants game on his car radio. It was the fifth inning, San Francisco ahead, five to nothing. Boring. He flipped the dial over to the Oakland A's game across the Bay...just to get the score.

A bit later at AT&T Park in San Francisco, the Cubs went quietly – naturally – in the top of the seventh inning. The Giants did not score in their half of the inning. That was the signal for Beault to leave the game and walk into Willie Mays Plaza. He did and took a bullet high on his chest and another ripped across his arm. Down he went. Real blood, Beault blood, seeped into the Tim Lincecum sleeve from his shot arm. The shooter's car raced off. Grenville's cohorts, from hiding places, rushed over to him at the sound of the gunfire and pulled him over to a waiting car.

Nadine was sitting in the back of the KSFG mobile TV van on 4th Street sipping coffee talking with her cameraman and sound tech when her cell phone rang. "This'll be it," she said. "Hello, Grenville."

"Nadine, Basil's been shot."

"Okay, that's our signal. We'll head right over and get video and sound. We're thirty seconds away. Thanks."

"Nadine, Bas has been shot."

"Heard you, Grenville, we're on the move."

"Nadine! I'm sorry. Bas was shot tonight. He's alive and getting good care..."

"Oh, God, What, why, how? Where is he?"

Grenville told her where Beault was being driven for gunshot wounds. She and her crew hurried there.

A short while after Jaguar Beault's body was removed by his friends from where he was gunned down at the ballpark, police units arrived, an ambulance, reporters and various onlookers. Gunshots at the home of the San Francisco Giants would tend to draw a crowd. Police took statements that were very unhelpful. A shooting without a victim. The ballgame in the stadium went on and the crowd in Willie Mays Plaza disbursed. The Cubs lost.

Nadine was at Beault's bedside in an emergency room at San Francisco General Hospital, a few minutes drive from the Giants ballpark. Beault was alive. He was tethered to IV tubes and beeping machines. Nadine held his hand, the one on the arm that was not grazed by a bullet. Nadine was calm now, knowing her love was not in danger. She did, however, feel Beault's outrage that Mickey Truke used live ammo and not the blanks he promised. "We should have shot him when we had the chance," he said to Nadine, who shook her head disagreeing.

"I'm back to tossing him off the bridge," she said coldly.

"I'll drive the car," Grenville volunteered.

45

A sampling of the Menzies family watched the news at eleven and took note of a shooting at the Giants baseball game...how the victim was hurried away by bystanders with no identification forthcoming. The family members drew their own conclusions. They knew who the target was. Zelda said, "That Truke twerp did okay. Shot that busybody private copper and we don't have to pay for it." Her husband smiled. Other Menzies clansmen and clanswomen nodded their agreements. "June, you did good, honey, bringing this guy in," Zelda went on. "This assassination operation could prove to be very lucrative. Money, money, money." She rubbed her hands together.

Bruce Menzies was not so sure. "You know, mother, this is risky business. Here in the states, this is called a capital crime. You go to the electric chair for murder."

"We didn't pull the trigger, dearie, so don't worry."

"Mother! That doesn't make any difference. We would all of us be just as guilty as if we did do the trigger-pulling."

"Brucie, you always look on the dark side of things. What do the kids say? Take a chill pill." Zelda laughed at this and liquid slopped down her blouse. She was drinking.

"But..."

Zelda stopped Bruce. "But nothing, honey, they can't put thirty of us in the electric chair over this dead bloke." Then she added, "We wouldn't all fit." She laughed until she coughed. She swallowed some more of her drink to clear her throat.

"Down in Texas..." B-rt started.

"Besides," Zelda said, not paying attention to B-rt, "we don't plan to get caught, do we?"

There were – generally speaking – eight males in the Haight-Ashbury Wild Bunch, sometimes ten, sometimes six. Four, twelve, who knows. They didn't keep a roster. The count often had only to do with who was able to toss some coin on a table. They had to eat. And that rent bugaboo.

Tonight there were seven lounging around the two-bedroom apartment just north of Haight Street on Clayton not far from the small Post Office station. The television set was on. Flip, flip, flip. Channel surfing by one of the males. "There's nothing good on this damn thing," a Wild Buncher commented on the evening programming.

"Turn the channel. Maybe there's something on another channel," somebody suggested.

"That's what I am doing. I'm turning the channel. Whaddaya think I've been doing?" He turned it again and the new station flashed a bulletin. A shooting at AT&T Park where the Giants play.

"God, look at that," said a gangly twenty-something with long hair, the not-so-successful start of a red beard and a wardrobe selection that looked like discards from a junk store...after a fire. "Some guy got wasted right in front of the stadium."

"Let's do what we did before," another lounger said. "Let's say we done it. Another tough-ass killing." He laughed. "What's his name can post it to that Facebook thing so everyone'll know we mean what we say about what we can do."

"Kill the man!" came from a voice on a mattress in a corner. The sentiment was way out of context and stumped most in the room. "Right on!" said one of the others anyway.

The forty-something leader came through the door and into the apartment, making everyone jump. "Jesus," somebody said to him, "don't do that, you scared us. Where ya been?"

"I been out, that's where I been. And don't be scared of a door opening. It happens every day somewhere. You sissies."

"Did you see that a guy got popped over at the ballpark? We was saying we ought to call the news and tell them we done it. You know, a pro-type killing. It'd be like free advertising. We got to get a move on if we want to make any money out of this shit. We could put it on...Wobber could put it on that Facebook thing."

"I'll think about it," said the skinny forty-something. "I'm running this outfit," he scowled.

"Ooooooh," came a murmur.

"Where is Wobber? He ain't here?"

"Guess not. Ain't seen him."

The leader said he was boss and so he was going to sleep without posting the kill because he was boss. He wanted to show everyone else who the boss is.

Moments later, the door opened again to let in another of the Wild Bunch. Guys jumped. A door had opened. This time in walked Harold Wobber who gazed at the Bunch and said, "What's makin you jump?"

"Don't come blasting through the door. It scares us," a Buncher said. Wobber shook his head. The guy went on. "You hear about the shooting at the ballpark?"

Wobber said no, but he knew that it was the night for Mickey Truke's staged assassination of Jaguar Beault. On a phone call out of sight of the Wild Bunch crew to hear if the plan was working, Wobber learned from Blough that the whole thing had gone all wrong and that Beault was actually shot but was going to survive it.

"We're going to call the news and say we done it," another Bunchman said. "We got to get the word out there that we are a killing outfit. We need the money."

The leader said, "Maybe we're going to call the news and say we did it or maybe I'm not. I said I was gonna decide that."

Wobber laughed. "Didn't you guys already take credit for a hit that wasn't you? You think anybody's going to believe us now? I don't think so."

"Oh, he's right."

"Maybe he is and maybe he isn't," the leader said. "Maybe we *can* take credit for this one."

"Oh yeah?" Wobber said.

The leader let a big grin cross his face as he nodded. The apartment went silent.

"You capped this guy?" Wobber asked idly.

"Maybe I did, maybe I didn't. What's it to you?" the leader answered, still smiling. "And where were you tonight?"

"I like girls. I went looking for girls. You ought to try it sometime," he challenged. The leader scowled at him. "And it's nothing to me if you cap somebody. I'm guessing you got a good reason. Or you get paid some mean scratch for doing it. If you're good at it, you roll in the dough." After a moment, Wobber added, "Unless you go through it like piss down a drain." He sat down into a mattress and closed his eyes.

"What do you know about it?" the leader inquired. "You ever..."

"I know the part about pissing it down a drain."

"How much?"

"How much! How much did I piss down a drain? Like I'm going to know that."

"No, no, how much did you...how much for a righteous capping?"

"Sorry, misunderstood you. Don't know nothing about here in Frisco, but when I was in...well, let's just say it should be in the high five figures."

The leader started counting on his fingers. Another Wild Buncher exclaimed, "High five figures? Jesus fucking Christ. We're getting that much? Holy crap! That's bitchin."

The leader stopped counting. "High five figures, huh? Really? That sounds like the big leagues."

"Big leagues? You capped somebody, for Christ sake. You didn't steal his wagon." Harold Wobber looked at the leader. "Just for the fun of it, how much did you get?"

"That's nobody's business but mine."

Wobber smirked. "That little, right?" A few of the HAWB gang sat up. Wobber smiled and said, "Hold out for more next time."

There was no talking in the room for a bit. Then Wobber said, "Who'd you do? Somebody's girlfriend, boyfriend?"

"You heard about it just now on the news. It was that guy over at the baseball park who they said was a detective here in the city."

"You killed a cop?" Wobber exploded, sitting up. "Are you nuts?"

"No, a private dick. Some asshole named Jaguar something."

"Jaguar? With a name like that he deserved to die." Everyone laughed. "How come you killed him?"

"I had a deal with someone." The rest of the Wild Bunch started to talk, ask questions. How come they didn't know about this? What was this guy holding out on them? The leader said, "Cool off, I was gonna tell you. When the time was right." Maybe when he was a hundred miles away and holding a fistful of money.

Wobber looked at the leader. "And you got paid peanuts. Don't seem smart to me, but I wasn't a part of it, so I can't say why you caved into this guy who hired you for so little. You sure this Jaguar guy is dead."

"Two caps right into his ass. He sure as hell is dead. Bam, he went right down." The leader wrinkled his droopy face. "You think I shoulda got more?"

"No kidding. You're makin me think you didn't get paid very much. You wasted somebody. A private dick. He'll have buddies who won't like what you done. Holy shit! I just thought. Can you trust this guy you had a deal with? He gonna keep his mouth shut about you? Keep his mouth shut about all of us? If things get squirrely? You better hope so." Wobber glanced up at the leader.

The leader was sweating. "God damn. I could be fucked."

"All of us could be fucked. You better get it squared away with this guy. By the way, do you know why he wanted this dude dead?" Wobber asked.

"All he said was that his family was going off the deep end and he was scared they'd end up in deep shit. They were hired to do this guy, but he didn't want the family anywhere near the thing. They had someone lined up for it, you know, to do it, but this guy wanted someone else. Me. Oh shit."

Wobber squinted. "How'd this guy find you? You know him?"

"No," the leader said, "he said he saw our name in the paper and tracked me down."

"Sounds like a load of crap to me," Wobber mused.

"Me too now. Oh God. Oh shit," the leader cried.

"Well, at least you got your money."

"No I didn't, not yet. He said he'd pay me when it was all over."

Wobber flopped back into the mattress and laughed. The leader shouted, "I am so fucking screwed. I kill a guy for hardly anything, and now I won't get a penny from this asshole."

"Always get your money up front," Wobber advised. Then he said, "Who is this guy anyway?"

"Says he's in that Lots Melemdez Banana. Remember when they said they done the guy in Sausalito? The one we said we did. Doesn't make any sense to me now. He don't sound like a spick to me. Sounds foreign though. Like some English snob. I don't know how he tracked me down." He stopped and said, "This is turning into a train wreck. We gotta turn things around. How can we turn things around?" No one in the apartment had an answer to that.

Wobber said, "Where'd you toss the piece?"

"What?"

"The gun you used. Where'd you get rid of it?"

"I didn't. I got it right here?"

"Holy crap. You are nuts. You don't cap a guy and then run around with the gun you used. You might as well wear a tee shirt that says "I'm the killer and here's my gun to prove it."

"What should I do?"

"Get a bag," Wobber told him.

"A bag? What for?"

"We'll put the damn thing in a bag and I'll walk it over to the park and toss it in one of them lakes they got there." Wobber was standing.

"You think that's the thing to do, huh?"

"Have you ever heard of fingerprints? Have you ever heard of ballistics? They call that shit evidence. And if they find evidence on you for a capping, they haul your ass in and put a needle in your arm and send you to the next world."

"Oh my God."

"Put it in the bag and give it to me. I'm saving your ass."

"Oh my God."

Wobber, careful not to touch the gun, folded the top of the bag over.

"Should we post the shooting on our Facebook?" someone asked.

Everyone looked at the leader. He looked at Wobber. Wobber thought for a few moments before answering. "Why not? If we're gonna be in the hit business, we gotta get the word out there like some of you said." He laughed. "On the next one, though, we'll ditch the goddam gun right away. And get the money up front."

Wobber sat down at the laptop and had the Facebook posting done in about five minutes. "There, that's it. Back in business." He looked at the leader. "How many more guns you got?"

"Three more. I think they work."

Wobber laughed again. "You think they work, huh. Not worth shit if they don't work." He put on a jacket to cover the bag and left the apartment.

46

While the Haight-Ashbury Wild Bunch was churning like a popcorn machine with highs about the prospect for easy money and then lows about the fear of capital punishment and hiding evidence, Blough and Headley were walking into a San Francisco General Hospital emergency room where Beault was lying on a bed.

"Always trying to be the center of attention, eh, Beault?" the captain said. Beault answered by raising the corner of his lip.

"Hi, Nadine, Grenville," Blough greeted the others. "Thanks for calling." A doctor followed the two detectives in. "You attending?" Blough asked him. The doctor nodded. "Filed a gunshot wound report yet?" The doctor said no he hadn't. He thought the admitting station was taking care of that. Blough looked to Headley who left the room. "We're police, doctor," he said, flashing his badge, "we'll take care of that notification. The lieutenant's doing that now." The doctor said that suited him and he busied himself over the patient.

When the doctor finished and was leaving the bedside, he said, "You are a very lucky man, Mr. Protherington."

Grenville harrumphed and said, "What is the old adage, 'luck is the residue of preparation and perspiration'? Or in this case the residue of how big a dumbass Truke is. I am going to kick his tail from here to Palo Alto when I see him."

"Why Minister Protherington," Blough said gravely, "is that what Jesus would do?"

Grenville considered. "No, he wouldn't. You are right, Joe." He paused again. "Jesus," he added, "would kick his tail from here all the way down to San Jose."

"Hold that thought, Grenville, you might get your chance. I called Ben Franklin and told him to find Truke."

Nadine's cell phone rang. She had seen the sign in the lobby that cells were to be turned off. She ignored the sign. "Hello," she answered. Grenville's cell phone rang seconds later. He also had ignored the sign. "Hello," he answered.

Beault and Blough looked at each other as the two phone conversations proceeded. "Must be all my fans calling to wish me well, don't you suppose, Captain?"

"If you say so, Mister Private Eye."

Grenville's call ended first and the small group waited until Nadine signed off her call. She said you first to Grenville who reported that he just learned that the Haight-Ashbury Wild Bunch was claiming credit for the shooting...on their Facebook page. "My friend has been watching them and the Bandas to see what was going to get posted. Sure enough, the Wild Bunch jumped on the chance to show off. He said the posting said they shot someone with the name of Jaguar Board," Grenville laughed. "My friend tells me the HAWB is probably setting records for brain-dead behavior."

"Credit for a hit they didn't make," Nadine said. "We know Truke did it. What's their game?"

"We've been over this," Beault said quietly. "They want to look legitimate."

"That's so, I suppose," Blough agreed as the lieutenant came back into the room and nodded to the captain, clearly meaning the gunshot wound was officially reported. "You know what else?" Blough continued, "I can tell you now that tonight Sausalito has arrested that Johnson woman for killing her husband. She had her hubby whacked." The others perked up. "And get this, she's going to be good for the three hip-hop hits in the city. Some kind of turf warfare or power grab in the rap industry. We've got them cold. What a shocker, huh?"

"Congrats, Captain," Beault said.

"Real police work in action. Usually does the trick," Blough smiled.

"Never a doubt," Beault smiled back.

"Your tip about the gasoline receipts for her car on the night of the killing was the turning point," Blough said to Beault. "Sausalito police ran that down, pulled some other records, talked to some people, kept a close eye on her, then put her through some hell. She broke. Then she named a name. Keep this quiet. My team went out to round up the woman's co-conspirator. He's not in custody yet."

"Your turn, Nadine," Grenville said when Blough was finished. She explained that her night editor at KSFG called to ask if she had heard about a shooting at the ballpark and would she know anything about it. Nadine convinced the night editor to leave a message for Xerxes Stone – her daytime editor – to assign someone in the morning to report the death of Jaguar Beault, a San Francisco private investigator. No one else, she told the night editor, would have that name, at least correctly, and the station could have an exclusive for the morning newscasts.

"I'm going to die?" Beault joked. The laughter stopped quickly when Ben Franklin appeared at the door.

"Where's Mickey?" Grenville snapped.

Ben dropped his head then brought it up. "I know you're mad. So am I. But there's an explanation. It's a lousy one, but it'll tell you what happened." At this, he reached behind the wall out to the corridor and pulled Mickey into the room by his jacket. "Talk," Ben ordered.

Blough and Headley started to laugh out loud. Everyone looked at them. "What?" Nadine said to them.

"This is going to be funny, I can just tell," Blough answered.

"Funny," Headley repeated.

"What are you two up to?" Grenville said, raising his voice.

"Not a thing. Let's hear Truke's story," Blough said.

"I am so sorry," Mickey almost whispered. "Uncle Ben told me you were shot...with real bullets." Grenville started toward Mickey but was intercepted by Dick Headley.

"I didn't shoot you, Beault," Mickey said, choking his words. "I was sitting in my car in an alley where I wasn't going to be hassled waiting for the seventh inning. I'm about three or four blocks away from the

225

ballpark. I have the radio tuned to the game. The Giants scored three runs in the first inning and two more in the second. Then nothing happened for a few innings. It got boring. So I turned the radio over to the Oakland game...just to get the score there. That game was pretty exciting and I listened. I guess I lost my train of thought with the A's rallying and all.

"Then it got to the seventh inning, you know, my cue to drive by the ballpark and fire those two blanks at you. Only it's the A's game. I pulled out and drove down to King Street and headed to that Willie Mays Plaza place. I slowed down and looked. You weren't there. I know I didn't miss seeing you. I knew you would be wearing that Tim Lincecum baseball jersey and be right out there where we would do this thing. But you weren't there. I went on past and drove around a couple of blocks to come back again. I figured you were just a minute or two late. When I went by again you weren't there again. And a lot more people were filling the plaza.

"It was right then that the announcer gave the score as Oakland seven, Boston six. Oh, shit, I thought. I flipped the radio back and heard the Giants announcer, oh shit, I heard him say he'd be back after these commercials with the Giants ahead five to nothing as we head to the top of the ninth. I am so sorry. But who shot you?"

Everyone in the hospital room stared at Mickey. No one said a word. Captain Blough was smiling and about to answer Mickey when his cell rang. He had also seen the sign about no cell phones in the hospital and was not intimidated. He was a guy who carried a gun and a badge. He raised his hand to the small group in the room. "Yeah." Then he listened and said, "No, don't worry, Beault's gonna be okay." He listened some more. "Thanks for the heads up earlier, and good work," he said finishing the call. He looked around the room. "This is what I've been waiting on. Those dumb shit Wild Bunch dumb shits really did it. Just like they posted on their Facebook. My guy called me a little while ago to say he was sure one of the Bunch did it. Now he has confirmed it more or less. It musta been a last minute deal they struck with some dumb shit from the Los Menendez Banda dumb shits. They got it arranged with one of the Bandas who didn't want his Menzies family involved. Oh, Bas, he's glad you ain't dead."

"Tell him so am I."

"You gonna make an arrest," Grenville asked.

"Right now it's only braggadocio, no more. My guy says it looks good. He got the gun and we'll do our thing on that. In the meantime, he's going to sit tight on these guys and see what else he can learn."

"Braggadocio?" Nadine said. "Haven't heard that one in a while."

"We move in different circles, young lady," Blough told her.

Ben listened to Blough's report and then took Mickey by the arm and walked him to the door and back out into the corridor where Mickey was heard to say again, "I'm sorry, Uncle Ben." After a moment, Ben walked in and reported, "He's sorry. That's about the story of his life."

"Wait," Beault called. "Ben, bring Mickey back in here, will you? I've got a question for you two." Ben glanced around the hospital room with a curious look on his face but did as Beault asked. Back in the room, Mickey looked terrified.

"Hi, Mickey," Beault said. Mickey nodded. "Ben," Beault said, "who hired you to assassinate me out in Lincoln Park?"

The room froze. Mickey looked at Uncle Ben. Uncle Ben looked at Captain Blough. Captain Blough looked at Beault and laughed. "This ought to be interesting," the captain said.

"Come on, Ben, I have a right to know," Beault said. "Besides, I got nothing else to do for a day or two."

"But if I..." Ben's voice cracked. "But if I tell you...oh...if I tell you, I'll be in so much danger."

"More than you are in now?" Grenville asked.

"Oh, Jesus, I can't. It'll come back on me," Ben huffed and puffed.

"Better you than Basil," Nadine added. Blough smiled. Headley smiled. Mickey hyperventilated.

"I can't," Ben decided.

"Why?" Beault asked.

"I'm afraid."

"Of what?"

"Of what you'll do?"

"All I want is a name. I have no plans. I've been meaning to ask you. You know, just trying to tie up loose ends."

"Tell him, Ben," Blough instructed.

Ben slumped into a chair no one else was using. He put his head in his hands. "Why is this happening to me? My whole life is going down the tubes." Mickey hung his own head.

"Tell him, Ben," Blough said again.

Ben looked up. "His name is Budlong Crabbe."

Beault let out a hoot and then winced at the pain on his chest. "Ouch," he complained. Then he snorted, "Mr. Smith!"

"You know him?" Ben asked.

"Sure." Then Beault related how Budlong Crabbe – calling himself John Smith – tried to hire him to off his wife, how Smith had chased after the purported riches in the Madagascar Pigeon statue, how the whole thing blew up in his face along with others and how he'd earned prison time. "I thought he was still in the lockup," Beault said.

"He is," Blough assented.

"Doesn't that make him kinda out of reach? Ben, why are you afraid?" Beault pressed.

"I'm...I..." Ben looked up at Captain Blough. "I just didn't think it would be wise to give up a name under these circumstances. The name of a person who likes killing." He sighed. "What the hell do I know anyway? I'm a first-rate fuck-up. Oh, sorry, Miss Berry."

"Call 'em as you see 'em, Mr. Franklin," Nadine said to him.

"Maybe I'll go see Mr. Smith," Beault said. "He's over in Folsom, isn't he?"

Blough looked at Headley who said he was. Then Headley motioned to Blough to step into the corridor. A few moments passed and they came back in. "New plan," Blough said. "Ben, we can address everybody's fears with a suggestion from Dick."

"Oh yeah?"

"Ask your friend in Chinatown to put the word out that Beault and all of Beault's family and friends are off limits."

"How will that do anything?" Ben asked.

"I'll take a wild guess here and say that Mr. Sun has influence that can reach right into Mr. Smith's cell in Folsom. Influence that will convince Mr. Smith to, uh, you know, mind his manners."

Grenville was laughing out loud. "My heavens, Joe, you are a cunning s.o.b."

"Me? No way, not me," he said and pointed at Headley. Then Blough turned back to Ben. "Do it. And soon."

Ben Franklin got the message.

47

Just after Harold Wobber returned to the apartment after tossing the gun...well, you know, following his absence to toss the bag into a Golden Gate Park lake (the gun, duh, wasn't in the bag)...a knock on the door scared the shit out of the HAWB. "What! Who is it? Whaddya want?"

"You got a call on the phone downstairs," a voice said.

"Who is it?" the HAWB leader said.

"I don't know. I'm not your damn secretary. It's the middle of the damn night. Get a move on."

"Oh, okay, yeah, okay, be right down."

"Who would be calling now?" asked a twenty-something as skinny as the rest. He hadn't been shaving either.

"Well, I don't know now, do I?"

"Go find out."

"Kee-rist! I'm going. Didn't you just hear me? I'm going."

"So go."

He went.

"Hello."

"Well?" came an Australian-accented voice on the phone.

"Well what?"

"How'd it go?"

"Just like I said it would go. I shot him. Jaguar Beault is dead."

"I think it's pronounced beault."

"Wha...who gives a rat's ass how it's pronounced? Now he's pronounced dead." That came with a laugh. "You like that? Pronounced dead? Funny, right?" No response on the other end of the line led the

HAWB leader to ask, "When you going to pay me? And I think I should get more. I was talking with a guy…"

"I'll let you know." Click.

The leader trudged back up the stairs and slammed through the apartment door scaring the shit out of the rest of the HAWB.

"Christ! You scared us," someone exclaimed.

"Don't be so jumpy. You're tough guys. Act like it."

"Who was on the phone?" someone else asked.

"None of your fucking business."

"What—is—your—problem? I'm just asking. Was it the contact?"

The leader grimaced. "Yeah, yeah, it was my contact." He emphasized my.

"So, are we jake with him?"

"Hell yes I'm jake with him. I did my job." He scratched his stomach. "God, I'm glad you got rid of the gun," he said to Wobber. It was the gun that Wobber had handed off to his friends in the police department. "You scared me shitless tonight with all that crap about fingerprints and ballistics and a needle in my arm. Damn, now no one can prove I, uh, we did that dude." No one could prove it except the below-average intellects in the Haight-Ashbury Wild Bunch who were as frightened as their leader. Oh, and the policeman in the room.

48

The doctor entered Beault's room and went to his bedside. Grenville asked him when Basil could be released. "Actually," the doctor answered, "we shouldn't need to keep him long at all. Maybe this morning. I'd like to watch him for a few more hours. He lost very little blood and he's got no broken bones, which is lucky. I'm guessing the bullet up here glanced off the bulletproof vest you were wearing and scraped across the skin here." He looked around the room. "Why were you wearing a bulletproof vest? Not that I need to know, being a medical man, but... just, I mean, curious."

"That man over there," Beault said pointing with his un-shot arm at Lieutenant Headley, "is my apparel consultant. He insisted. He knows how to give good evening wear counsel. When he does, I follow orders." Headley shrugged and nodded.

Nadine broke in. "You mean I can take him home?"

The doctor looked at his watch. "In about three hours, maybe at six a.m. if there are no complications. He's doing fine. It's like he knows what it's like to be shot." Grenville laughed at that comment.

Almost everybody had an opinion where to take Beault after someone said he should be bedded away from his own home because there might be another attempt if word got out he was alive. Ben Franklin's offer of a B&B he owned in Half Moon Bay was decided on. "I owe you, Beault; I owe you big-time for not strangling Mickey and for keeping me from doing more idiotic things."

Grenville drove Nadine to the Victorian where she packed clothes and other essentials. Her mother was there in charge of Alana. They jumped back in the car and returned to the hospital.

Nadine and Grenville could hear Beault snoring quietly when they neared his room. Asleep, good, they thought. Inside, Blough and Headley and Ben Franklin were still waiting for six. The doctor followed Nadine in and asked, "Does he always snore like this?"

"How would I know, doctor?" she asked innocently.

"Oh, I'm sorry, I thought you and he were..."

Nadine patted the doctor's arm. "Just kidding. Actually, I don't hear it very often. I'm a real heavy sleeper."

"Well, anyway, if he keeps it up he ought to be checked. Maybe it's his adenoids."

"Thank you, that's a fair warning."

"You're on TV, aren't you?" the doctor said. "I think I've seen you on the tube. The news, right?"

"The news, right."

"Yes, my partner is a real fan. Says you come up with the big stories. There was that real big one when the cops, er, police arrested all those unusual people in the park. Something about a strange bird. My partner was there."

Nadine looked at Grenville and asked the doctor what his partner's name is.

"Jim Gedmon. Do you know him?"

Nadine said she met him recently and pointed at Grenville and said, "He knows him real good."

"Oh yeah? How do you know Jim?"

"He's in my congregation."

"In your...are you...you're that guy?"

"I'm some guy."

"I should have put that together. Protherington. You don't hear that name very often. Oh, Jim loves your church."

"I don't remember seeing you there," Grenville looked at the doc.

"I don't go."

"You're not a believer?"

"Ha-ha. My friend, I do two things. I work in an emergency room in a downtown San Francisco hospital treating trauma victims about a hundred hours a day and I sleep. For the past year and a half I have basically seen two things. One, bloody wounds, broken bones and desperate people, and two, the backs of my eyelids. Some day I hope to have a real doctor job, you know, prescribe pills and golf on Wednesdays."

"I understand," Grenville said. "Well, you're always welcome at church between your two chores. What's your name?"

"Hess, Dennis Hess."

"Dennis Hess, M.D. Okay. And good luck," Grenville said.

49

The sun, hinting at a new day at six, was still too low to throw shadows from the city's tall buildings as Grenville pulled up in front of the hospital entrance where he helped Beault out of a wheelchair into the car. Nadine got in. Blough and Headley said they'd be in touch. Ben said the B&B was expecting them.

The drive to Half Moon Bay took less than an hour through the city and down the coast at a leisurely pace. On the way, Nadine hauled out her phone and said she had to alert a few friends who are going to learn of her betrothed's death. "I don't want people panicking when they see the news. I'll call, let's see, I should keep the list real short. I've already told mother. I'll call, oh, Dagmar first. She is going to get calls at the office. Does Ping know?" she asked Beault who said he doubted it. "I'll call Ping. Oh, you know who else? Miriam." Beault tried to laugh but it hurt.

On the way, Nadine got a call from her editor – Xerxes Stone – who offered sympathies and condolences over the sad death of her beloved Jaguar Beault. She thanked him for his kind thoughts and told him to go ahead on the eight a.m. news to confirm that the dead victim at the ballpark shooting was indeed Jaguar Beault. She told Xerxes to attribute the confirmation to a reliable source, not to her. Stone said he planned to have Rosalinda do the story live from Willie Mays Plaza. Nadine, of course, was acquainted with Rosalinda.

Stone also told Nadine that Rosalinda was heading over to Sausalito where a news conference called by the chief of police there and the Marin County District Attorney was scheduled for noon. He added that he felt there was a break in the murder of Jeremiah Witherspoon.

"Could be," he said, "they've pinned it on that weird Los Menendez Banda gang." Nadine held the phone out from her ear and glared at it. "Okay," she said, dropping the connection. Even in the face of death so close to the KSFG television family, the journalists kept their eyes on the news ball.

The drive to Half Moon Bay was also just the right amount of time for Beault to talk over an idea with Grenville and Nadine that he claimed might bring the mystery to a happy ending. They liked what they heard the recovering gunshot victim saying.

On arrival in Half Moon Bay there was also time to get acquainted with the spacious unit in the B&B before the eight o'clock KSFG news hour. The three of them watched the morning anchors, Stan and Joanne, say they would be going to AT&T Park momentarily for a special report on "last night's" shooting. They also said a press conference was scheduled for noon in Sausalito where developments were expected on the recent murder there.

KSFG sent its attention to the ballpark where the reporter proclaimed that she had an exclusive report identifying the "deceased dead man" at AT&T Park last night was none other than San Francisco private detective Jaguar Beault. She turned her head slightly as she spoke the sad news to fend off a tear, then she flicked her head again to cast some hair off her left eye. She described the scene at Willie Mays Plaza where the shooting took Beault's life. "Right here where I am standing," she added unnecessarily. When she was finished with her report she signed off with, "This is Rosalinda Maria Velasquez-Stone sending things back to our KSFG studios. Back to you, Stan and Joanne."

"What a bimbo," Nadine said, which made the Protherington brothers laugh out loud, Beault wincing again at the pain.

"Velasquez-Stone?" Grenville asked.

"She's married to Xerxes. It happened recently. I think they ran off to Reno to do it. They deserve each other."

As Grenville was leaving, Beault said thanks for the ride. Grenville said, "You owe me gas money."

The news conference in Sausalito got under way about twenty minutes late because the mayor had to return home and change his white shirt to blue when a staffer advised him it looked better to the TV cameras and lights. Less glare, he was told. When the mayor stepped to the microphone, he waved. Nobody waved back. He made all the comments television viewers did not need to hear and reporters wished could be banned by a constitutional amendment. Finally, he introduced the Sausalito police chief, a woman of average height and way-above-average appearance dressed in her Class A blues. The Marin County D.A. joined her at the podium where they announced that Donna-Ellie Donna Johnson, nee Knight, widow of Byron Johnson, was under arrest for his murder and would be arraigned in the next few days. The District Attorney made a very broad outline of the evidence against the Widow Johnson. He said he could not be more specific at this time. Then why in hell did you call a press conference, reporters wondered.

In the Haight, one of the skinny dudes living in the apartment on Clayton yelled at the television set to show his anger about being one-upped by some Sausalito cop chick. "We did that shoot," he shouted.

"No we didn't," another one said.

In South City, Scott and Zelda Menzies were watching, too, eating the last morsels of their lunch. Zelda said to Scott, "Back to square one."

In the Castro, Grenville was on the phone with Jim Gedmon who was watching the news on TV where he worked. "You can," Grenville asked him, "talk to the Haight-Ashbury Wild Bunch and Los Menendez Banda through some digital means to make it look like they are actually talking to each other?"

"Sure. Web sites, Facebook, tweets, sure," Gedmon bragged. "Facebook might look like the best bet. And it'll look legitimate, too. Facebook is a snap to pervert."

"My brother and I hope your plan can work out there in the dark, you know, for selfish reasons. Will it, will it work?"

"Because," Gedmon queried, "though it is devious yet cleverly ingenious, it will bring these misfits to good old American justice leaving you and your brother – and me – free of any culpability in the event that statutes or ordinances or privacy concerns are violated?"

"What makes you say that, James?"

"I know you, G.P."

"Ha. God'll get you for that." They heard each other laugh.

Grenville pressed, "Well?"

"Well what?"

"Answer my question."

"What question?" Gedmon said.

"Will it work?"

"Oh, my digital drama. Yes." Then Gedmon added, "Unless it's no."

"I'm betting you will do it just fine, Jim. Oh, hey, guess who I met. I met Dr. Dennis Hess. He treated Bas for those gunshot wounds."

"I know, he told me."

"Great guy. Holy Mary Mother of God, though, he needs a break. What a schedule he has. He looks overwhelmed. I suppose that goes with the job in an E.R. He sure seems to be a good physician."

"Let's hope we never have to find out personally like the way your brother did."

"I see your point," Grenville agreed. "When can you come by so we can go visit with Bas and set our little game in motion?"

"Whenever you say. Oh, by the way, you know how the Wild Bunch is taking credit for killing your brother? On their website? Out in front of God and everybody? How can they be so obtuse? Even if it was true, and I can't abide that, why do they parade a capital offense so blatantly? It's going to be a pleasure to torpedo them."

Grenville said, "Jim, it looks as though it is true. One of them shot Basil. Captain Blough has some inside dope on that."

"Gutter snipe HAWB asshole pricks," Gedmon said.

In San Francisco, the police chief had a press conference and announced that the same Widow Johnson was responsible also for the assassination deaths of the three hip-hop entrepreneurs in his city. He said that just this morning after hours and hours of exhaustive legwork and probing, SFPD homicide division detectives had taken into custody one Irving Leslie Jones as the actual shooter in all four killings. Mr. Jones, the chief revealed, had a business relationship with Mrs. Johnson. He did not grin as he said that. He also said you might know Mr. Jones as a local rapper who calls himself 2Krool4Skool. It was a headline writer's dream.

During the question period of the news conference in San Francisco, Rosalinda Maria Velasquez-Stone shouted twice at the chief who appeared not to hear either one. When the questioning ended, she hurried to corner San Francisco's top cop. She was a reporter on the trail to a hot story. She stopped the chief and turned to the camera. "Sheriff," she said, catching her breath, "how did you find these murderers" – alleged murderers, he corrected her – "alleged murderers so fast?"

"Solid police work. In San Francisco and in Sausalito," he complimented his neighboring resort. "And I'm not the sheriff, I'm the chief of police."

"Oh, sorry about that," she apologized. Then recovering, she said, "Will you ask for the death penalty?" looking smartly into the camera.

"That's not up to me. That's a decision for the prosecution."

"Oh," she said. Then "This is Rosalinda Maria Velasquez-Stone reporting from police headquarters where the, um, the police have announced the capture of the murderer – alleged murderer – of four people. Now back to you in the studios, Stan and Joanne."

Anyone still tuned into KSFG's coverage of the dramatic announcements heard, "It's Brandon and Tiffany, Rosalinda. Stan and Joanne went off the air a few hours ago."

In Half Moon Bay, Nadine looked at Jaguar Beault and at Grenville Protherington. "Do I look that cabbage-brained when I do a live spot?"

"No. No, of course not, no, not at all, no," the two brothers answered together, stumbling over each other's quick denials. Nadine glared at them.

In the Haight another underfed Wild Buncher yelled "shit" at the TV. "I thought we done that one, too."

"No, we didn't," another one said.

In South City, Zelda Menzies uttered, "Oh balls."

In San Francisco, Mickey Truke asked, "2Krool4Skool? Why can't I come up with a neat name like that? The Jackal had one, this asshole has one, and me? Nothing. The name Mickey doesn't exactly strike fear into people's hearts." No one answered Mickey because he was alone.

In the Bed & Breakfast in Half Moon Bay, Beault and Berry and Grenville smiled. "Captain Blough does it again," one of them said.

In Chinatown, Sun Shin Wong sipped tea and rolled his eyes at the enigmatic ways of popular entertainment and its resort to violence to conduct business. "So old-fashioned," he muttered.

50

"You still owe me that shoot-off, Mr. Private Eye. Lying here with gunshot wounds is no excuse," Dagmar smiled at Bas as she entered the front room of the B&B. Ping Bodie was a step behind, which did not surprise Beault or Nadine or Grenville.

"Any time, Annie Oakley, that is if I can get a permission slip from my doctor," Beault said. "You know, don't you, that I am invalided?"

"Mrs. Protherington-to-be, does he frequently hide behind these little owies?" Dagmar asked Nadine. "Does he use them as a way to get around simple challenges? Are you marrying a fraidy-cat?"

"He has his moments, Dagmar. This just isn't one of them," Nadine said.

Dagmar reached down to the lounging Beault and gave him a kiss on the cheek and smiled into his face. "I owe you so much, Bas. You captured those two kids. You got them off the streets. The way I hear it, they aren't going to hurt anyone for a long time."

"I got lucky, Dagmar. I was lucky that they were so confident they could pull the same thing so soon after what they did to you. I was lucky they are such lame-o's."

"But, Bas, what you did for my boys. Talking them out of taking matters into their own hands. I know they would have done some terrible things to those two criminals."

Beault said, "I was really afraid they might find the two punks. I'm just glad it worked out this way. Except of course what you had to put up with."

Dagmar reached down again and gave Beault another kiss on his cheek. A few tears trailed down her face onto Beault's.

Bodie came over to the sofa where Beault was sitting. He stood looking down. "I...when...I..." He stopped.

"Ping, it's not near as bad as it looks. The resourceful Dick Headley talked me into that big Kevlar vest again. Coulda been worse, but it isn't. I'll recover real quick."

"I know," Ping said, "it's just that I've seen you like this before and it rips me apart. What Leticia did to you and now it's happened again. I can't get it out of my head."

"Ping, it's over and we have to move on. I know that's easy for me to say, but you've got friends around you who are willing to help." Beault looked at Dagmar who, on cue, smiled.

Nadine said, "Who's for coffee?"

Dagmar and Bodie got the low-down on Beault's medical progress from Nadine. Dagmar answered questions about her own progress from getting smacked across her face by the bus robber.

"That is a nasty welt on your chin," Grenville said.

"A cicatrix from the battlefields of San Francisco," Beault agreed. "The hazards of riding the public transportation of our city," he said with a grin.

"I suppose next you will tell me to take my chances by driving in the city," Dagmar argued. "No, I'll stick with the bus. It's safer than roads, especially now that I decided to keep my fingers around my gun that you so cleverly retrieved for me."

Bodie stiffened at that and stared at Dagmar.

Beault exclaimed, "Dagmar, I told you that's a dangerous idea. Any number of things can make that plan go real bad for you."

Bodie rasped quietly, "That is for darn sure."

"I had a long talk with my boys. We defined just how I would do it. Wanna hear how?" she asked.

"No," Beault said.

"Fraidy-cat."

"Meow."

Bodie shook his head. Dagmar saw that and smiled at him.

Changing the subject, Dagmar told Beault that a television station called – "Channel five or seven, can't remember which – and they want to talk to you about that vandalism epidemic on the cars you are investigating. The Neighborhood Watch captain had told the reporter that you are the one to answer any questions. I told the reporter you were dead. He said when. I told him. He said he didn't know that. I told him it was all over the news, likely as not all over his own station's news reports as well."

Dagmar smiled. "I said if he didn't have any luck at his own station confirming the sensational shooting death of Jaguar Beault, the notorious San Francisco private investigator, outside a San Francisco Giants baseball game at prominent AT&T Park – you know, I said to him, a real big news event – he could call KSFG and they might have some video tape about it." Everyone laughed.

"Then I called the nice Neighborhood Watch captain to remind him of your untimely death. He asked me if I knew of any other private eyes who could take over for you. I said I'd let him know after your funeral and a proper period of grieving. What a knucklehead."

After a soothing visit when the recent victims consoled each other, Dagmar and Bodie left Half Moon Bay.

Around that same time, Jim Gedmon followed Grenville's directions and headed across the hills from the Silicon Valley on the 92 Freeway right over the San Andreas earthquake fault into Half Moon Bay and then to the B&B. Fog framed the evening. Fog. It is why lots of people call the quaint beach town Half Moon Gray.

Gedmon, Grenville and Nadine drank a Chardonnay. Beault, lying back into several soft pillows on a couch, sipped tea. Grenville gave the other two a quick background report on Gedmon's cyberexpertise. There was his fascination as a teen, a degree from Stanford, federal stints, and now the private sector. Gedmon corrected Grenville at that and said there's no such thing as a private sector. "Not anymore, that is," he said. "I can make just about anything public," he chuckled. "But I don't. That would be wrong." He chuckled again.

So it was that on this fog-framed evening on the Pacific Coast south of San Francisco, the quartet committed a small conspiracy. Gedmon would stage-manage a schoolyard tiff through cyberspace between Los Menendez Banda and the Haight-Ashbury Wild Bunch.

"I may have to use language more suited to the gutter than to your pulpit, G.P.," Gedmon said. "Will that trouble you?"

"No it won't. I prefer to think that kind of language will befit the way the people in those two organizations actually talk," Grenville said. "What I can't imagine is how you will learn the unpleasant words you'll be employing. Certainly you do not know them yet," he said, "unless you have heard them on a golf course."

"Excellent point," Gedmon said, then he snapped, "I know, I'll go down to the docks and hang around the bars and listen to the argot of the seafaring crowd. I understand they talk in tough terms."

Nadine looked on in wonderment of these two. Beault said, "Stop, you're making my wounds hurt."

"Jim," Grenville asked, "how will you make it look like the two gangs are talking to each other?"

"Good question, G.P., and it's all very simple. I will activate an inter-facebook robotroid app that will look like a port into a cloud. Then I'll pre-snap an iPad tablet connector to a text-laden twitter account using a false name. I can choose any blog formatting I want by downloading an android from the web. Then I'll..."

"Whoa, whoa, whoa," Grenville interrupted. "That's way over my head." He didn't notice Beault and Berry were smirking. Then he did. "What?" Then he looked at Gedmon. "What?"

"It's a technical world we live in now, G.P.," Gedmon told him. "Not that technical, however. That was just gibberish. I'm yanking your chain. You know, you're pretty easy to get to with this stuff."

"Gibberish? My chain? I'm easy? I thought you knew what you were talking about."

"Sounded good, didn't it?" Gedmon laughed.

"Yes, very good, very funny," Grenville nodded. "One thing though, James, I'm bigger than you and stronger than you and faster than you and I could kick your ass right now if I thought it would do you any good."

"That's not an accepted act of Christian love, Mr. Minister. Besides, Miss Berry here would have one heck of a news story. Like man bites dog. Minister puts a whuppin on his parishioner."

"It still might be worth it," Grenville mumbled and laughed.

Beault said, "Grenville, do you really want to know how James is going to pull this off? Wouldn't it be better – safer – if you and me and Nadine are left in the dark? Let James just go about his business. Besides, he has that undercover cop to protect. Don't forget what Joe told you about blowing his cover."

Grenville thought. Then he agreed. "Yeah, I see your point." Then he paused again before saying, "I still should kick your butt, Jim. On the other hand, maybe I'll use you and your sinful ways in a sermon next week."

Nadine said, "Be sure to confess to your congregation in that sermon that you are the one who is behind putting James up to these sinful ways."

"Everybody's ganging up on me," Grenville vamped.

Almost simultaneously, members of the now-disgraced Los Menendez Banda and the ill-reputed rag-tag Haight-Ashbury Wild Bunch were in separate locations licking their wounds from the crescendo of news that neither gang had had a role in the notorious hip-hop murders. This assassination gig, both camps reasoned, was not so easy to get into successfully as it had first appeared. Gunning down Jaguar Beault at AT&T Park was a notch on the bedpost for the HAWB leader, but it didn't bring any cash or any leads to real jobs for pay. They'd have to think long and hard on just how to make that hit mean something. Thinking, however, was not their forte. And that put them in a dead-heat tie with the people populating Los Menendez Banda.

Making things worse for these two enterprises was a story of the hip-hop murders in this very morning's edition of the San Francisco Chronicle covering about sixty column inches. Los Menendez Banda got the first part of a short paragraph while the Haight-Ashbury Wild Bunch got the rest. The paragraph simply pointed out that the two claimants to the killings were apparently just opportunists.

"Just what you would expect from a Socialist newspaper," said one of the Menzies boys in South San Francisco.

The "snot-nosed" reporters, one of the HAWB gonzos called them.

"We should blow up the Chronicle building," another of the under-fed Wild Bunch volunteered in the Haight apartment.

"Yeah," said another, "but where is it?"

All the Wild Bunch guys thought about that. Then one said, "Isn't it over in Berkeley or Oakland or somewhere?" No one, other than the new guy who had a way with computers, knew.

Someone else said, "Wouldn't we need something to blow it up with. Dynamite like. Do we have anything like that?" No one knew. Wobber, lounging back on a pillow, closed his eyes so he would not give away how mind-boggled he believed these people to be.

"What's a Socialist newspaper anyway?" came from another voice in the Menzies household down in South City.

51

Jim Gedmon plopped down in a chair at his home office desk, uncapped a Negra Modelo, wiped his damp hands dry, chomped off the end of a fat cigar, did not light it because his doctor partner did not tolerate smoking, stretched out his arms and cracked knuckles on both hands, unsleeved his laptop, flipped open the monitor, powered up, then said, anticipating his upcoming encounters with Los Menendez Banda and the Haight-Ashbury Wild Bunch, "Reach for the sky, you yellow-bellied four-flushers." Quickly he turned this way and that to see if anyone heard what he said after he realized he spoke the words out loud. No one was there to hear him, which gave him leave to also say out loud, "Now to work."

When the work was finished, Gedmon was manager of a Facebook page he titled "L-M-B" for public consumption, although the official domain name was Los Menendez Banditos to avoid any conflict with the digital reality of the Los Menendez Banda site. Likewise, he managed another page he named "H-A-W-B", or Haight-Ashbury Willowy Bunnies. In both cases, the registered names were buried in officialdom. A third site he named Jameson Appletree. That was his own site to interface with the others, legitimate and, well, not so legitimate.

Gedmon referred to a slip of paper with an e-mail address on it. He wrote a note to that address. The note was read a few hours later by Harold Wobber on his password-protected e-mail account on the laptop in Haight-Ashbury.

In the meantime, Gedmon had also located the real Facebook sites already set up by the wannabe assassins. The HAWB site did admit to the assassination business with its deluded claims about the hip-hop hits, but the Wild Bunch did not use the site to actually solicit business. In the end, Gedmon concluded Wobber was busy deceiving his roommates and that they were all too green to recognize how easy it was to penetrate their lives and how narcissistic they were as they asked Wobber to reveal utterly useless information about themselves.

"I should be ashamed of myself," Gedmon murmured as he worked his way around the keyboard. "This will be easier than shooting fish in a barrel." He stopped for a second and wondered who in the world would shoot fish in a barrel. Or why. And what were the fish doing in a barrel in the first place. Questions for another day.

The digital challenge for Jim Gedmon was laughable. That work went easily and fast. But what messages should he use to involve the two targets without tipping his own hand was the solution he needed to devise. For one thing, the two targets were below average in technical smarts and would have to be led down the road by their noses until they saw good reason to buy in. On the HAWB side, he had Wobber collaborating. That was fortunate. For another thing, the Banda crowd may be too wary – afraid – to be drawn into a scenario where they would agree to play chicken. Throughout this, however, Gedmon had Beault's plan. He decided to call his spiritual guide and say he was ready to act.

Grenville listened. "I'll talk it over with Nadine and Bas to make sure they are still in agreement on this."

Nadine and Bas – Jaguar Beault – said, "We are. We'd better talk it over with Joe to make sure he is comfortable with the skullduggery." Joe Blough and Dick Headley were at the B&B.

Captain Blough said, "I'm good with it. What do you think, Dick?" he asked Lieutenant Headley, who answered, "Let's do it."

Blough recapped. "So this unnamed computer dude is going to get these two moronic outfits thinking they are talking to each other leading to a race for some supposed riches. Then we step in and grab them ending their aspirations in the crime field."

"He admits, Joe, that we'll need some luck along the way," Grenville said. "Just think, though, how tempting it is going to be for them when they see a potentially big payoff from it all."

"I suppose that's right," Blough said, and then he looked at Nadine. "That part's not my call; it's up to you and your lesser half," he said, pointing at Beault.

"We've talked it over and we're good with it, too," she said, holding Beault's hand.

Grenville said, "I'll call my guy and tell him to get moving on it. Then I'll call the congregation jocks together and set up a game. It'll be like old times."

"The lieutenant here came up with a great idea earlier to bring the risks down to where we can manage them fairly easily," Blough said. "It's not shock and awe, more like shuck and jive. I think you'll like it. Incidentally, Grenville, I know your computer guy wants to stay in the shadows, but tell him from me that he's doing a great job."

"Thanks, Joe, he'll appreciate that."

"And have him give my best to his friend, Doc Hess."

"Huh? Wha...how..."

"Grenville, my daughter is in your church. She knows how to read people. She's got her mother's great brain cells. She has Jim Gedmon figured out."

"But..."

"But nothing. It doesn't go past here. All right, everybody, we have work to do. I have a call to make to one of my officers. Dick has a recruiting job to do. Grenville has some messages to deliver. And...and...somebody has a call to make to Mickey Truke. Who wants to do that? Who wants to alert that idiot?"

After a long pause, Beault sighed, "Me. I'll do it." After another pause, he said, "Where's my gun?" It got a laugh.

52

J im Gedmon sat down at his desk and did the beer bottle thing and the un-lit cigar thing and the laptop thing and the knuckles-cracking thing. He smiled. "This is so cool," he said out loud, not caring this time if someone might hear him.

He opened his sites and typed from Los Menendez Banda to the Haight-Ashbury Wild Bunch:

The truth comes out and it shows that you Haight-Ashbury Wild Bunch douche bags are a clueless mob of apes. Stay out of the way of Los Menendez Banda. We rule the killing fields of San Francisco.

He hit send. He sat back. The cigar would have been primo but for Doc Hess' inviolable admonition. The beer tasted great. Then it came. The response from HAWB:

Who the hell are you?

Instead of passing that response over to the real LMB page, one he knew originated from Harold Wobber's fingers, as arranged, Gedmon typed:

You are a lying pack of dogs who claimed to kill someone you didn't. Los Menendez Banda, you are full of shit. Take it from the Haight-Ashbury Wild Bunch. We know what we are doing.

Now he had to wait. Was the Banda crowd on-line? He heaved a big sigh as he saw it after a short time:

What are you talking about?

Well-well, I got their attention, James thought. More typing to LMB:

Everyone knows the worst you assholes do is roll homeless people for their shoes.

Back came:

What is your problem.

Gedmon answered, typing to the LMB:

You fucking spics! We don't roll homeless people for their shoes. That's something you wetback pussies do. Why don't you go back to where you came from.

Comeback was:

Get a life, mate.

What went forward instead to the LMB from Gedmon was:

We're not going anywhere. Come to Haight-Ashbury so we can drop the hammer on you. Do you ever come out of your hole?

Gedmon almost apoplexed when he saw the response from South San Francisco:

Eat fucking shit! We'll show you a ass-kicking make you dingoes crawl back into your hole.

They're buying it, James thought. He could envision Wobber sitting at a laptop and coaching his Wild Bunch buddies along. James forwarded the Wobber response. He didn't need to make up his own. Even more exciting was what came back from the LMB:

Look over your shoulder we're right behind you.

Then:

Fuck off! We've had enough of your bullshit.

On that one from Wobber, Gedmon decided to use it but that it was time to attach the kicker to the LMB:

We've got bigger things to do than squash Mexican jumping beans like you. Watch the headlines assholes. We're in this for the big money. Don't get in our way.

James was in a daze, a happy one, as he bandied the real messages and his fake messages to and fro like a shuttlecock from legitimate Facebook pages to phony ones to meet his needs. Then the next one from the LMB:

The headlines? The ones that say Los Menendez Banda eats you for lunch?

That brought a quick return with more tempting from Gedmon writing as the HAWB to the Banda:

Stay the fuck away from the Beault money and the Beault dame. You got that? Stay the fuck away unless you want to end up in body bags. We offed him, we get his money.

James made a decision. Time to act. He wrote out a final text. It read:

You better take this serious. We mean business. If you show up at Kezar on Saturday for the football game Beault's queer brother is putting on by his sissy friends to honor his dead brother we will eat you for lunch. We are grabbing Beault's woman's daughter so the woman will have to fork over the money he got from that bird thing. So stay away. This is a done deal.

He hit send – click – and send – click – and the identical message went to the real computers at Los Menendez Banda and at the Haight-Ashbury Wild Bunch. Then he closed down the sites he had created, making them go dark. He called Grenville. "It's done. It went pretty damn well, I must say. Wouldn't hurt, though, G.P. for a prayer or two."

"Thanks, Jim, all of us really appreciate what you've done. You have another fan, too. Captain Blough says thanks."

"He knows it's me? Am I in trouble?"

"He's known all along, I think. Says his daughter had you pegged for a cyberstar. And, no, you are not in trouble."

"His daughter, Francine? That sweet thing from church? Sees right through me? Damn, I'll never figure out women."

"That's an advantage, Jim, that we have. We'll never need to."

"Things looking good for Saturday?"

"Lots of stuff to do. It'll be a hell of a game and a great party afterward even if those nitwit gangs don't show," Grenville laughed. "See you there."

53

Zelda Menzies coughed and gagged. "They're going to try to grab that reporter's daughter and get her money. I say we go do that. But how? How'd we do that? Where would we do that? I'm not thinking straight. Goddamit!"

Scott Menzies said, "Calm yourself. We've got a trump card."

"Do we? What is it?"

"That birdbrain Truke. We'll send him over to the park on Saturday. Him and his guns. He takes out these Wild Bunch cockroaches while the rest of us are grabbing the little girl on the sly."

"He can handle it? His part?"

"He told me he can. He will. He's a shooter. He owes us for lying to us about the kills he said he made. If something does go wrong, we are in the clear. We're just unarmed innocent bystanders if we play our cards right. Truke will be the one holding the gun. Our trump card," Scott said. "Even as we are edging away with the lass. It's covered."

"I hope so."

"Don't forget, we'll have enough hands on, uh, hand, to camouflage it when we grab her. Nobody will try to stop us. Especially those poofs playing their game."

"I hope so."

The leader of the HAWB, underweight and long-haired, which hardly set him apart from his compatriots, looked over Wobber's shoulder at the laptop and screamed, "Those fucking beaners are going to grab the Beault woman's daughter. They're after some money. Why didn't I think of that?" The shouting woke up the only two other Wild Bunchers in the room at the time.

"What's goin on?" one asked.

"I said those fucking Los Melendems assholes plan to snatch that guy's chick's daughter for...oh, the hell with you. Shut up. I have to figure this out."

"What's to figure out?" Wobber said. "We show up, too, and blow 'em away, grab the daughter ourselves and we're home free. The woman'll pay big to get her back. Then we all just disappear with our cuts of the dough. Who's going to stop us? Those fags playing football? Not on your life."

"Makes sense," the leader said.

"Damn right it makes sense. You said you got three guns, right? Let me have 'em," Wobber offered, "and I'll work 'em up clean and get 'em loaded. I know my way around them."

"What did you do before you showed up here?" the leader asked.

"You do not want to know. You do not want to ask," Harold Wobber said. He stared at the leader.

"Point made. Get the guns ready."

54

The football game was pegged as a memorial event for the dead Jaguar Beault. Grenville's friends set up the big field for the game just outside historic Kezar Stadium as they had when Beault took that bullet from Mrs. Smith as he solved the mystery of the Madagascar Pigeon. The players agreed to start the game at eleven o'clock. There was no debate. Eleven was as good as any other hour.

Shirts and jackets and ice chests outlined the playing area. Boxes of goodies for lunch were stashed near the barbeque pits. Ballplayers kept arriving in twos and threes by car and bikes and on foot. Guys were stretching, jogging, tossing a couple of footballs around. Nobody was dropping them. They looked like they belonged here. Way out on the edges of the park a small cluster of men eyed the ball-playing interlopers. Others stopped at the cluster from time to time, spent a moment or two, exchanged something, and then moved on. Grenville said to no one in particular, "Drug dealing."

Someone answered, "That pisses me off."

Grenville nodded, "Me too." Then he looked across the field. "Oh, look, here's an audience." Eight wheelchairs rolled toward the football field. Oldsters, apparently, wrapped up against the San Francisco chill. Coats on, blankets over their legs, woolen and broad-brimmed hats, all pushed by other men and women overdressed against the cool in the air. The procession stopped a safe distance back from the field's sidelines. That was sensible against a potential wayward running back or downfield pass. Otherwise, a nice Saturday diversion for some seniors. It was about ten-thirty.

It was also a Spare the Air Day. Your author has heard it referred to as a practice prescribed by authorities whose job it is to dream up the reasons. Spare the Air Day is a Bay Area sop, others say, to the eco-fanatics who see it as a movable feast. When visibility in the region falls below thirty-five miles or so, the authorities proclaim. They proclaim that residents refrain from burning their wood fireplaces. What do you suppose the tree-huggers say about that? Wood burning? Chop down trees just to burn the branches? Jaguar Beault, our hero and a Green Party advocate, says don't even cut the wooden things down in the first place. What's with that anyway, he wonders. Go solar, set up wind farms. How about a Spare the Forest Day, Beault protests.

Also, the proclaimers proclaim that San Franciscans turn to other modes of transportation than their cars on Spare the Air days. A few people do. Cars do not jibe with San Francisco's progressive power structure. The power base looks askance at the traffic and the pollution. They do not, however, look askance at the parking meter and public parking lot revenues or the revenue from parking and traffic tickets written all over the place...so some critics say. The proclaimers want to promote, you know, Muni buses (if you are not in a hurry to get someplace), BART (when it is up and running) bicycles (for the city's daredevils), walking (if you are willing to put your life at the willfulness of those damnable autos), Segways (if you have natural balance).

By the way, those parenthetical comments reflect the testimony of the critics. None of those radical opinions about the citizenry thereabouts should redound to Jaguar Beault. He is merely a humble resident of the City by the Bay. Blame others for these extremist views.

The air today for the football game was pleasing in the popular Golden Gate Park. Yes, there was something up there. It looked mostly like fog. San Francisco has fog occasionally if you did not know that. Also attending today's activities was a live feed van with KSFG-TV markings on the side. Nadine Berry was not in it. Rosalinda Maria Velasquez-Stone was inside with two cameramen and a soundman. The three technicians were trying to orient the reporter on how a football game in a public place was likely to proceed. She said, hey, she had seen football on TV before. Oh, okay. They all got out of the van parked up on Stanyan and headed to the field of play.

Grenville noticed the four journalists coming his way, but then, out of his peripheral vision, he saw five of the drug dealers walking over toward the field. He turned his back to them and scanned the area. He had nearly thirty congregants from his church and other friends who planned to play in the game. He could see them take notice of the newcomers. A few edged closer, tossing a ball back and forth. Others stealthily went around to the backside of things.

"You planning to play something here today?" the lead walker called out to Grenville's back.

Grenville turned to face him. "Yes, football."

"Not today. This is our turf. Why don't you take a hike."

"This is a public park, mister. Me and my friends just want to have a friendly day out."

"You're that queer church guy, ain't you?"

"Why, yes, you are right about that." Now Grenville was joined by four of his friends.

The two cameramen saw something promising and began shooting. The sound guy aimed at the scene. Rosalinda was looking into a little makeup mirror.

"So take a hike, sissy boys, before we run your asses off of here." The druggie was talking big.

The smallest of Grenville's nearby buddies walked over to the big mouth and said, "Run my ass off first."

The bigger guy looked down and said, "This won't be a fair fight, you little pansy."

"I know," Grenville's friend answered. And it wasn't.

The druggie reached in and grabbed Grenville's friend's replica jersey of Ken Stabler, the old Oakland Raider quarterback, with both hands intent on pushing him to the ground. Instead, "Stabler" windmilled both his arms up under the druggie's arms knocking the grip off his jersey. Then the druggie took two quick jabs to his midsection and two more to his chin. Down he went. Unseen by his associates, several football-playing friends of Grenville Protherington had slipped up behind the action. When the drug dealer went down, his associates made moves forward. "Bad idea," they heard from their rear. They stopped, looked around and chose surrender as the better part of joining in the fray.

Two cameras and a sound recorder were performing professionally. Rosalinda was brushing her hair.

Three of Grenville's friends, two ex-pro football linebackers and a retired deputy sheriff, looked at the fallen drug dealer. The deputy sheriff said to the unpunched druggies, "Pick up your buddy and come along with us." The three escorted the five guys back to their drug-dealing spot under a tree. It was a fair distance so Grenville was unable to hear what was said. From the miming, however, it looked as though the linebackers and deputy persuaded the four unhurt dealers to show them their wares. Whereupon Grenville deduced that the wares were dumped onto the ground and scattered and shuffled under by the feet of the linebackers and deputy.

Two cameras and a sound recorder had dutifully stepped along with the guys. Rosalinda turned around and began looking for her two cameras and sound equipment. She couldn't find them.

Grenville also deduced that one of the dealers offered some sort of objection because one of the ex-linebackers shivered him so hard with his forearm the guy dropped like a log cut from a tree. When one of the dealers appeared to be reaching into a case for a gun, the deputy leaped on him, disarmed him and kneed him between his legs. Another bad dude lying on the ground. The deputy made sure he got the guns from the other dealers. More miming ensued, leading to the two unhurt dealers pulling out their dicks and peeing all over the drugs in the dirt. The two ex-linebackers and the deputy sheriff pointed to the ground where the urine was needed most. Following another short miming and one-sided physical interactions, the dealers limped away.

The cameramen and soundman were laughing uncontrollably. Rosalinda was looking this way and that trying to see her colleagues. She could not locate them. She brushed a couple of hairs off her face.

The ex-linebackers and former deputy sheriff walked back to Grenville. "Shitheads," one of them said. Grenville laughed. The deputy said, "I know it might be unethical, but I took their guns and their money, too. A few thousand dollars. Thought what we do is to give it to today's winning team and they can vote for a charity to give it to."

"That's awful of you, what you did just now."

"What, Grenville?"

"You ended that sentence with a preposition."

"Sorry," the deputy said, laughing.

Grenville walked over to the KSFG technicians and said hello, etc. "Get some good footage?"

"Oh yeah," one of the cameramen agreed. "Great stuff. We always do when we come out here and watch you play football."

"Where's your reporter?" Grenville asked.

"In a different galaxy," the soundman said.

More players arrived at the ball field, more stretching, more passing footballs around. Two captains were named and they chose sides. Someone rode up on a sexy racing bicycle decked out in colorful togs wearing a safety helmet and dark glasses. "Gonna play football?" he asked Grenville.

"No, this is a Tupperware party. Need any storage items?" They both laughed.

The biker began to ride off, then he stopped. "I did not see that little scuffle your friends just had, Minister," he called back.

"What little scuffle would that have been, Captain?"

"The one I'll probably see on the news tonight. How do you do it? You know somebody in the television business?" They laughed again and Joe Blough rode away.

The first half lasted about forty-five minutes. This did not include television commercial timeouts, although there were the insipid questions from sideline reporters – well, one reporter in this case – who didn't know much about football. Rosalinda stood back from the playing area and went to various people to get reactions and descriptions. She smiled her engaging smile into the cameras as she listened to the descriptions of the game from players taking a breather from the action. Then when it was time to ask another question, she flipped her raven hair from her forehead and said something the player did not understand. Very generously, the player answered as best he could because he knew that the reporter was a co-worker with their good friend Nadine Berry.

The only interruption of any note, apart from water breaks, was a three or four minute argument over what the score was. Grenville settled it with an arbitrary answer. "Jackass," someone yelled out at him. There was no connection between that shout out and the simultaneous arrival of Mickey Truke. He approached from behind the row of wheelchairs on the sideline. The invalided chair-borne seniors looked at him. More than a dozen members of the Menzies household followed him by about twenty yards. They slowed and stopped and spread apart in a phalanx. Moments later, eight Haight-Ashbury Wild Bunch dropouts walked out of the trees on the other side of the field heading toward the football game. Three of them held pistols down along their sides.

The two team captains decided now was as good a time as any to declare that it was halftime.

"Where's the baby bitch?" the HAWB leader called out. He showed his gun.

Mickey Truke stepped between two of the wheelchairs. He was holding a gun. "You have made two mistakes today," Mickey called over to the oaf. "One, you came here. Bad move. Two, you called her a bitch. Worse move."

Two cameramen separated and moved strategically to each side of the field. The soundman followed one. Rosalinda froze.

While the HAWB leader was asking, "Who the hell are you?" all of the ballplayers headed off the field.

Then Mickey answered. "I am the guy who is going to make you regret your mistakes."

"You tell him, Mickey," Bryce Menzies called out from behind the wheelchairs. "And where's the girl?" Bryce added hopefully, edging toward the crowd of seniors in wheelchairs and where he saw a baby carriage.

"She's right here," Nadine Berry said to him, turning around from the baby carriage she had pushed in with the wheelchairs. It was empty, but you already deduced that, didn't you? Why wouldn't it be? Alana was at her grandmother's. One of the cameramen skipped toward the carriage. He had not deduced Alana's absence. Why would he, he was busy filming news events, not in on the clever planning by Nadine's fiancé. Off to the side, Rosalinda looked around. "What?" she said. Bryce kept edging in until he heard some shouting.

"The little girl is ours," the Haight-Ashbury Wild Bunch leader yelled. He raised his gun and fired at Mickey who returned fire. All the Menzies behind Mickey hit the dirt, Scott and Zelda slower than the rest. They had old knees and rickety movements. All the Menzies, that is, except Bruce, who, when he recognized the HAWB, began putting distance between himself and the football field. That separation was growing as he sprinted away. Two plainclothes policemen following him were faster than he was. One of the cameramen was also pretty swift even with a big camera on his shoulder. That separation, the one between the two officers and Bruce, was shrinking. Then there was no separation. Bruce was rolled up on the ground imitating a fetus. The cameraman was pointing his camera down and laughing.

Back at the sporting event, shots were going back and forth between the three armed Wild Bunchers and Mickey Truke. As the four guns went cap-pow-pop-bam-cap-boom-pop, someone yelled, "Damn, they can't hit a thing." Bryce was flat on his face.

The bicycle rider watched the action from the north end of the field, straddling his parked bike. He pushed off and pedaled on toward the field of combat. The single cameraman now at the scene was shifting his aim from here to there in an experienced manner. After less than a minute of shooting, the field went silent. No more shells. Seven of the eight Haight-Ashbury Wild Bunch dunderheads were looking down to see if they had taken any bullets. No blood. Rosalinda was looking out from under a picnic table.

At this moment, Jaguar Beault, dead these past days, climbed out of a wheelchair and walked out toward the Wild Bunch. He was wearing his Tim Lincecum jersey...the orange and black colors of the local team and, today, the red blotches of dried blood from the night he was assassinated. The forty-something Wild Buncher gazed at Beault. "You! Hey, you're dead. I shot you," he yelled in Beault's direction. People who were not bending over with laughter at the idiot's public admission of attempted murder were shaking their heads at the moron's complete lack of self-awareness.

Beault called back, "What's that you said, you shot me?"

"Yeah, at the baseball place. I..." He stopped. He looked at his gun with a curious glance and then pointed it at Beault, squeezing the trigger and shouting, "I'll get you now." Click. "Damn!" Click-click-click. "I'm out of bullets."

By now, the several temporarily invalided seniors had leaped out of their wheelchairs, tossing blankets and hats, joined by the kind people who had pushed them in, all flashing badges revealing them as San Francisco policemen and policewomen. You knew that too, didn't you? It was sort of obvious unless you were dimwitted members of the Wild Bunch or inexperienced and misguided immigrants from Australia who thought that, well, who knew what they thought.

Dust all over her pretty clothes, Rosalinda was up and about asking people their reactions to today's shootout at Kezar Stadium. A few of them bothered to answer.

Seven Wild Bunchers were handcuffed and read their Miranda rights. One of the Wild Bunch cried out, "Why aren't you arresting that guy?" pointing at Harold Wobber. "He's the one who handled the guns. He's the one who's guilty."

Someone standing nearby told him, "He's a cop, you simpleton. Are you completely hopeless?"

"A cop? He said he was a killer. He's one of us."

"He musta been lying to you, and lying is wrong, but he'll get over it."

All the Menzies clan who were present were in handcuffs, too. Captain Blough said he would sort out the charges later. He also said the South City police were raiding the Menzies residences and rounding up the rest of the clan. A clean sweep.

Two cameramen and a soundman scampered around the crowd capturing sight and sound. Rosalinda was trying to get dirt out of her hair.

As the police were beginning to lead the felons away, Scott Menzies yelled out, "Wait a mo, wait a mo. All that shooting. Nobody got killed. What's up with that?"

"Blanks," Captain Blough explained.

"Blanks? In all the guns? How can that be?"

"Well," the captain said, "that fellow there is a police officer who convinced the Wild Bunch that he should be responsible for the guns. He's been undercover in that crowd for a short time. He loaded their guns with blanks. I don't want to sound disrespectful, but the Haight-Ashbury Wild Bunch? You could put all their brains in a demitasse cup and still leave room for a bowling ball."

"But Truke, what about Truke? He is an assassin," Menzies complained.

Mickey, standing by and showing his gun, said, "Blanks. Didn't want to hurt anybody. And I'm not an assassin. I flunked that course."

"Oh, sheepshit," Scott Menzies uttered.

"Is that an Australianism?" Blough asked Scott Menzies. "Sounds like one to me." No answer. "Step over here with me and the lieutenant," he ordered. Out of hearing from the others, the two police detectives held a lengthy conversation with the Menzies patriarch, who mostly listened. His wife, Zelda, was at his side. She listened, her face a blank. When the talking ended, the Menzies pair nodded stoically to the two cops. Blough turned to some of his officers who were waiting just steps away.

"Get all of them out of here," the captain directed his men. Then he saw someone. "Hey, Josh, come on over here, please."

The beaten-down-looking undercover cop said, "Hi, Captain, I like your uniform. Captain Bicycle."

"And I like yours," Blough retorted, looking at the disheveled undercover cop. "Come meet some people." Blough introduced Josh Randall, recently known as Harold Wobber, to the bystanders.

"You're the undercover co...policeman at the Wild Bunch, right?" Grenville told him. "Good disguise."

"Not as good as yours."

"Sorry?"

"You disguise yourself as – what did I hear you say, a man of peace – and then you dropped that deadhead with a single blow."

"Oh yeah, in the Haight. You saw that?"

"I was watching. Those guys had given me a ration of crap a couple of times. I had to take it from them so I wouldn't blow my cover."

"We didn't see you," Beault said.

"You weren't supposed to. That's why we call it undercover work," he laughed.

Beault and Grenville looked at each other. "We didn't see him," Grenville said.

"What is this all about?" Blough asked.

Beault described the incident on Haight Street for the captain, how he and Grenville used corporal punishment to educate Frankie. Blough gruffed. "We're crime stoppers, not criminals, street hooligans, brawlers, er...oh, hell. You knocked him on his ass, huh?" Everyone smiled at the police captain.

"Josh, what are we gonna do with that lame bunch, the Wild Bunch?" Blough asked Randall.

"I've been thinking," Randall said, "except for that shooting at Mr. Beault here, they are guilty mostly of being feloniously stupid. Let's tell their dippy leader that he's going down for attempted murder and kidnapping. The kidnapping is a bit thin, but when we tell him it's federal and he'll go away forever plus a week, he'll cop to the attempted murder in seconds. Goodness, he just copped to it here a minute ago, didn't he? We could easily get him to take twenty years. The rest of the Bunch? They'll evaporate into the fog and won't cause much trouble if we have the right kind of...uh...you know...counseling session. Whaddya think?"

Blough looked around at his little crowd of friends. "Josh calls it a counseling session," he said. Then he added, "Josh Randall has detective written all over him."

Beault asked, "Do you mean if he's in different clothes? Like those nifty pedal-pushers you are wearing?"

Blough said, "Take your ass any day on a bicycle. Wanna race?" The challenge was not accepted.

The almost constant breeze in San Francisco scattered the smoke from the expended blank shells, masking violation of the Spare the Air Day. The noise from the shooting spree brought scores of people from neighborhood shops and apartments to the park. They saw a spirited second half of the football game. Another argument about the score of the game spiced the afternoon. The game resumed after the shoot-out because no winner had been determined. And winning was the reason for the game.

Captain Blough, Lieutenant Headley, Mickey Truke, Jaguar Beault, Nadine Berry and Grenville Protherington stood together near the row of empty wheelchairs. "We get a lot accomplished on this field, don't we?" Blough said to the group. "First, that pigeon statue thing and now this. It was a great idea your mister had," he said to Nadine.

"Bas knew he wasn't going to be able to play an active role in it," Nadine said. "He still hurts some from those two bullets. So he sat feeling sorry for himself for a few minutes then put his thinking cap on." Beault moaned. The others pretended they were sympathetic.

"Confucius say thinking cap sometimes too tight. Yield bad ideas," Sun Shin Wong said, startling the group.

"Didn't see you coming, Mr. Sun, oh, and Ben Franklin. Hold on, did Confucius really say that?"

Mr. Sun laughed and bowed slightly. "Probably not, Captain."

Blough introduced Sun Shin Wong to the Protherington brothers and to Nadine. Beault said, "It is nice to meet you, Mr. Sun, and to give me a chance to say thank you for your help along the way. Ben has shared so much from what you were able to learn. It meant a lot to us."

"It is my pleasure, Mr. Beault," Sun answered.

"I see you settled matters here," Ben said.

"Yeah, and in more ways than you might expect," Blough teased.

"What?"

"I don't know if you are aware, but our public servant, Richard Headley here, is a keen student of U.S. history. He's a practical guy, too, so he came up with a clever answer to the Los Menendez Banda mess. And we can thank Ben Franklin for that."

"How's that?" Ben asked.

"The famous Benjamin Franklin petition."

"Again, what are you talking about?" Ben wondered.

"Oh, come now, Ben," Blough said. "The famous...Dick you tell him."

"I just proposed we do the same as in the petition to King George," Headley began. "It said, let me paraphrase, that since transporting felons to America from England really did not work as intended, you know, for the better peopling of the country, and because it actually worsened matters, we should, like Franklin proposed, remit the Menzies bastards back to where they came from."

Ben gawked at Headley. "I never..."

"Not you, Ben," Headley agreed. "The original Benjamin Franklin. It was a sensational idea, but the petition to the British Parliament not surprisingly fell on deaf ears."

Blough picked it up from there. "Dick and I just had a heart-to-heart with those two old Menzies farts. Dick described the Franklin proposal. He outlined the odious penal alternatives here in California for his kinsfolk if they stayed around and slogged through the expensive – and inevitable – trip to jail. Instead, Scott and Zelda have elected to repatriate themselves and their whole tribe to Australia. They are, however, leaving behind Bruce, who was the family traitor who hired the Wild Bunch to kill Beault."

Everyone stared at the lieutenant. "Score one for a founding father," Headley said.

"Anyway," Blough said to Ben and Mr. Sun, "you missed all the excitement. But since our intrepid journalist, Miss Berry here, just happened to have her TV truck on scene when we started – I don't know how she does it – you can catch the highlights on the KSFG news tonight. Maybe it's that wunderkind editor of hers, the one with the strange name. And he assigned that up-and-coming reporter, Rosalinda Maria Velasquez-Stone, to do the interviewing. I've seen her on TV. She's a rising star." Blough looked at everyone with a dead-serious face.

"Oh no," Ben responded, "Wong and I were over there in those bleachers. We saw everything. Mickey made me proud."

"Thank you, Uncle Ben. Maybe *this* was my lucky day."

"No, son, not lucky. Just darned good."

Off to the side of the park, Rosalinda Maria Velasquez-Stone, KSFG television news reporter, recapped the day with a three-minute description of the shoot-out. She barely mentioned the colorful encounter with the drug dealers and the football game. Later, in the editing room, the three minutes was edited down to about twenty seconds of nearly intelligible commentary.

Epilogue

Basil Protherington and Nadine Berry had a date set for their wedding, that small, intimate ceremony at the Congregation of Brotherly Love in the Name of Jesus Christ in the Castro. Grenville Protherington would be the officiating minister. A short list of invited guests began to grow. Then it grew some more. ("You have to invite these people. They're like family.") Then the list outgrew the capacity of the church in the Castro. Where then? It needed space for maybe a hundred well-wishers. Crissy Field? No, too hard to control the crowds using the open area for fun and exercise. The same for Golden Gate Park.

Captain Blough told the couple that his daughter, Francine, said a really romantic wedding would be on the surf on Ocean Beach, at low tide, of course, the little waves lapping around their feet and ankles. Do it at sunset as the colors in the sky provided a rainbow canopy over the special rite of matrimony. Nadine and Basil said that was a possibility and they'd think about it. Later, Francine said to her dad, "Pop, did they think I was serious? Gad, they are such old fuddy-duddies. They can't take a joke."

Then an idea. Nadine and Basil talked it over. They were holding hands. How about the Legion of Honor in Lincoln Park? In the open area before the entrance. Up from the circular pool and the grassy expanses in front.

Perfect. They kissed. They kiss often.

It was a casual dress affair. It was outdoors. It was overcast and cool. It was...is...San Francisco. People were milling about on the lawns, down around the pool, up on the stairs, on the expanse outside the main entrance, making the event somewhat less intimate than origi-nally planned. Congregants from Grenville's church volunteered to be unofficial ushers so that the crowd would not get unwieldy. Good luck with that. The nuptials were scheduled for noon. Sun Shin Wong had generously provided a sumptuous buffet along a line of tables featuring lunch favorites from a variety of the restaurants he owns. It smelled really good.

Before noon arrived, two police cars rolled up, one behind the other. The forward one announced its arrival with three screeches from the siren. "Rip-rip-rip." That got the attention of all the wed-ding guests. Two mature gentlemen from the guest list walked down a grassy slope toward the police cars as an officer emerged from each unit. The cop in front took charge. He looked to be about sixteen years old, lean and eager. He was older than that. "We've had a citizen complaint of a big demonstration here," he said to no one specifically. "What is going on?"

"It's a wedding, officer," one of the two mature gentlemen answered.

"A wedding? You can't do a wedding here."

"It's all right, officer, it..."

"No, it's not all right. I just said it's not all right. You can't just have a bunch of people out here to a public place and put on a wedding. You have to have a permit, er, probably, and you need traffic control. Look at all those cars parked down there." He looked around. "You'd need port-a-potties, too, for all these people."

"But officer..."

"Don't interrupt me, mister, aren't you listening to me?" The officer's partner outside the other police unit stood back watching things. He hadn't spoken. He looked to be about fifteen years old. He wasn't.

The mature wedding guest got a little annoyed. "Look here," he said, "you ought to cool down and let me explain."

"Hey, mister know-it-all," the officer said, "I'm doing the explain-ing. We're following up on a serious citizen complaint. We're the police, that's what we do." The wedding guest smiled. "You think this is funny?" the cop challenged. "You and all these people have to leave."

The wedding guest was wearing gray slacks, a blue dress shirt with no tie and a windbreaker for use against the cool breeze. When he put his hands into his pants pockets to contain a rising rage, his windbreaker parted in front and a holster on his belt was revealed. For the first time, the second officer spoke. "Gun!" he shouted. Both officers drew their weapons.

The other mature wedding guest who came down the grassy slope was dressed similarly as the first. He slowly drew his own windbreaker apart to reveal his own holstered gun. "Another gun," the first officer yelled. "Hands above your, uh, heads," he almost stuttered.

By now a few dozen wedding guests had slipped down to see what was going on with the police.

"What in hell is this? You look like mafia," the first officer said. He was clearly nervous, likely in a situation new to him on his beat. He and his buddy were pointing their 9mm handguns.

"Mafia?" the wedding guest repeated. "I don't think so."

"This is San Francisco, mister, you can't carry a gun in San Francisco. Unless you…"

"Unless what, patrolman?"

"Unless you got a permit. And even then…"

"Let me show you something," the guest said reaching to his back pocket.

"Freeze! Hold it right there," the cop shouted. "I want to see your hands."

"I just want you to see what I have. It's not a weapon." He turned his rear end around toward the policeman and slowly pulled out a black wallet. "Here," he said handing it over. "Read this."

The officer warily reached for the wallet and opened a flap. He read. He looked up at the wedding guest. "Oh dear God," he gulped.

"What?" the other officer asked. "What is it?"

"Joseph Blough, Captain, San Francisco Police Department," he read aloud. "Is this you? Are you him? Oh dear God." The officer's mouth dropped open. The other officer repeated, "Captain?"

A very handsome woman stepped down next to Captain Blough. "Joe, what's going on? Why do those officers have their guns drawn? Is there a problem?"

"No, Dominique, there's no problem," Joe said to his wife.

"Make them put their guns away then," she said.

"Officers," Joe directed, "you should holster your weapons now." They did. Then a young woman stepped down next to Mrs. Blough asking, "Mom, what's the matter?" She was very pretty, a younger version of Dominique. The first officer stared at her.

Dominique said, "There's no problem, Francine. Dad's handling it."

Captain Blough said, "What's your name, son?"

The officer looked back at the captain. "My name?" He acted as though he couldn't remember his name. "Uh, uh, sir, I..."

"Just your name, officer. It's not hard to do."

"Yes, sir. Oh, it's Silvestri, Charlie Silvestri."

"Good, and you?" Blough said, looking over at the other cop.

"Danny, uh, Daniel Wong, sir."

"What precinct?"

"Richmond Station, sir, over on Sixth."

"Pete McIntyre's shop."

"You know him, sir?"

"Of course, we went through the academy together. Pistol Pete McIntyre. I still don't get it how he got his bars before I did. He'll be so glad to hear that we've all met."

"Oh God. Sir? I apologize for saying..."

Blough kept talking. "How long have you been on the force, Charlie?"

"Seven, sir, seven months."

"What about you, Danny?"

"Six, sir, six months."

"New blood on the beat protecting and serving the citizens of San Francisco," Blough said to the other mature gentleman, who said, "I think they are making Captain McIntyre proud."

Blough said, "Oh, by the way, meet Lieutenant Richard Headley. He works for the same police department that you two young officers do."

Silvestri and Wong gawked at Headley. "You're Dick Headley?" one of them said. Headley nodded.

Blough smiled at the two young cops. "And look here, Captain McIntyre gave you your own units to use on patrol. That's Pete all over, giving you young officers a load of responsibility." He smiled again.

Officer Silvestri gulped. "Uh, sir, are you going to say anything to our captain?" he inquired. He looked at Danny and glanced at Francine.

"About what?"

"Well, sir, about today."

"I don't know. I'll have to think about that." He paused. "You know what's funny? I'm having breakfast with Pete Monday morning."

"Oh God," Silvestri moaned.

Another wedding guest stepped down to the police presence, slipping between some other onlookers. "Grampapa!" Danny Wong blurted out.

Mr. Sun looked over at the second officer. "Ni hao, Danny," he said, "on duty today, I see." He looked at Blough. "Captain, is there anything wrong?"

"No, Mr. Sun. These officers were drawn here by the big crowd for Beault's wedding..." Dominique elbowed Blough. "I mean Nadine Berry's wedding. I think they've learned something, though. Did we learn something here today, officers?"

Silvestri turned to look at Danny Wong. They shrugged.

"Anything, officers, anything at all?"

"Well," Danny started, "I think we learned that we have a lot to learn."

Blough looked at the other mature and armed wedding guest and said, "Lieutenant Headley, they think they have learned today that they still have a lot to learn. I think they mean about police work. That seem like a fair thing to conclude?" The lieutenant said he believed that the two young officers had made a good start on that today.

Mr. Sun smiled and said, "Danny's always been a quick study."

Francine said to her dad, "Maybe these policemen" – here she looked at Silvestri – "would like to stay for the wedding. It won't take long and they could eat here. They have to stop for lunch anyway."

Blough looked at his daughter, looked at the officers, looked at his wife who smiled, looked at his watch. "Thirty minutes, that's all." Francine quickly grabbed Silvestri then Wong and pulled the two cops up toward the food.

Headley called after them. "Officers, wouldn't it be a good idea to turn off your lights, close your doors and secure your patrol cars?" The two cops came back and did just that, grinning like idiots.

Grenville walked down. "Police business, Joe?"

"All taken care of. It's all over. We're ready for a wedding," the captain said.

The wedding guests watching the police action turned and strolled back up the grassy slope and walkway and found spots to hear Minister Protherington begin the marriage rite. He spoke lovingly of his brother and of his new sister, Nadine, and of his new niece, Alana. Beault – Basil – promised his undying love for Nadine who did the same for Basil. Alana held a pillow that presented a pair of wedding bands to the newlyweds. Grenville finished the formal readings and pronounced the two married under the laws of the State of California and in the eyes of God.

"You may kiss the bride," Grenville said to Basil who began to lean in to do just that when Grenville stepped between the newlyweds and said, "in a few minutes."

Basil jerked his head to Grenville. "What?"

"There is a tradition," Grenville said solemnly and loud enough for all to hear, "in the Congregation of Brotherly Love in the Name of Jesus Christ that when we join a man and a woman in matrimony, the male guests at the wedding are entitled to share a first kiss with the bride before her new husband has done so." Beault stared at Grenville. "So please step over there and wait your turn, Basil." Grenville said this as a long line of men began forming.

"Tradition?" Beault asked. Then he snapped, "There is not!"

"Tradition," someone called out. "Tra-di-tion," someone echoed. "Tra-di-tion," more called until it was a chant. "Tra-di-tion, tra-di-tion, tra-di-tion," the air filled. Followed by a lot of laughing and cheering.

"You," Beault accused Nadine. "You were in on this from the beginning, weren't you?" Mrs. Protherington answered with a huge smile.

Then the newlyweds kissed as the wedding crowd applauded loudly. What the two did later that night is none of your goddam business. And stop being so freakin nosey. Show some class.

Almost The End...Turn The Page

Afterword

Two months after the Protherington wedding, a sinister confab was under way in a bierhaus in Munich in Germany in a steady evening rainstorm between a bartender huddled across the bartop secretive-like with a woman who had slipped onto a stool and ordered a peppermint schnapps. Her drink of choice. They spoke of naughty things. Not yet overly defined were the who or the when or the where or the how of the naughty things, but the two nevertheless pressed on sure in their minds of the why – money. The what was a sketchy what and a dopey what as described to the woman by the bartender. Swifter above the neck than the bartender, she recognized it was dopey. But money... hmmm. You might have questioned the what had you been there as part of the scheming, only you were not. So you cannot fully appreciate the pair's sinister aims. Not to worry. You will learn for yourselves what the what was and what the how was and what the where was, all that stuff, when you follow our stouthearted private eye in his most trying assignment yet, coming in the next Jaguar Beault Thriller. It is entitled, *The Nuclear Armageddon Endgame*. Look for it. It'll be along as soon as all the words are written down...and at a very reasonable price.

Now This Is The End...
...Yet A Prelude To Another
Jaguar Beault Thriller

www.ingramcontent.com/pod-product-compliance
Lightning Source LLC
Chambersburg PA
CBHW062136170626
46813CB00002B/720